The Way You **Hold Me**

Also by Elle Wright:

The Wellspring series
Touched by You
Enticed by You
Pleasured by You

The Pure Talent series
The Way You Tempt Me
The Way You Hold Me

Published by Kensington Publishing Corp.

The Way You **Hold Me**

Elle Wright

Kensington Publishing Corp.
www.kensingtonbooks.com

DAFINA BOOKS are published by

Kensington Publishing Corp.
119 West 40th Street
New York, NY 10018

ISBN-13: 978-1-4967-2579-0
ISBN-10: -1-4967-2579-4
First Kensington Mass Market Edition: December 2020

ISBN-13: 978-1-4967-2580-6 (ebook)
ISBN-10: 1-4967-2580-8 (ebook)

10 9 8 7 6 5 4 3 2 1

Printed in the United States of America

For my besties, Tasha and Lina.
Thank you for everything. Love you!

Acknowledgments

The cast of characters that make up Pure Talent are so dear to me. I loved writing them so much. Skye and Garrett gave me the flux initially, but I found myself cracking up at Skye and her antics. I also found myself swooning at the patient way Garrett handled her. He is a true hero, who loves his heroine.

Writing this book was a bit different because I decided to bring in a therapist. Therapy has helped me in my own journey and I knew Sasha would help Skye in hers.

I hope you enjoy this story as much as I do.

First of all, I want to honor God, who has kept me through everything. He specializes in things that seem impossible.

To my husband, Jason, I can't imagine my life without you. Thank you for *holding* me through life's trials and tribulations. Thank you for loving me the way you do. Your support means everything to me.

To my children, Asante, Kaia, and Masai; I love you all so very much. Thank you for inspiring me. Keep being who you are. Keep God first.

To my family and friends, thank you for your unwavering support. My life is brighter because of you. Thanks for being #TeamElle!

Everybody needs a Sheryl Lister in their lives. To my sis, thanks for being you. Love you!

Thanks to my street team, #EllesBelles! You all hold me down. I truly appreciate you.

Special thanks to my Book Euphoria sistas. Love y'all.

I also want to thank Priscilla C. Johnson and Cilla's Maniacs, A.C. Arthur, Brenda Kidd-Woodbury (BJBC), MidnightAce Scotty (MidnightAce Book Bar), King Brooks (Black Page Turners), BRAB (Building Relationships Around Books), Orsayor Simmons (Book Referees), Tiffany Tyler (Reading in Black and White), Shannan Harper (Harper's Court), Wayne Jordan and Romance In Color, Stephanie Perkins (The Book Junkie), and the EyeCU Reading and Social Network for supporting me. I truly appreciate you all.

And to my readers . . . thank you for rocking with me! You're the bomb! I couldn't be doing this without you.

Thank you!

Love,
Elle

Chapter One

"I feel like my entire life is an overthought."

Skye Palmer let out a nervous laugh and shifted in her seat. A soft charcoal-gray plush chair. It wasn't the infamous chaise longue she'd expected her therapist to have. After all, she'd seen enough scenes—in movies or on television—of distraught people entering clean, nondescript offices to blab all of their troubles to a stiff person paid to listen and write prescriptions.

Making the decision to see a therapist, to reveal pieces of her life and detail her struggles to a stranger, had been difficult. Skye had always been the person who helped others, not the person who *needed* help. Somewhere along the way, though, she'd lost herself. She'd wrapped herself in the cloak of hurt, disappointment, and bad decisions. She'd suffocated under the weight of gut-wrenching heartache. Bitterness had replaced contentment. Doubt had replaced hope. So when her bestie, Zara Reid, encouraged her to take this step, Skye agreed.

Instead of feeling frazzled or even nervous, Skye felt calm. Still, she couldn't bring herself to embrace the peace she'd felt or the warmth of the woman silently watching her, waiting for her to complete her thought.

"How so?" the doctor asked finally.

Skye swallowed and gave the woman another quick once-over, noting the clinical psychologist's professional—yet relaxed—appearance and demeanor. Instead of a "Plain Jane" or a "Blah Betty," the woman before her was gorgeous, with smooth, brown skin, thick curls, and long legs. Again, she wasn't sure what she'd expected when she decided to make the appointment.

Dr. Sasha Williams stared at her, a polite smile on her lips and her black-rimmed glasses perched low on her nose. She'd come highly recommended from Skye's good friend Paityn Young, and had made room on her schedule that morning to meet with Skye. The least Skye could do was talk. *Right?*

Except, it had been fifteen minutes since she'd arrived, and Skye had only made the one comment. She *should* be talking. She'd paid for the session. Hell, she'd prepaid for several sessions.

"I . . ." Skye didn't know what the hell to say. *Damn that Zara for suggesting I do this.*

Skye's gaze swept the room. The ample space was impeccably decorated with warm colors, slate hardwood floors, a beautiful rug in the center, a vintage desk, and a matching loveseat. Artwork on the walls added a calm to the room. The owner had obviously spent time and money on the details. And if Skye didn't know anything else, it was her job to notice the tiniest of details. Even the smallest thing could derail a client's career, and she was paid to pay attention to everything, to be five steps ahead in every situation.

The bookshelf to her right boasted a variety of titles, from classics like *Little Women* and *The Hobbit* to titles by Toni Morrison and T. D. Jakes. Several textbooks about a wide range of subjects from psychology to anatomy also lined the shelves. Scattered on the table next to her were a few issues of *Essence* magazine, along with P*sychology Today, Vogue*, and the *Atlanta Tribune*.

Skye's attention drifted to the Allbirds flats her therapist wore, the ones she'd been tempted to buy herself a week ago. "I like your shoes," she grumbled.

The beautiful doctor crossed her legs at the knee. "Thank you."

The clock to her left ticked ahead, each second echoing in the room, reminding her that she only had twenty more minutes to get something meaningful out. Blue Atlanta skies were visible out of the window ahead, which could be deceiving if one were expecting a warm day. The December temperatures were low for this time of year, a balmy forty degrees. If she were outside, though, she was sure she'd find Midtown bustling with people getting ready for New Year's Eve.

Speaking of New Year's Eve . . . "Thanks for seeing me today." Skye smoothed a hand over her lap and clasped her hands together. "I appreciate you fitting me into your schedule on the holiday."

The doctor shrugged. "It's not a problem."

"This is my first time."

Dr. Williams smiled. It wasn't a tight smile. It wasn't an annoyed grin. It was genuine, sincere. Like she actually meant it. Yet, she didn't say anything.

"I guess I don't know what to do," Skye admitted. "Which is different for me."

"Whatever you need to do is what we'll do."

Tears burned her eyes. *Oh God, don't you dare cry, Skye.* She took a deep breath and let it out slowly. But one of those damn tears slithered down her cheek, like a cold, slimy snake. She wiped it away quickly. Glancing up at the doctor, she said, "I didn't mean to do that, Dr. Williams."

"Call me Sasha."

Sighing, she peered up at the ceiling to regain her composure. Once she'd taken a few seconds, she met the woman's unwavering gaze again. "Sasha."

"Why didn't you mean to cry?"

"Because I don't cry." *A lot.*

"Is it because you think you're not supposed to?"

Skye shrugged. "I've shed enough tears. Too many. I'm not going to cry anymore." *Yeah, right.*

Sasha tilted her head, assessed her with kind eyes. "Someday, I want to talk about why you feel you're not entitled to show emotion. For now, though, I'd like to focus on why you feel your life is an overthought. It's obviously on your mind."

Skye's watch buzzed and she peered at the screen. *Carmen*. The second time her boss had called her this morning. "Excuse me." She grabbed her phone and opened the Messenger app. Rolling her eyes, she typed out a hurried response. "I'm sorry."

"No problem."

"Overthought." Skye swallowed, attempting to continue her initial thought. "My life is an overthought because I can't stop overthinking everything I do. It's excessive and stifling. I feel frozen in indecision."

"At work?"

Shaking her head, Skye said, "No. Never at work. I'm good at what I do."

"Publicist at Pure Talent Agency."

"Yes."

"Do you love your job?" Sasha asked.

"My job is fine." Skye swallowed the lump that had formed in her throat. "It's everything else."

Nodding, Sasha said, "Tell me about it."

Skye opened her mouth to speak, but snapped it shut. What would she say? She'd already given the practiced response—*work is fine, I'm good at what I do, blah blah blah.* If she was honest with herself, though, she might be able to admit that work was part of her problem. Because she wasn't satisfied, she wasn't fulfilled, she wasn't challenged. But those feelings paled in comparison to the loneliness, the regret she felt about her personal choices.

"Skye, how about we start with a task?"

I can do that. Skye perked up. "What are you thinking?"

"Based on your questionnaire, and the little bit you've shared, I think it would help break the ice if you could focus on a small project before our next session."

Leaning forward, Skye asked, "What would that be?"

"Think about one thing that you're hesitant about, one thing that you tend to overthink."

Garrett.

The top of her list of regrets was always Garrett—her first love. They'd burned hot and heavy while together and blew up spectacularly when it ended. Well, not exactly. It just felt like a bomb had gone off in her chest, hollowed her out, and left her empty. The breakup itself was pretty tame. There were no hysterics, no broken glass, no harsh words. But it still hurt like hell, worse than any pain she'd felt before then, and even after. And that was saying a lot, considering her history.

She had no one to blame but herself, though. Because she'd walked away from him, even though it had ripped her apart. He'd done nothing but love her, take care of her. And she'd walked away without really even telling him the reasons why. Then she'd blamed him for it, not verbally, but in her actions toward him. Since he'd moved back to Atlanta, she'd kept him at arm's length. She'd mostly avoided one-on-one interaction with him at events and treated him with cool indifference when she did speak. He didn't deserve it, though. Yet, she couldn't stop doing it. Every. Single. Time. Hell, it was probably some sort of twisted self-defense mechanism she'd turned on its head. She didn't know. Hence, the need for therapy.

"Next time you're faced with this thing—or person—don't think about it," Sasha continued. "Don't tick off a list of pros and cons, don't question your motives or anyone's perception of you."

Damn, she's good. Skye had already started thinking of the reasons why giving it another try would or couldn't work, what he would think if she admitted she was wrong to break up with him all those years ago. *Does he even find me attractive anymore?*

"Allow yourself to feel your emotions in that moment and do what you really want to do," Sasha said. "Is that something you think you can try?"

Skye always loved a challenge. Even if it felt impossible. "Sure, I can handle that." She glanced down at her buzzing watch again. Once again, it was work. Because work never stopped for Christmas, for Thanksgiving, and definitely not New Year's Eve. "I have to go." She stood, wrapping her scarf around her neck and donning a pair of shades.

Sasha rose from her seat. “Two weeks, same time?”

“Yes. Thank you.” She gripped Sasha’s outstretched hand and squeezed. “It was good to meet you. Thanks again for seeing me on such short notice.”

“I look forward to working with you.”

Skye nodded and rushed out of the office. Frustrated, she pulled her phone from her purse to call her boss—who’d called her three more times since she’d responded to her text that she was unavailable.

“Skye, thanks for finally calling me back. I’ve been trying to reach you.”

“Hello, Carmen. What can I do for you?”

“We have a problem with Paige.”

Paige Mills was a popular actress and one of Pure Talent Agency’s biggest clients. Usually when she had a problem, everyone jumped to her attention. Holidays were no exception.

“What’s going on?” Skye asked.

“I need you on a flight to Los Angeles next week. The details will be on your desk when you get back to the office after the holiday.”

“But, I have—”

“Skye, this isn’t up for discussion. Everything will be finalized when you get back in the office.”

Except Skye hadn’t planned on going back to the office after the New Year. For the first time in her professional career, she’d scheduled a vacation to do nothing in particular. Her goal was plain and simple—stay home, go to movies, chill with herself and her family.

Closing her eyes, she took a calming breath. “Carmen,

you know I'm scheduled to be on vacation next week. Can someone else handle Paige? Like her personal publicist?"

"No," was the short, curt reply. "And I don't have time to explain to you the reasons why that won't happen."

It was just like the older woman to disregard Skye's plans. The two had never gotten along, but Skye wasn't one to play the "I'm your boss's only niece" card. Even though her cousin, Xavier Starks, had offered on more than one occasion to step in and say something.

Massaging her temples, she bit back the curse itching to burst forward. She swallowed. Hard. And tried again. "Is this something I can handle *after* my vacation?"

Skye was no idiot. In fact, she'd spent a lot of time educating herself on a myriad of subjects outside of her chosen career, from horticultural science to Nietzsche to wine. She could talk to anybody, anywhere, at any time, about any subject. Since Carmen was promoted several years ago, Skye had attended every single conflict management training course she could stomach. Each of them had left her feeling extremely inept. Because no matter what she did, she still didn't like the woman yapping on about work like it wasn't New Year's Eve.

She wanted to tell her boss where she could stick her foul attitude, she yearned to give Stupid-Ass-Know-Nothing Carmen a piece of her mind in Tagalog *and* in English until she begged for mercy. And, damn it, she wanted to tell Uncle Jax exactly how that heffa had treated her since she'd traipsed into the office and told Skye she didn't care whose niece she was.

"Skye?"

"Yes," she bit out.

"Did you hear me?"

She didn't. "I'm sorry, can you repeat that last thing?"

"I said, I'm going on medical leave for two months, starting now. You're in charge. I'll leave my notes on your desk."

Skye's mouth fell open. "But—"

"Happy New Year."

Then Carmen was gone. And Skye was screwed.

Skye purposely arrived at Xavier's and Zara's house for their New Year's Eve engagement party half an hour before the ball dropped. After that phone call with her boss, she'd screamed in her car for two whole minutes. Once she'd effectively released her tension, she headed home to put her boss and work behind her and focus on the task at hand.

It had taken her hours to find the right dress for the occasion. Then it had taken her even longer to get the nerve to leave her condo. Because tonight was the night she would make her move. Tonight was the night she wasn't going to overthink her past or her future.

"What's up, cousin?" Xavier greeted her with a kiss on her cheek as he always did. Raised more like siblings than cousins, Skye had never known life without X. Her adoptive father and his father were brothers, and they'd grown up in the same Brentwood, Los Angeles neighborhood. Now they worked together at Pure Talent.

"Hey, X." She noted several familiar faces in the room. "Party is lit."

"We have a lot to celebrate."

Grinning up at him, she nodded. "You do."

Skye couldn't help but be happy for her cousin and her bestie. She'd seen the two of them fall for each other despite their own personal reservations about love and relationships. She'd rooted for them as they slowly realized their lives didn't work without one another. And she would be there with them every step of the way going forward.

"I need your help, though," he said.

She frowned. "What's wrong? And why didn't you warn me about Carmen?"

"Trust me, it was a shock to us, too." X had recently stepped into the role of heir apparent to the Pure Talent empire, so she knew he'd been privy to the details about her boss's leave. "We got the email this morning. I called you, but you didn't answer."

Skye grimaced. Her cousin was one of the calls she'd missed during her session. "Sorry."

"Zara explained where you were, so you're good. It's short notice, but I figured you'd be happy."

"I don't know how I feel," she admitted. "She's the head of publicity. Am I ready for this?" *Do I even want it?* "And her desk is a mess. I'm going to have to fix her shit."

He squeezed her shoulder affectionately. "You got this, Skye. I have no doubt. And if *you* do, I'm here to help."

She couldn't help but smile. There was never a time X didn't have her back, even if he didn't agree. Growing up together, a mere block away from each other, had ensured they would be present in each other's lives. But it hadn't stopped there. They'd built forts, played video games, and transitioned from precocious kids to determined teens to successful adults. They were family, but they were friends, confidantes. And she loved him dearly.

"Thanks, X. You're always there for me."

"That never changes." He smiled. "Now, I need you to find your girl. She's around here, panicked."

Skye looked for Zara among the crowd and instead spotted a waiter carrying several flutes of champagne. She snagged a glass and turned to X. "Why?"

"The wedding."

"Ah. I'm not surprised." Her bestie was many things, but event planner wasn't one of them. "I got you."

He bumped shoulders with her. "Thank you."

Skye scanned the room again, telling herself she was searching for Zara. Not Garrett. "Where is she?"

X glanced around the room. His eyes lit up when he spotted who she assumed was Zara behind her. "Over there." He pointed toward the bar. "Talking to Garrett."

Turning slowly, she caught a glimpse of her best friend before focusing on the man that had haunted her dreams more nights than she'd even want to admit. He was dressed casually, in black slacks and a black shirt. His brown skin glowed in the dim lighting. He laughed at something Zara said, before taking a sip of his amber-colored drink, most likely cognac. Neat. At least, that's what he used to enjoy.

Before she could stop herself, she headed over to them, Sasha's words echoing in her head, playing on an endless loop. *Don't think about it, just feel, just do.*

"Skye, where the hell have you been?"

She stopped in her tracks, recognizing the male voice immediately.

"I know you're not going to walk up in here and not speak to me!"

Skye turned slowly, ready to shoot her best guy friend with her fiercest scowl. The smirk on his face let her know he didn't give a damn what she had in store. And the arch of his brow told her he knew exactly where she was headed when he'd intercepted her.

Grumbling a curse, she rushed over to him. "Why are you so damn loud, Duke?"

"I mean, damn. Can't get a call back? A hug? A Happy New Year? A *go to hell*?"

"Hi," she grumbled, noticing the three women standing close to him, eyeing him like he was prey.

Dressed in a crisp, white dress shirt unbuttoned at the collar and rolled up at the sleeves and fitted gray slacks, Duke Young didn't look like any personal chef she'd ever seen. In pure Duke fashion, his beard was trimmed and his wavy hair was mussed to perfection.

"Amihan." He grinned, holding out his arms. "Hug. We're supposed to be celebrating."

Amihan was her middle name, and it meant "northeast monsoon" in Tagalog. It was also her great-grandmother's name. As an Afro-Filipina woman, she was proud of her heritage. But only her mother called her Amihan, or Ami. Duke did it when he was trying to play the big bossy brother role he liked to play so much.

When she was a kid, her mother used to tell her stories that make up what is called Philippine mythology. According to the folklore, Amihan was a birdlike creature—the first of the universe—responsible for saving humans from a bamboo tree. For some reason, that story always made Skye feel special.

Unable to pretend to be mad at him any longer, she laughed and shoved him playfully. "I can't stand you."

"Hey, I figured I better stop you before you do something you'll regret." He pointed one finger at each of her eyes. "I know that look in your eyes."

Smacking his hand away, she told him, "Shut up."

"You look good enough to be dangerous tonight. Where's your date? Weren't you supposed to bring Kenneth?"

"His name is Keith, and we're just friends." Initially, she'd thought about bringing Keith to the party. They'd met at a fundraiser several weeks ago, and had gone out a few times. But she didn't consider them serious, even though he'd expressed interest in becoming more than friends.

"Friends, huh?" Duke studied her with narrowed eyes. Silently.

"Stop looking at me like that," she hissed. "You get on my nerves."

"Why are you so defensive?"

"Since you're so nosy, Keith and I decided not to ring in the New Year together. We're meeting for a nice breakfast tomorrow. An *innocent* breakfast."

"That's lame."

She smacked his shoulder. "Shut up. You're holding me up."

Chuckling, he held up a platter of mini desserts. "Try one of these."

Duke made a pretty good living as a personal chef, and had been hired to cater the party.

Skye bit her lip and mulled over the choices. "Did you make them?"

"What do you think?"

"Hm. I'll take"—she picked up a chocolate one—"this one." She popped it into her mouth. Groaning, she nodded and gave him a thumbs-up. "So good."

Duke set the platter down. "Thanks. Hug?"

Skye shook her head and finally gave him a hug. "You think you're slick," she whispered. "You just don't want those women to come and holla at you. I'm not playing your fake girlfriend tonight."

He barked out a laugh. "Damn, I can't get anything by you."

Pulling away, she pointed at him. "See! Dirty. Dog. I have to go."

"I can only be me."

Waving, she walked away. "Bye, Duke."

"Be good, Skye," he shouted.

Composing herself, she made a beeline for Zara—who just happened to still be standing with Garrett. X had joined them as well.

"Z-Ra, hey." Skye's voice came out more breathy than she'd intended. She hugged her friend.

"Hey, hun," Zara squeezed her hand.

"Garrett," Skye said in a clipped tone. The same tone she'd told herself she wouldn't use the next time she saw him.

Damn, Skye. She'd promised herself that she'd do better, that she wouldn't treat him the way she'd been treating him. The terse, one-word reply wasn't called for—at all.

With a heavy sigh, she amended her greeting, this time in a softer tone. "Hi, Garrett."

He smiled. "Hello, Skye. How are you?"

I can do this. "I'm well. You?"

"Good."

Step one complete. On to step two of Operation: Do Not Overthink. Turning to Zara, she said, "You look amazing."

Zara grinned. "Thanks. Can you believe I let X pick my dress?"

Now, that shocked the hell out of her. With wide eyes, she asked, "What?"

"I know, right? I must be in love."

"Hey, I did good," X said.

Skye laughed. "Damn. This has to go in the record books. Let me look at you, girlfriend."

Zara waved her off. "No, I'd rather check you out."

Skye twirled, giving Zara—and Garrett—a full view of her outfit. It was their thing. Whenever they dressed to impress, they checked each other out. But Skye didn't need Zara to tell her she looked good. After countless changes, she knew she rocked out her look. Not that she was conceited or anything. The short, black-and-white sequined dress she'd chosen fit perfectly, accentuating her greatest assets and showcasing just the right amount of skin. And judging by the way Garrett was looking at her, she'd bet he agreed.

"You like?" Skye asked. That question was for both of them. Only one answered.

"You're a hottie." Zara elbowed Garrett. "Isn't she stunning?"

I love my bestie.

"Definitely," he whispered. "You look beautiful, Skye."

Shit. She pressed a hand against her stomach to calm the flutters. No one had ever said her name quite like Garrett did. The low rasp of his voice, the way it seemed to roll off his tongue coupled with the accompanying heat in his eyes . . . No wonder she tended to overthink everything with him. Her need to protect herself was a valid response to the way he made her feel. Because she always felt like she was teetering on the edge of regret and arousal, anger and desire around him.

"It's time!"

The loud announcement interrupted the moment, and

guests scrambled to grab drinks or find loved ones as the room erupted in the countdown.

Twenty.

Skye shot Garrett a sidelong glance. But he wasn't looking at her anymore. His attention was focused squarely on his glass.

Fifteen.

Sighing, she gulped her champagne down.

Ten.

Well, it was now or never.

Five.

She set her glass down on the bar. His eyes met hers. He smiled.

One.

He opened his mouth and said, "Happy New—"

But before he could finish the salutation, she reached up, gripped his collar in her fists, and pulled him into a kiss. *Happy New Year is right.*

Chapter Two

Honey. Tongue. Lemon. Teeth. Peppermint. Soft. Champagne. Warm. Nectarines . . . Cheers? Confetti? Happy New Year?

Garrett tried to pull himself back to the present. He really did. But the woman in front of him, the woman who'd kissed him like she was still his, the woman who'd haunted him with her presence *and* her absence, wouldn't let go of him. Her mouth on his, her breasts against his chest, her soft moans mixing with his low groans . . . *This has to be a dream.* Because his reality wasn't this sweet, this perfect.

The cute, soft purr she let out made him want to peel her dress from her body and make slow love to her all night. He felt her pull away, but he wasn't ready to let her go. He wasn't ready for this to end.

Cradling her face in his hands, he pulled her closer, enjoying the feel of her skin beneath his fingers. She sagged against him as he kissed her with a passion he hadn't felt since . . . the last time their lips met. Years ago. This wasn't over. Not yet. *Not ever.*

Vaguely, he heard the roar of laughter surrounding them. He knew it wasn't the time and place to get reacquainted with her, but he couldn't help it. He wanted her. Hell, he always wanted Skye Palmer. And he had no doubt he would forever want her.

Yet, his heart and his mind warred with each other, pulling him out of the moment. Because she wasn't *his* Skye anymore. A few days ago, she'd barely spoken two words to him. They weren't good, they weren't even friends anymore. Despite the surge of emotions threatening to consume him, he knew he had to stop. No matter how good it felt to have her in his arms, he knew he needed to let her go. Reluctantly, he forced himself to pull back.

Garrett wanted to dive back in, nibble on the corner of her mouth, touch every part of her until she begged him never to leave her. From the moment Skye had arrived, he hadn't been able to keep his eyes off of her. She looked like a sexy little nymph in black and white sequins. Her low-cut dress fit like a glove, and her long legs in those damn heels made him bite back a groan.

Zara had tried to keep him focused on their conversation about business, but it was no use. He couldn't look away, not as she chatted with X and Duke, not when she tasted the mini dessert, and definitely not when she ventured toward him. If he didn't know better, he would have thought she was playing with him, twirling in front of him the way she had for Zara earlier.

Now she stood before him, her eyes closed, her fingertips on lips still swollen from his kiss. He brushed his thumb over her chin and smiled. He wanted more time. He wanted a chance to talk to her, to tell her everything he could never say. But he knew his bubble was about to pop. Three, two, one . . .

Skye's eyes popped open. A blush worked its way up

her neck, to her cheeks. Her tongue darted out to moisten her lips. And he was laser-focused on the motion. *So beautiful.*

"Gar . . ." She cleared her throat. "Um, Happy New Year."

Then, she ran.

His instinct was to follow her, but he knew Skye. Going after her would only make her run faster, and he didn't want that. Time had passed, the years had flown by. But he'd spent years memorizing everything about her, from the mole on her earlobe to the way she nibbled on her thumbnail when she was in deep thought. The days, months, and years away hadn't changed the fact that Skye was still the same woman he'd fallen in love with during a *Star Wars* marathon. And she was still the same person who'd walked away.

Garrett watched Skye disappear down a hallway and scanned the nearby area. Not surprisingly, he was met with many pairs of curious stares. Zara smiled sadly at him, before she took off after Skye. Duke followed Zara shortly after.

A moment later, a glass of cognac was in front of him, held by X. Snatching it away, he downed it, slamming the empty glass on the bar top.

"You good?" X asked.

Garrett nodded. "What do you think?"

He hadn't been *good* in years, and it all started when his mother and stepfather died in a car accident, leaving him to raise his ten-year-old sister. Alone.

"That was . . ." X made an unusual, more like uncomfortable grunt. "Yeah, I'm not even sure what to say about that."

"You and me both."

Garrett couldn't help but notice the faces still staring at him, still waiting to see a reaction. There weren't many who knew of his history with Skye, but there were a few in attendance who did.

"Well, Happy New Year, bruh?"

Chuckling, Garrett shook his head at his boy's attempt to lighten the mood. "Man, shut the hell up."

"What?" X shrugged. "Listen, it's very rare that I'm at a loss for words. So, I'm just going to say that it's fucked up. Because I know how you feel about her."

Garrett had learned a long time ago that family was a heart thing, not a blood thing. He'd received more support from Xavier and the Starks family than he'd ever received from his own mother. And he never knew his father, so . . .

Hard to believe he'd hated X on sight when they'd met as freshmen at Morehouse College. Xavier had strolled onto campus with a chip on his shoulder, which Garrett delighted in knocking off. With his fists. He couldn't even remember why they'd fought that day in one of the study lounges, but once they'd come to blows, that was that. They became friends while nursing split lips and bruised knuckles, then brothers when they pledged the same fraternity.

The rise and fall of his relationship with Skye was well-known to their close circle, but Xavier had remained steadfast throughout. Even though he was Skye's cousin, he'd always tried to stay impartial and didn't hesitate to tell either of them if they handled things wrong.

X clasped his shoulder. "If you need to talk, holla at me."

Garrett waved one of the waiters over and asked for another cognac. Because . . . drunk was on the menu for the rest of the night. "I'm cool, bruh. It is what it is. No big deal."

It wasn't a lie. He'd categorize it as more of an affirmation. If he continued to tell himself it didn't mean anything, that kissing Skye wasn't a big deal, maybe he'd somehow be able to forget about it. *Doubtful.*

X raised a brow, signaling he knew Garrett was full of shit. "Whatever you say, bruh."

It was no secret Garrett hated lies *and* liars. Maybe it was because his mother had lied to him throughout much of his young life. And her "small" lies somehow turned into big lies, which always tended to affect him in detrimental ways, like losing scholarships due to the falsification of income.

"I need another drink," Garrett grumbled.

"Good idea. Then I can get on task."

Frowning, Garrett asked, "What the hell are you talking about?"

Scratching his forehead, X said, "We were supposed to ask you all together, but since that probably won't happen . . . I guess now is as good a time as any to ask you to stand up with me at the wedding."

Garrett raised a questioning brow. "Wedding? As in tuxedos, photographers, and dancing? What happened to Vegas and the Hunk O' Burning Love Wedding Chapel?"

Once X had decided to propose, he'd been adamant about just going somewhere and getting married. His friend was sure Zara wouldn't want a wedding. Which was true. But what neither of them had counted on was their parents' wishes. So, wedding plans commenced shortly after the proposal.

X waved him off. "Yeah, I don't even want to talk about it. Zara is frazzled and cursing under her breath every time we're in the same room with my parents. Christmas morning with her mother and sister was even worse."

"Even with Rissa getting married, too?" Zara's sister was engaged as well, and right in the middle of planning a huge Los Angeles wedding.

"We're in the sunken place right now. Nothing and no one makes sense. Everyone is all about weddings."

Garrett shrugged. "Well, I'm not surprised. You shouldn't be either. You know your mother is not going to let you get married in Vegas."

While Jax and Ana Starks were surrogate parents to many, including Garrett, they only had one biological child. Ana would never be okay with an elopement for her "baby."

"I'm trying to rein her in on that budget, man." X rubbed his head. "She's going crazy with the details, talking about exotic flowers from South America. And she wants to incorporate Liberian traditions into the ceremony and reception. On the flip side, Zara's mother wants to cater. Every night, we get a call about something, and it hasn't even been a month yet."

"Good luck with that. And you know I'll stand up with you. Just don't expect me to plan a bachelor party. That's not in my wheelhouse."

"It's cool. You know Duke already has plans." X glanced at his watch. "You can go now."

Garrett nodded. In every situation, he'd always given Skye at least fifteen minutes to process things. Then he'd go after her. So, he did. He weaved through the room, greeting people with nods as he made his way toward the hallway. They really did need to talk.

Just as he rounded a corner, he spotted Zara closing the front door. He didn't need to ask the question. He knew Skye was gone.

Zara grinned at one of her guests and caught his gaze.

Sighing, she approached him, sad smile firmly in place. "Garrett, I—"

"Zara, we don't have to do this."

"I'm sorry. Skye—"

He finished her sentence. "Left. Your sad smile pretty much told me what I needed to hear."

"The good news is you gave everyone a good show."

Unable to help himself, he barked out a laugh. "You've been with X too long."

She shrugged. "What can I say? I love his sense of humor."

"Is she okay?" Because Skye being okay mattered to him. It always had.

Zara nodded. "She *will* be fine. You will, too."

"Whatever you say."

"I'm so serious." She grinned. "I feel like the tides are turning."

"Don't get carried away."

It had been a little over a year since Garrett had made the decision to leave Houston, after spending years building his crisis management practice. One day, he realized his hometown didn't have what he needed anymore. He'd uprooted his life to be there for his sister, to give her stability. But Maxine had moved to Tuscaloosa, Alabama, to attend college years ago, and there was no reason for him to stay in Houston anymore. Moving back to Atlanta had been a logical step. His friends, his surrogate family, and Skye were in Georgia. And Max was three hours away at University of Alabama. Win-win.

Initially, he'd hoped to reconnect with Skye in a genuine way. Maybe they wouldn't be lovers again, but he wanted to at least reestablish a friendship. But that didn't turn out like he'd hoped. In fact, that kiss was the closest he'd gotten to her since he'd come back.

"So, listen," Zara said, pulling him from his thoughts. "I don't want you to think this is a bad thing, though."

And he officially didn't want to talk about Skye or the kiss or New Year's Eve or anything other than cognac. Neat. "Zara, I—"

She squeezed his arm. "No, seriously, it's not bad that Skye left. It's not even bad that the kiss happened. Sometimes you don't even recognize what you want until you realize what you've been missing."

Garrett frowned, wondering if he'd missed something. Had she been talking while he was tumbling down Hope Springs Eternal Lane? "I don't even know what that means."

"Garrett, you're the crisis manager. You know when someone's in crisis mode. I'm no expert, but I think it's very telling that Skye bailed. Maybe that kiss shook her. Mark my words, that won't be the last time it happens." She patted his shoulder. "Get another drink. The night is still young."

Garrett had worked every day as a crisis management attorney, helping organizations and clients prevent, prepare for, manage, and reduce damages in crisis situations. But he was having his own damn crisis and didn't know how the hell he was supposed to fix it. Or even if he could.

What the hell am I doing here?

Using her key, Skye opened the door, stepped inside the apartment, and turned on the light. The place was quiet. If she didn't know better, she would think no one was home. Immediately, she noticed the clothes strewn on the floor in a trail leading down the hallway toward the bedroom.

Her stomach fell. The last place she needed to be was in this apartment, the last thing she wanted to see was in that bedroom. Closing her eyes, she kicked the black lace bra at her foot away from her.

Shit.

Skye picked up the poker near the fireplace and walked to the bedroom door. With a heavy sigh, she turned the doorknob and pushed it open. “Get the hell up!” she yelled, raising the poker in her hand.

On the bed, the man and woman bolted up. The woman screamed when she spotted Skye.

“What the hell is this?” Skye barreled toward the bed. “What are you doing in my apartment? With her?”

“What?” the woman screeched. “This is your apartment?” She jumped up, naked as the sky was blue.

Skye looked away for a second before turning furious eyes on the man. “You bastard. How could you do this to me?” She swung the poker toward him.

The terrified woman screamed again.

“I’m sorry, baby,” he said, rolling off the bed. “Don’t hurt me again.”

Skye pointed at him. “I’ll deal with you later.” She whirled around on the woman. “You!”

“Oh no.” The woman clutched a pillow to her bare chest. “I didn’t know he had a woman. Please . . . Don’t hurt me.” She backed out into the hallway, a shaky hand warding Skye off. “I’ll leave. I won’t even look at him again. I promise.”

“Why shouldn’t I kick your ass up and down this apartment?” Skye pointed the poker at her. And for the first time since she’d grabbed the metal weapon, her mask almost slipped. “Who the hell are you?”

“Nobody. I’m nobody. Listen, I’m not a hoe. I don’t do

this. I only came home with him because I thought he was single. You have every right to be mad." The woman pointed toward him. "At him. He's the cheater. He lied." The woman scrambled to pick up her dress. She slid it on haphazardly, never taking her eyes off Skye.

"Get the hell out of here!" Skye crashed the poker into a glass on top of the counter.

The girl yelped before she picked up her pumps and hightailed it to the door.

Skye followed, grabbing the bra with the poker and tossing it to the frazzled woman. "Don't forget this shit."

The bra landed in the woman's hair, right before she stumbled out of the apartment. The lady recovered quickly, jumping to her feet and bolting away.

Skye walked over to the door and closed it. Dropping the poker to the floor, she sighed heavily.

A loud clap sounded from behind her. She turned to find Duke standing in the middle of the room, jeans hanging low on his hips, his curly hair messy, and a devilish smirk on his lips.

He barked out a laugh. "Brava."

When Duke had texted her that morning, asking her for help, she'd hesitated because she didn't want to talk about Garrett or that damn kiss. But she couldn't not help Duke, even when she thought he was wrong as hell.

Covering her mouth, she giggled. "I needed that." She bent down and picked up his shirt, throwing it at him. "And put this on."

He slipped his T-shirt on. "You killed that performance, Skye."

She took a bow. "I thought so, too."

"The poker was a nice touch." He approached her, pulling

her scarf and shades off. "Did you have to break my nice glassware, though?"

"You deserved it. For once again bringing a random woman home that didn't know how to leave."

He shrugged. "Hey, it always starts promising. Then takes a turn for the worst. Thanks for coming in for the save. I owe you."

"Breakfast. Bacon, eggs, and hash browns. Get to it."

Duke smiled and headed to the kitchen. "Not a problem. What happened to breakfast with Kenneth?"

"Keith," she corrected. "Why do you insist on calling him Kenneth?"

"Because you're not serious about him. I can't figure out why you're wasting his time."

Duke was right. Skye had decided that morning to let Keith down easy. There was no point in prolonging the inevitable. She simply wasn't interested in exploring anything more with the media mogul. They weren't compatible on any level.

"Well, I'm not anymore," she said. "I called him this morning, wished him a happy New Year and a happy life."

Duke laughed. "It's about time. I never trust anyone who wears his pants too high at the waist."

Giggling, Skye slid onto a bar stool while Duke made quick work preparing her meal. "You're crazy."

He set a glass of orange juice in front of her. "How was your first therapy appointment?"

Eyeing him curiously, she wondered why he'd asked her *that.* On her way over, she'd mentally prepared herself for the onslaught of questions about her behavior at the party. Although Zara and Duke had rushed to her side last night, neither of them had uttered a peep about the kiss. They'd sat in silence as Skye babbled on about overthinking and bad choices and full lips. And now that she was there, he'd chosen to ask about therapy? Not the kiss. Not Garrett.

Instead of drinking the juice he'd given her, she picked at her fingernail. "I guess it was okay." After a few seconds, she glanced up to find him watching her. "What?"

"You know therapy only works if you actually *do* something during your session. You can't expect a breakthrough if you don't put in the effort."

It was just like Duke to tell her the hard truth. Plus, he knew something about therapy. His parents were world-renowned marriage and family counselors. Active listening, cognitive dissonance, and congruence was normal dinner talk for them.

Rolling her eyes, she took a big gulp of juice. "I just couldn't bring myself to talk much."

"Why? I can't get you to shut up."

"I hate you," she grumbled.

"No, you don't." He cracked an egg into a bowl, whisked it, and poured it into a pan. Next, he laid five thick slices of bacon into a second frying pan. "I'm not making hash browns. I don't have time for that. Want a pancake?"

Skye frowned. "No."

"I have a flight to catch."

"I know," she whined. Skye had offered to drive Duke to the airport. Her friend was headed to Michigan to visit his family.

"Is it Sasha?" he asked, shifting the discussion back to therapy.

When she'd mentioned her appointment to him yesterday, he'd given his opinion on Dr. Williams. Sasha had spent a lot of time with his family because she was close to his sister, Paityn.

"No, she seems great. It's me. I can't seem to get out of my own head."

"Which is why you're seeing her in the first place."

The smell of bacon wafted to her nose, and her stomach growled. For some reason, Duke fried bacon better than anyone else. Even her mother. "True. But you're right, if I can't open up, how is this going to help me?"

He opened the refrigerator and pulled out a container of pre-sliced fruit. "You'll find a way. You always do."

"She gave me an assignment."

He transferred three pieces of pineapple—her favorite—to a plate. "Right up your alley."

"It's like she knew me."

"She's good like that."

She eyed Duke, wondered if there was a history between him and Sasha. "Duke, did you and—?"

"Don't ask questions you don't want to know the answer to."

"Ugh, you make me sick. I can't wait for you to settle down with one woman." She held up one finger for emphasis.

He winked at her. "Never."

"Whatever. When it happens, I'm going to laugh at your ass, because she's going to put you through it."

He put the bacon and eggs on her plate and slid it toward her. "Eat."

Picking up a piece of pork, she bit down into it and groaned. "I swear, you're a bacon god or something."

He chuckled. "It's a gift." Leaning against the counter, he pinned her with his gaze. "So tell me more about this assignment."

"You saw it last night. She wanted me to pick one thing to not overthink."

"Ah, so that's why you kissed the hell out of Garrett."

She tossed a napkin at him. "Be quiet. I knew you'd find a way to bring that up."

"Shit, it was impressive. Good show."

"I guess." She munched on a piece of fruit, and tried not to think about that kiss or Garrett's mouth—or Garrett's cologne. Or Garrett, period.

"Think you made a mistake? Did you open up a locked box that you can't close again?"

There wasn't much Duke didn't know about Skye. They'd met as kids and had bonded over their mutual love of Slurpees and Daryl Hall and John Oates. They'd seen each other through some very dark times, and he'd remained one of the most important people in her life.

She swallowed. "Maybe."

"Or maybe it's time to talk to him. You've spent a long time acting like you don't care, when I know you do."

"It's been over for a long time."

"So why is he an overthought?"

She hated when Duke was right. Hated it. "I don't know. Shit. That's why I'm going to therapy. I'm a hot ass mess."

"You'd be less of a mess if you'd just have a damn conversation with him. It's not that hard."

Skye had talked to Duke ad nauseam about Garrett, and never liked the advice he'd given her. "Of course, it's not that hard to you. You're Teflon. I'm . . . cotton. Things soak in, drench me. If he rejects me, or hates me, or laughs at me, I'll deflate like a balloon."

"Stop being so damn dramatic. The man let you kiss him in front of women who would've actually given him some and not run away like a damn scaredy-cat."

Ouch.

"And he liked that shit," he continued. "If he didn't he

would have stopped you." Sighing, he tapped the countertop with his thumb. It was a Duke quirk, a signal that he was thinking. Usually something profound or downright sweet followed. "Listen, you have a lot to offer any man. Garrett would be a fool to let you walk away from him again. But you're not giving him a chance to prove that he wouldn't."

See. Profound and sweet. "It's not about that. It's about facing what I did to burn our relationship to the ground." And admitting the damage might be irreparable.

"So face it head-on. Whatever that looks like, do it."

He sounded like Sasha.

"I hate to see you second-guessing yourself all the time. You're doing it with work, with your relationships. And you always fix everybody else's shit. Spend some time on you. Self-care. Your parents are good. Zara's good. X is good."

She smiled. "What about you? Are you good?"

He scoffed. "I'm perfect. I keep telling you not to worry about me. I always land on my feet." Walking around the island, he wrapped an arm around her and pulled her into a hug. "I just want you to be happy. Then, maybe I can finally move to L.A."

She leaned into his embrace. "I love you, too. Thanks for being you."

Chapter Three

"Roll tide! Roll!"

Garrett rolled over and grumbled a curse, covering his head with a pillow. It was too early for screaming.

"Bama strong!" Claps followed a brief chorus of the University of Alabama fight song. "Come on, G! Get up!"

The sheet draped around his waist was being torn away, and he gripped it for dear life, because he didn't want his little sister to be traumatized by his morning wood. "Don't, Max."

He tossed one of his throw pillows toward her voice, cracking up when she let out a loud grunt. *Ouch.* The hangover that had swooshed in the moment his sister entered his room shouting at some outrageous decibel made him cringe. He needed Advil or another shot. Stat.

"You hit me in the eye, G!"

Before he could finally open his eyes, something smacked him in the chest hard. He traced the ridge of the object now lying at his side and realized it was a shoe. Pushing it off the bed, he shifted the pillow to the right and cracked one extremely tired eye open. *Shit.* He squeezed it shut again. Because his sweet little sister had opened all of the blinds and the sunlight nearly took him out.

"I need something for this headache." He let his pillow fall back over his eyes and prayed for the pounding to stop. He hadn't thrown back that many drinks since his early twenties. *What the hell was I thinking?*

The sound of footsteps retreating out of the room echoed like a loud gong in his ears. Garrett wanted to crawl into a quiet hole, away from sunlight, away from noise. A few minutes later, he felt her next to him again.

She lifted his hand, pushed a glass into it. "Here."

He opened his other hand and she dropped two pills into his palm. At this point, he didn't care what she'd given him. He needed his head to stop pounding. Lifting up his pillow slightly, he took the medicine and gulped down the water.

She grabbed the glass. "What did you do last night? Wait, better question, what were you drinking last night? I wish you'd open your eyes so you can see yourself. And your house."

Too many questions, too much noise. "Please," he groaned. "Don't shout."

"I'm not!" she yelled, before bursting out in a fit of giggles. He imagined his sister bent over, holding her stomach as she laughed at his expense.

"Get. Out."

"You're still in your clothes, G," she said. "I have to take a pic of this, just so that I can send it to you every now and then to remind you of this moment. I might even put a cute little filter on it and post it on Snap."

He pointed toward her voice. "You better not, Maxine Renee Steele-Pratt."

"Full name, G? Really?"

Garrett always had a hard time asserting authority with his sister. Then again, he never really had to. She was a good girl and had rarely been in trouble. "Max."

"Remember when I snuck out and got drunk with my friends after the homecoming dance senior year? You told me that liquor never solves problems."

He remembered that night very well. Max had just been dumped by that little punk Felix. And she'd cried on his shoulder because she couldn't understand why. Still . . .

"When I finally open my eyes, your phone better not be anywhere in sight," he ordered. "The difference is I'm grown as hell. You were a kid."

"Fine," she mumbled. "I won't take a picture."

A moment later, he finally peered up at her, trying to focus on her and not the pain shooting down his neck. *What the hell was I thinking last night?*

Max blessed him with a bright smile and did a swan dive onto the bed, much like she'd often done as a kid with wild hair and braces. Nothing much had changed since then. His cute, cheeky sister was now a beautiful woman. But she was still a ball of energy with wild curls. Only now she had straight teeth and a silver nose ring.

And . . . *Shit.* The mattress vibrated for what seemed like twenty long seconds, intensifying his pain.

"I'm here," she said matter-of-factly. Rolling onto her back, she sighed. "I made it. Aren't you happy to see me?"

"Extremely." And he meant that. He just didn't expect to *see* her so early. With a grunt, he scooted over to give her room. "I thought you weren't coming in until midafternoon."

She giggled. "G, it's one thirty."

His eyes widened. "What?"

"Yes!" She sat up, maneuvering her legs in the crisscross-applesauce position he was quite familiar with, since he'd had to attend every spelling bee, every scout meeting, every parent-teacher conference, every school competition, every swim meet. "I thought you'd have breakfast for me. I looked in the cabinets and you have no food. No cereal, no milk, no eggs. Please tell me you haven't reverted to takeout and dining in at swanky restaurants every night. I saw a Pop-Tart in your cabinet. A Pop-Tart!" She pointed at him. "You know those are no good for you. I need you to get it together. You promised."

Garrett sighed. The conversation he'd had with Max a few months ago still rang in his ears. He'd mistakenly told her about the physical he'd had when the doctor told him he had high blood pressure. It wasn't a surprise, since the condition ran in the family. But she'd made him promise to do better, to eat healthier, to work out more.

He wasn't out of shape by any means, but he recognized a few areas that needed improvement. Specifically, his penchant for eating late and the snack drawer in his office, full of chips. Oh, and his craving for a Pepsi every day. And coffee. *So, I have to step my game up.*

"I know," he said. "I'm going to do better. It's my resolution for this year."

Pursing her lips, she hit him with a pillow. "You don't make resolutions. Remember?"

"True," he admitted.

Garrett had never spent the last part of one year affirming what he would do or no longer do the next year. When he wanted to change, he took the necessary steps to implement change. Simple as that.

"I'm just worried about you," Max said, picking at a loose thread on the old sweatshirt she always traveled in. It was a present from him, the first piece of clothing he'd purchased for her after their mother died—for favorite-team day. Of course, it was too big and the wrong team.

But when she could finally fit it, she wore it until the letters faded.

"I'm fine, Max. Honestly. I joined a gym, I've added more green vegetables to my diet. By the time my next annual appointment rolls around, my BP will be back to normal."

Max blew out a shaky breath. She bit down on her lip, like she had something on her mind, like something was troubling her. And he always wanted to fix it.

Raising a child, being the father-figure to an impressionable tween girl hadn't been his ideal way to spend his twenties and early thirties. Garrett had worked hard in school and managed to graduate with minimal student loans without his mother's help. After completing his first year of law school, he'd received the news of his mother's unfortunate passing and dropped everything to move back to Houston.

The transfer to University of Houston Law had been fraught with many roadblocks and countless setbacks, but he'd been able to switch programs. His full-time law school program turned into a part-time program because he had to work to support them. And his three-year plan morphed into five hard years. He'd taken side jobs so Max could do extracurricular sports and attend residential coding programs in the summer, and he'd adjusted his own goals so that she could excel in hers. But they made it. And looking at her now, healthy and happy, he couldn't regret the sacrifices he'd made.

"G, maybe I should move to Atlanta after graduation."

He tilted his head, narrowed his eyes on her. "Why? The plan was Berkeley."

Shrugging, she changed positions, hugging her knees to her chest. "I don't know if I want to go that far."

His shoulders fell, because he knew where this sudden change in plans came from. The worry, the fear of losing him like she'd lost their mother. Even though he hadn't had a good relationship with Ma, he never disparaged her to his sister. He wanted to preserve the few good memories she'd had of Geraldine Steele-Pratt. "Max, no. You're not moving to Atlanta, not for me. I keep telling you not to worry about me."

Losing both of her parents in one night had been traumatic for Max, so he understood her reasoning. He also understood her desire to be close to him. After all, he was her only living family member. But he hated the thought of her changing her strategic career plan to be with him.

Despite all the odds against her, Max had graduated as valedictorian from her high school. She'd been accepted to every single college she'd applied to, and was awarded full scholarships from all but two of her top choices.

From the time she'd received her first computer, she wanted to be a computer engineer. He still remembered when she strutted into his bedroom at twelve and said she wanted to move to California so that she could work for Apple. Since then, she'd developed several apps and had plans for her own start-up company specializing in app development and design.

"No," he repeated, shaking his head. "You'll finish your undergraduate degree at Bama and go to Berkeley like we planned. Period."

Max sucked in a deep breath. "I'm still thinking, G. I'm just not sure right now. You always said I should follow my heart. Right?"

Every. Single. Time. His sister had perfected the art of throwing his words in his face. He couldn't argue with his own logic, especially when he believed it wholeheartedly.

Which is why he'd left his full life in Atlanta, law school, and Skye to go home and raise a scared ten-year old girl who'd just lost her entire world in a drunk driving accident. And he'd never regret that choice.

"Do you think you could make hamburger pie today?" Max opened the refrigerator and started putting away groceries. Since he still didn't have his car, he'd had groceries delivered.

"Is that healthy?" he asked, with a smirk. "Because all that greasy meat and cheese can't be good for you."

Max shot him a sidelong glance. "Don't do me like that." She giggled. "I will grant you a cheat day if you make me a hamburger pie."

He wrapped an arm around her shoulder and squeezed. "I got you, Max. I bought everything I need to make it for you."

Max did a fist pump. "Yes! I can't wait."

Garrett wasn't a chef, like Duke, but he could make a few things. He'd had to learn fast when he moved back to Houston. Starting with simple recipes from an old book his mother had, he'd worked his way up from boxed macaroni and cheese with chicken tenders to casseroles to sautéed shrimp with lemon butter sauce over linguini noodles. Eventually, she'd picked up an interest in cooking and surpassed him in skill. But he still enjoyed cooking for her.

They finished putting away groceries in silence, while the television played in the background. The Sugar Bowl would come on in a matter of hours and he wanted to be done with dinner before it started so they could relax.

Max pulled the mustard and mayo from the fridge. "Want me to make you a sandwich? You should probably eat."

The headache was gone, so he could actually think straight. Food sounded good. "That's fine. Cheddar cheese, mayo, and tomato. No lettuce."

She bumped his shoulder as she stepped up to the island where he was laying out the ingredients he needed for dinner. "I know, silly. Do you want your bread toasted?"

"Sure." He peeked at his vibrating phone. "Wait. No. Don't toast the bread."

Picking up the phone, he read the text from X. His friend had filled in several blanks during an earlier phone call. Like where Garrett's car was. Apparently, X drove Garrett home when he fell asleep on the pool table. *Not my best moment.*

Xavier and Zara planned to drop the car off on their way to dinner. He responded, thanking his friend, and set the phone down. Max's arrival that morning had kept him from thinking about last night and Skye. He was curious, though. The thought of calling her, just to check on her, had filtered through his mind several times. He told himself that it had more to do with his knowledge of her, of her propensity to overthink her decisions to the point of obsession. It had nothing to do with how warm she felt against him, how soft her skin felt under his fingers, how sweet she smelled, how she responded to him. How she'd *always* responded to him, like he was the answer to her prayers and her problems. *Nope, it has nothing to do with that.*

Max walked two plates of sandwiches and chips to the kitchen table, and took her seat. "I figured today could be a total cheat day. Tomorrow, though, we're on the treadmill in the morning."

Laughing, he joined her with two bottles of water. "I'm ready. When do you have to go back to school?"

"Next week." She bit into her sandwich.

"How was Christmas with Brianna's family?"

Max grinned. "Good. It felt good to be back in Houston."

His ex-girlfriend, Brianna, had played a major role in their lives when he moved back to Houston. They'd graduated from the same high school and she'd stayed in the same area to teach elementary school. Since she was Max's teacher, she'd stepped in to help him care for her when his mother died.

Rekindling their innocent teenage romance had been the furthest thing from his mind when he'd moved back home. Yet, after he'd witnessed the fierce bond between Max and Brianna, he'd given it a try. Needless to say, things didn't work out how he'd expected them to.

While Brianna was a beautiful woman, a wonderful, nurturing mother-type figure to Max, the chemistry was off. He would often find himself wanting to stay at work to avoid dates or canceling dinner at the last minute for various reasons. In the end, she'd ended the relationship, telling him that she knew he wasn't in love with her and she wanted to be free to find her true love. He couldn't fault her for that, and had wished her well. Now, she was married with two kids of her own.

"She's pregnant again." Max took a sip of water. "They're having another girl."

He smiled, genuinely happy for his friend. Because that's what they were. Friends. "That's good. Think she'll try for a boy after this?"

Max shrugged. "I don't know. I'm just happy she's happy. She's so cute with her belly."

"I bet."

"Why didn't it work out with you and Brianna?"

He eyed her with a frown. "I don't know. Why do you ask?"

She set her sandwich down and twirled the plate. "I guess I just wonder if you'll ever find someone that you can love."

Been there, done that. "I do love people. I love you."

Rolling her eyes, she said, "I know that. But if I'm going to move to Cali, I want to know that my big brother is good."

He let out a heavy sigh. "Max, one thing I want to make clear is my commitment to you following *your* dreams. I don't want you abandoning your plans to be here with me because you think I'm lonely." Even though he probably was. "The reason I worked so hard is for you. I wanted you to have choices, I wanted you to be able to go to college and not worry about anything but your grades. So far, you've excelled in everything, you've been such a joy in my life."

Reaching out, he placed a hand over hers and squeezed. "Don't worry about me," he continued. "My practice is exceeding expectations." The business generated from Pure Talent alone helped him pay his operating expenses and more. "I have friends." X and Zara were like family, and they'd spent a lot of time together since he'd moved to Atlanta. Not to mention, he had an entire network of Morehouse classmates that he kicked it with. "I date." Just not the woman he wanted to date. "I'm fine."

Max turned her hand over and squeezed his. Nodding, she sighed. "Okay, if you say so."

"Good. Enough about me. Tell me about you. Are you dating?"

She slipped her hand from his and shifted. "Um . . ." She scratched her ear. "I kind of have a boyfriend."

He blinked. “What?”

Max hunched her shoulders. “Yeah. I really like him, G. He’s such a gentleman. And he treats me with respect. He’s a nerd, like me. But he’s a nerd that likes football.”

Garrett held up a hand and she gave him a high five. “That’s half the battle.”

“His name is Damien. I call him Dame. I want you to meet him.”

He paused, sandwich midair. “Really? It’s like that. How long have you been dating?”

“Four months,” she mumbled, biting into a chip.

His mouth fell open. “Four months? Why didn’t you tell me?”

“Because . . . You’re G. I can’t talk to my brother about my sex life.”

“No.” He shook his head. “We’re not . . . You’re . . .” *Damn, my little sister has a sex life?* The urge to kill that nerd boy welled up inside him. “Are you sure you want to be having relations with anyone?” Because he couldn’t bring himself to utter the word out loud. Because Max needed to stay a virgin until she was married. No matter how illogical and unrealistic that was.

Max gave him an incredulous stare. “G, I’m not a vir—”

“Don’t finish that sentence. I get the point. Since we obviously can’t have a conversation about this, I hope you’ve talked to someone responsible about the particulars, i.e., protection. No little nieces or nephews anytime soon.”

“Of course. Brianna has always had an open-door policy about sex.”

Garrett swallowed. “Okay.” He nodded. They ate in silence for a few minutes before he asked, “Damien, though? That’s a pretty evil name. Who’s his daddy? I hope he’s not the devil.”

Max laughed. "G!" She shoved him playfully.

Shrugging, he said, "Hey, it's a legitimate concern. You've seen the movie. I'll beat someone's ass for you, but I'm no match for the devil."

Giggling, she shook her head. "I can't with you."

"Okay. Fine. If you're happy, I'm happy."

Max stood and hugged him tightly. This feeling . . . the unconditional love he felt for her made everything he'd had to endure worth it. Now that he knew she was okay, maybe he could concentrate on life. And love.

"I love you, G." She kissed him on the cheek.

"Love you, too."

Chapter Four

“How the hell do people go through life without knowing simple shit?” Skye shifted loose papers around and stacked files on Carmen’s desk. “Or taking care of easy things like writing down a phone number or creating a press release for a client. You will not believe some of the crap on this desk. Stuff that should have been taken care of weeks ago.”

“Do you need help?” Zara leaned forward and picked up one of the files. “Because this is straight bullshit. What I don’t understand is how she was able to cover for so long. Something had to fall through the cracks.”

Skye glanced up at her friend. “I don’t get it.” She tossed a stack of Post-its with doodles on them. Nothing of value, but they cluttered the desk. She needed to get organized so she knew what to tackle first. “This office needs to be cleaned from top to bottom. I’ll have Kyra set that up when she gets back from maternity leave. I don’t trust anyone else to manage that project.” Her boss’s assistant had recently had an adorable baby girl and was expected back in the office next week.

“Good.” Zara closed one of the white file boxes and wrote on it. “This is crazy.”

Carmen left a freakin' mess. They'd been there for two hours, sorting through stuff that didn't matter and trying to find things that did. Skye didn't know what she would have done without Zara. When she'd stepped foot in the office earlier that morning, she'd taken one look around and sent an SOS text. Her friend didn't hesitate, and got there in twenty minutes—on her day off.

"Is it weird that I've waited so long for this opportunity and I'm not sure I even want it?"

Zara peered at her, concern in her eyes. "Really? I thought it was something you've always wanted."

In theory, it was. Skye once thought that her life wouldn't be complete until she was the director of publicity for Pure Talent. Yet, recently she'd been feeling stifled in her current position. The more she worked, the more she realized she might want a little more freedom than Pure Talent offered.

"I thought it was," Skye said. "I don't know. Maybe I'm just in a funk."

"Maybe, but I don't think it would hurt to take this time to think about everything in your life, reevaluate your career as well."

"We'll see." Skye decided she didn't want to talk about it anymore. Chances were she was in a weird headspace because of the changes in her life. Or she could just be reeling from starting therapy . . . *and kissing Garrett.*

Zara opened the small refrigerator in the corner. "What time does your plane leave again?"

"At 9:20." Skye scanned a document and added it to the *Important Shit* pile.

"Are you sure you don't want to stay at my house?" Zara had chosen to maintain her residence in L.A. because she and X traveled there often for work and because her family was there.

"I'm sure. I'll just stay at the Beverly Wilshire. That's where Paige is hidden away right now."

Skye had already talked to Andrew Weathers, who represented the movie star. The woman, who'd continued to amaze critics and fans with her convincing portrayals and genuine kindness, was expecting Skye first thing tomorrow morning.

"This entire situation seems so out of left field," Skye mused. "It's not like we aren't equipped to handle requests such as these, but Paige has worked with Catherine for years. I wonder why she's not using Davis PR."

Catherine Davis ran one of the most successful public relations firms in the country. The woman had clout in the industry. It made no sense that Davis's firm wasn't running point on this. And, of course, Carmen's ass had been vague as hell on the particulars. *I can't stand that heffa.*

"It is weird," Zara agreed. "Did you tell your parents you were coming to town?"

A couple months ago, Skye's parents moved back to Los Angeles. Her parents had decided to retire in the next few years. They'd implemented several changes so they could do so comfortably, and that included returning to her childhood home. After working for years, putting in long hours and missing out on a lot of life, it was time they enjoyed themselves.

"I called them yesterday. Momma wants me to stay there, but I'd rather not."

Zara snorted. "Trust me, I get it. I love my mother, but she never understands work. She loves to interrupt me when I'm on calls or returning emails."

"Exactly." Skye fed several sheets of paper into the shredder. "There's also the fact that she loves to meddle.

Always up in my business." The older she got, the more her mother talked about having little grandkids.

"I swear, that's what mothers do best. Knowing Mama P, she'd be in your closet every day, picking out your outfits."

Laughing, Skye pointed at Zara. "You know it. She'd fuss about all the dark colors."

No one who'd ever met her mother would guess she ran a successful fashion empire off first glance. On a regular day, her mom could be spotted in oversized sweats and a huge sweatshirt, with a pair of gym shoes and a hat. But when it was time to go out on the town or attend a gala, Marisol Pia Starks knew how to dress it up. And she also knew how to dress people of all shapes and sizes.

Marisol P Fashions had been a powerhouse in the industry, and it was because of the vision of a four-foot-nine Filipina woman from Manila. Growing up, Skye remembered sitting next to her mother and watching her sew until her fingers bled. From the time she could hold a pen, her mother taught her how to stitch fabric.

Every first day of school, every last day of school, every dance, every minor event, was an opportunity for her mother to dress her. Back in the day, arguments about Skye's choice of color or cut, length or material were daily occurrences in their house. It was clear from an early age, they had different styles. But she was proud to be the daughter of such an accomplished woman.

"You know what?" Skye asked, tapping a pen on the desk. "I'm convinced my mother has some sort of secret power. When I called her yesterday, she grilled me about New Year's Eve, like she knew something happened."

"Are we finally going to talk about this?" Zara said, plopping down on the chair in front of the desk. "Because, oh God, it's past time."

Skye giggled. "What is there to talk about? It happened."

"After ten years, Skye!" Zara smacked her palms on her jean-clad legs. "What possessed you to do it?"

Shrugging, Skye replied, "It was an assignment from Sasha. She challenged me not to overthink one thing."

"Care to elaborate?" Zara leaned back in her seat and crossed her legs. She studied Skye for a moment. "Of all the things that you could have chosen, from olives in your potato salad to brown shoes with blue pants to *Martin* or *A Different World* reruns . . . you chose to kiss the man that you have treated like absolute crap since he arrived back in town."

Skye blinked. "What?"

"Seriously, Skye. Just admit it. You've been angry, mean, and downright bitchy to that man for years. Yet, when it's time to throw caution to the wind, do something impulsive, you kiss the hell out of him. Why?"

If Skye knew the answer to that question, she wouldn't be going to therapy. One of the reasons she'd decided to see Sasha was because she'd recognized that her behavior wasn't logical. Garrett hadn't broken her heart, he hadn't cheated on her and dumped her at the altar. *That had happened later.* There was no reason for her to be pissed at him.

"He's here?" When Zara frowned, Skye rushed to explain her thought process. "It's the only explanation I can come up with. He's here, and he's not with me." Skye leaned forward, resting her elbows on the desk. "Which is stupid, right? We had a past, an awesome friendship that turned into a once-in-a-lifetime love. But circumstances out of our control limited our time together. I should be okay with that. I should be grateful that I was able to bask in real love, even if it wasn't forever."

Skye stood and paced the room. "But I don't know what it is." She wrung her hands in the air. "Every time I see him, I feel sad." *Or horny.* "He walks in a room, looking so good, and I want him. I want what we had. Then, I get mad—at myself. Because I ended the relationship, I flipped out and made a rash decision, I let him walk out of my life without a fight."

"Hun, you were twenty-three years old. Give yourself a break. And for goodness' sake, give Garrett a break."

Skye let out a frustrated sigh. "I know. I get on my own nerves." She laughed. Then she cried. "And I'm crying," she announced with a hard roll of her eyes. "Again."

Zara walked over to her and hugged her. "It's okay. It's just me. I won't tell anyone. I promise."

She glanced up at Zara. "I feel like I suck for treating him that way. Transferring my anger at myself to him is the only way I've been able to see him and not either fall apart or beg him to have sex with me."

Zara laughed. "Girl! I thought I was a hot ass mess when I started falling for X."

"You were a hot ass mess," Skye said. "But I love you anyway."

"I love you, too. But you have to do better. It's time."

"That's why I'm working on me."

Her friend raised a questioning brow. "At therapy?"

"Yes," Skye told her with a nod.

"You mean, the session when you didn't talk?" Zara narrowed her eyes. "That therapy?"

Skye muttered a curse. "I can see I talk to you too much. Stop being right. It's not your turn."

"I'm just sayin'. Get your shit together. Use therapy for what it's intended. Talk. Then talk to Garrett. Who knows . . ." Zara walked around the desk and picked up a stack of files. "Maybe you can finally get some."

"Wow!" Skye balled up a piece of paper and tossed it at her friend. "Getting some on the regular does not give you license to play me."

Her best friend stuck out her tongue. "Trust me, good sex changes everything." Zara gasped. "How about you not overthink seducing Garrett?"

Skye would never admit that she'd had that same thought, so she simply said, "No. I'm working on me. I won't be 'getting any' until I'm confident I can have healthy sex."

An hour later, Skye walked into Sasha's office. "Hi. Thanks for seeing me today." She plopped down on the love seat, not the chair. "I have to go to California tonight and I wanted to at least talk about what happened on New Year's Eve."

Sasha smiled. "That's fine. That's what I'm here for. Just so you know, I'm available to meet via video chat."

"Really?" Skye knew that more and more therapists were conducting therapy sessions online, and she thought it was a good idea. Especially for clients who traveled a lot for work. "Good to know."

"Just send me an email if you'd like to meet while you're away. We can work something out."

"I appreciate that. I'll reach out sometime next week."

"Great." Sasha crossed her legs. "Tell me about New Year's Eve."

"Garrett," Skye blurted out.

"Who is Garrett?"

"He's the one who got away. Well, the one I left." Skye gave a brief explanation of her relationship with Garrett, focusing more on how it ended and skipping over a huge chunk of their relationship because of the time limitations.

"When his mother died, he had no choice but to be there for his sister," Skye explained. "Being in a relationship with me would have complicated an already difficult situation. Breaking up with him was the hardest decision I've ever made. I lost sleep over it, I second-guessed myself many times. I even changed my mind and went to Houston to tell him how much I didn't want to be apart."

"What happened when you went back?" Sasha asked.

"He never knew I came. I saw him with a close friend of his from high school. I knew from previous conversations that she and his little sister, Max, were extremely close. When I saw them together, I felt like I was intruding on the moment they were having."

Skye remembered that Sunday morning as if it were yesterday and not a decade ago. She'd flown to Houston, intent on telling Garrett that she'd made a mistake, that she wanted to work it out. But when she'd arrived at the house, she saw them in the backyard together. Max was actually laughing. After everything that had happened, the sweet girl had a smile on her face because she was with two people who meant the world to her. Suddenly, it felt wrong to interrupt that moment, to interrupt the little slice of peace they had in the midst of so much sorrow. Skye had made the decision right there to let him go.

Skye swallowed past the lump in her throat. "I did it so he could give her the life she deserved. And probably because I was young and the thought of being a mother-figure to a tween was overwhelming."

"That's not abnormal, Skye. A lot of women in that situation would have probably made the same choice."

Skye also told Sasha about the conversation she'd had with Zara earlier. "So, when you said to pick one thing that

I constantly obsess about and try not to overthink it, I picked him. And I kissed him."

"Really?" Sasha asked. "How was that for you?"

The answer to that question was the reason Skye had run away from him after the kiss. "I was scared shitless."

"That's understandable. Do you know why you chose to kiss him? As opposed to simply having a conversation with him about your relationship?"

What is with everyone telling her to talk to Garrett? "Honestly, I kissed him because I wanted to see if it felt the same."

"Did it?"

"No, it didn't." Skye let out a shaky breath. "It was better. Far better than I ever expected or even remembered."

"Garrett?" His assistant poked her head into his office.

After a healthy breakfast of oatmeal and a run, Garrett had decided to go into the office and take care of a couple of things while Max went shopping with a friend of hers. Later, they'd head to the movies to see the latest Marvel movie.

He took his glasses off. "Yes, Tara."

"Julius Reeves is here to see you."

Frowning, he checked his calendar. No appointment. "Did he say why he was here?"

"No, just that it was an emergency."

Julius Reeves was one of the hottest black directors in the industry. His movies were packing theaters across the nation, transcending race and gender. But it was common knowledge the man was hard to work with—and an unapologetic ladies' man despite his marriage to Paige Mills, Black America's Sweetheart.

"Give me a few minutes."

"Sure. If you don't need me for anything else, I have that appointment."

"Definitely." He waved her off. "Take off."

"Have a good afternoon."

Garrett did a quick search for news articles that would give him an indication of the purpose of this visit. It didn't take long to hit pay dirt. Apparently, Mr. Reeves had pissed his wife off with his ways. Vloggers were reporting about a possible split, and a brewing scandal. Suddenly, everything made perfect sense.

Standing, Garrett walked out of his office and greeted Julius. "Mr. Reeves. Good to meet you. Garrett Steele."

The other man stood up. "Good morning. Call me Julius."

They shook hands and Garrett immediately catalogued the type of handshake he'd received. Which often told him everything he needed to know. His undergraduate degree in psychology had taught him a few things that had helped him excel in his career as a lawyer, but it was Jax Starks who once told him to pay close attention to how a man shook his hand. In Mr. Reeves's case, the weak and rushed handshake alerted him that all was not what it seemed with the director.

Garrett noted Julius's attire—dark jeans and a plain long-sleeved shirt. Nothing that would help him stand out in a crowd. Which meant he wasn't trying to be seen. Paparazzi probably wouldn't be thrown off for long, though. No matter how low-key celebrities tried to be, someone always spotted them. Garrett had seen it plenty of times when he hung out with X.

"My agent suggested I contact you," Julius said. "I'm looking to hire a crisis management attorney and I hear you're one of the best."

"May I ask who referred you?"

"Sebastian Hunter."

"Ah, I know Sebastian. We've worked together on several occasions. Come on in." He led Julius into the office. Once the other man took his seat, Garrett sat down. "What can I do for you?"

"There's an investigation, which may culminate in criminal charges. One of the production assistants has filed a complaint against me. For sexual harassment."

Garrett sat back and observed the man in front of him. Over the past few years, the number of sexual harassment cases had tripled. And he'd been very careful about the types of cases he took. The last thing he wanted to do was defend a man guilty of violating any woman, even if it paid.

"The woman was someone I had an affair with," Julius continued. "Which is not something I'm proud of, by the way. I love my wife. I don't want to hurt her. I'm the first to say I'm not perfect. I've been unfaithful in the past, but we've been working on our marriage. We recently had a recommitment ceremony. I want to do everything in my power to make sure I protect her. She's not happy with the latest public scandal."

"Can you blame her?" Garrett asked.

"No, I can't. The news of the affair was damaging enough." He sighed. "But this sexual harassment complaint . . . I didn't do that. It was consensual. She was a willing participant in the affair. And now that it's over, she wants to claim it was harassment."

Garrett listened while Julius gave him more information about the case. As he talked, Garrett knew he was being fed a whole bunch of bullshit. Still, other than adultery, he couldn't say the man was guilty of anything else.

He'd learned the hard way that looking or sounding guilty wasn't the same as being guilty. A former pro-basketball star had behaved in a similar manner, resulting in Garrett refusing to take his case. In the end, the basketball player lost his career and his life, only for the world to find out later the man was innocent. That case still haunted Garrett. It changed how he conducted business, colored his interactions with potential clients, and made him check his own personal biases at the door. Julius deserved the same consideration, even though Garrett's gut told him the man was full of it.

"Why not hire a PR firm?" Garrett asked.

"I have. But I felt like I needed something else, someone else. A different type of support. Make no mistake, this is a crisis and I need an expert."

"If I hop on, I want to make one thing very clear," Garrett said. "I'm not a criminal attorney. I won't represent you in a criminal case. I'm willing to step in, help manage the media, work to save your brand, and try to salvage your reputation as a director."

"I understand. My next movie is releasing soon. There's a press junket, media requests, interviews, panels . . . Everything you can imagine."

"That's to be expected."

"My wife is the lead in the movie," Julius told him.

Shit.

"I'm sure I don't have to tell you how tricky these appearances will be if we're not getting along and if these rumors spiral out of control," the director added. "I'd like you to be on hand, at least initially, in case things get heated."

"That's fair. When is the first event?"

"Wednesday. In Los Angeles."

Garrett frowned. "That's tomorrow."

"There's a movie premiere and panel," Julius explained. "I haven't seen Paige in days. This is important."

Garrett opened his calendar. He'd purposely limited his client appointments in January so that he could spend the month planning his year. Tomorrow was clear, but Max was still in town. They'd just made plans to go to Skyline Park.

"That may not work for me," Garrett said.

"It's short notice, but this thing kind of came up suddenly. Otherwise, I wouldn't ask you to move around your schedule for me."

"I'll have to get back to you."

"I'm not trying to be an asshole, but I need to know if you'll be there. My team is waiting for the information."

Garrett clenched his jaw. "Give me an hour. Does that work?"

"That will work." Julius stood and handed him a business card. "This is my personal cell. I'll be waiting for your call."

Standing, Garrett walked his potential client toward the front door. "I can't guarantee anything, but I will let you know my status as soon as possible."

Julius turned to face him. "Thank you."

Garrett locked the door once Julius left. When he entered his office again, he immediately dialed Max.

"G!" his sister chirped. "I might have gone a little crazy at the mall. Thanks for the Christmas money."

Chuckling, he shook his head. "I'm glad I could help."

"What's up?"

He heard shuffling in the background and a child's piercing scream. "Where are you?" he asked.

"At the food court in the mall. They had an Auntie Anne's.

Had to get a pretzel dog. This kid in front of me in line is a spoiled brat," she added in a whisper.

"I hope you know you're not a good whisperer."

"I don't care."

"Listen, something's come up with work."

"Oh no! Are you canceling Marvel on me?"

"No. Maybe Skyline Park, if you don't mind." Garrett did a quick search for a flight on his computer and found a pretty reasonable one, leaving tonight at ten thirty.

"Shit!" she hissed. "I mean, shoot. Sorry." He wasn't sure if she was apologizing to him or the mother with the loud-ass kid. "I was looking forward to that. What happened?"

"New client." He jotted down the flight number on a Post-it. "If I take the case, I'd have to be in L.A. tomorrow."

"L.A.? Tomorrow? G!" she whined. "How long are you going to be gone? And can I drive your car while you're there?"

"Two words. Hell. No. You're not the best driver. And I don't know how long I'll be gone. Do you want to come with me?"

She screamed. Then apologized again. "Yes. Count me in."

He barked out a laugh. "Okay. Meet me at the house. I'll make the arrangements."

"Sweet! See you soon. Bye."

Garrett spent the next twenty minutes preparing a contract outlining the specifics of his representation. When finished, he contacted Julius and let him know he'd take the case. Due to the time constraints, they agreed to meet tomorrow morning to discuss the details and he emailed the contract draft for review.

Julius agreed to reimburse travel expenses for Garrett

and Max. And before the call was done, he'd received notification that Julius had already paid the retainer. Once he hung up, he purchased first-class airline tickets, reserved a rental car, and booked the hotel rooms.

While he packed up his laptop and a few client files, his phone buzzed.

Max: Can you send me $40? I need a Cali mani/pedi.

Garrett chuckled to himself. That girl definitely knew how to scam him. He typed out a quick response: Check your account in two minutes.

A funny Will Smith GIF followed next, with a line of heart emojis. Shaking his head, he finished his tasks, contacting Tara to let her know where he'd be and emailing his associate attorney as well.

Going to Cali wasn't on his agenda for the week, but he couldn't help but feel like the trip was a game changer for him. He just didn't know why.

Chapter Five

DIRECTOR JULIUS REEVES
FATHERED LOVE CHILD WHILE MARRIED TO
PAIGE MILLS—WITH ONE OF HER CO-STARS.
CAUGHT IN PASSIONATE EMBRACE
ON THE SET OF NEXT MOVIE.

"Fuck." Skye reread the headline on the tabloid site again. The turbulent flight to L.A. late last night was bad enough, but waking up to this shit was worse.

"What's going on?" Andrew asked, pulling her from her thoughts.

"Ouch, shit." She cursed the hot coffee in her cup. She'd been so desperate for her favorite blend that she'd tried to guzzle it down before letting it cool a bit. "Sorry," she grumbled into the receiver. "Give me a second." Skye switched her cellphone from one ear to another and told the barista at the hotel café to bill her room.

As Skye waited for the receipt, she skimmed the article quickly. The salacious pic that accompanied the news confirmed what she'd thought all along. Julius Reeves was a fucking bastard. *Asshole.*

"Listen, Andrew." She took one bite of her banana and tossed the rest into a nearby trash bin. *Too soft.* "I don't know what's going on with you and Paige, but you're going to have to push that shit aside. Did you see the latest? Secret babies, passionate kisses on some remote island resort . . . I'm up to my eyeballs in this mess, and she's been asking for you."

Skye rushed toward the hotel elevators as Andrew tried to explain his dilemma. At this point, she didn't care about anything he had to say. She just needed him there. The shit storm brewing was going to get worse once Paige saw the latest headline—if she hadn't already.

Glancing at her watch, she groaned. She was late. And she *hated* to run behind. "I want to say I understand," she told him, "but I don't. Just get here." Ending the call, she typed out a quick text to her assistant, asking her to send her everything she had on Heather Franklin. The little home wrecker might regret messing with Paige after Skye was through with her.

Yawning, Skye scrolled down her unread messages. She'd basically been up all night working, researching the film, and familiarizing herself with the different events and appearances surrounding the movie release. Paige was busy as hell, and Skye would have to be there every step of the way.

"Skye Light!"

She recognized the nickname and only one person had ever called her that. She whirled around. "Max?"

"Hi!" The young woman barreled into her, hugging her tightly. "I haven't seen you in so long."

What. The. Hell.

Max pulled away and grinned. "How are you?"

Skye scanned the immediate area. *Am I being punked?*

She met Max's waiting gaze. "I'm well. Just . . . surprised to see you."

"Me too."

Once again, she looked around and wondered if Max was there with her college friends or her brother.

"Are you staying here?" Max asked.

"Yes. I'm here for a few days. Are you in LA with friends?" Maybe she should have just come out and asked if Garrett was in town, but she couldn't bring herself to do it. Normally, she could handle multiple things at a time, but adding Garrett to the mix didn't bode well for her sanity—or her hormones. Because she'd dreamed of him, of them together, every night since that kiss.

"We're here for business," Max said with a hard nod.

We? Skye swallowed, absently dropping her gaze to check her outfit just in case the "we" Max mentioned included Garrett. The navy-blue belted jumpsuit and boots she'd chosen for comfort missed the mark on sexy, but she knew she might need to run at some point during the day. Literally.

"It's so good to see you." Skye smoothed a hand over her hair. *Damn.* While her hair wasn't messy, it wasn't fabulous either. "It's been too long."

"Yeah." Skye didn't miss the sadness in Max's voice. "I must have asked G to call you countless times after he moved back home. But . . ." She shrugged. "I even thought about calling, but I wasn't sure you wanted to hear from me."

And now she officially felt like an ass. One of the biggest regrets about her breakup with Garrett was Max. When they went their separate ways, contact with Max had ceased as well, except for the occasional spotting at an event. Which was a shame since they'd gotten to know each other well over the course of the relationship.

"I would have loved to hear from you." Skye grabbed Max's hand and gave it a gentle squeeze. "I'm sorry . . . it was just hard," she added softly. "But I did miss you."

Max shifted her weight from one foot to the other and flashed another brilliant smile. "Missed you, too."

Skye studied the younger woman, noting the subtle changes in her appearance. Max was dressed casually, in skinny jeans and a blouse. The baby face and chubby cheeks were gone, and she'd grown into her freckles and her hair. But she was as lovely as she'd been at ten years old. "You look beautiful."

"Thanks. I'm a computer engineering major at University of Alabama," Max offered.

Skye knew that. She'd kept tabs on the beauty in front of her through X. First dance, first date, high school graduation and the countless awards Max had won . . . she'd been privy to the details and couldn't have been more proud. Despite everything Max had been through, she'd grown into a wonderful and accomplished young woman. And Skye had been rooting for her from afar.

"Not too far from Atlanta," Max continued. "And now that G is there, I visit more. I always hope you'll come around."

"Well, let's make it happen." Skye pulled out a business card and handed it to Max. "Give me a call next time you're in town. And we'll get dinner, catch up."

"I'd love that."

"I'm sure you have lots to tell me. School? Boys?" Clearing her throat, she added, "I mean, men."

Max smirked. "There's a lot going on."

"And I want to hear about it."

There was a moment of silence before Max said, "I've never forgotten what you told me."

Emotion threatened to choke her as a conversation she'd had with little Max filtered through her mind. It had been years, but it made her happy to know that she'd contributed positively to Max's life in some way.

"I'm glad." The elevator door opened, but Skye didn't step into it. Even though she knew she should. Even though she was late as hell. For some reason, she couldn't bring herself to leave Max again. "Because you're gorgeous."

Growing up as a biracial child, Skye had struggled to feel comfortable in her skin. The pressure from other kids to identify as either Filipina or black had caused severe anxiety. She'd also had a hard time dealing with the fact that she'd never known her biological father. Unsure where she belonged, she hated her light skin and wanted to be darker like her adoptive father and her closest family members and friends who were all black. Then she went through a phase where she hated her height and wanted to be shorter, like her mother.

Max had endured many of the same struggles as the daughter of a black woman and white man. The young girl once confessed that she hated when people called Garrett her "half" brother. She said it made her feel like she might not have meant as much to him because they didn't share the same father. Skye's heart went out to her, even though she knew that Garrett had never treated Max as anything but his sister. He didn't place labels on family, and neither did Skye. Family was family. Still, Skye knew the struggle, she knew the pain and confusion.

"Thanks." Max gasped and pulled out her phone. "Let's take a selfie."

Max turned around and leaned back. Skye looked into

the iPhone and smiled right before the flash went off. Without prompting, they both made a silly face and Max snapped another pic.

Laughing, Skye said, "You'll have to send me those."

"I'm posting them to IG." Max busied herself on her phone, probably making good on her declaration to share the pics. When she was done, Max hugged Skye. "I'll let you go. I hope your coffee isn't cold."

Skye took a sip, and shook her head. "Nope, it's perfect. Don't forget to call me."

They hugged again and Skye turned to push the UP button for the elevator and nearly smashed her coffee cup into Garrett's hard chest. "Oops." She stepped back and held her coffee cup out a bit. *Can't drop that.* "Sorry."

"It's okay," he said, a soft smile on those full lips.

And, *oh God*, that man was fine. The years had definitely been good to Garrett Steele. "Hi," she breathed.

"Hello, Skye."

It was never a simple *hi* or *hey* with Garrett. There seemed to be so much more behind the greeting. And he'd always greeted her with warmth, whether she deserved it or not.

The elevator door opened, and a couple stepped out, hand in hand. She watched them walk away, wide smiles on their faces and love written in their body language. Swallowing, she glanced up at him. Skye was far from short at five-foot-eight, but he'd always dwarfed her in height. Whenever she'd go anywhere with him, she felt safe.

"Skye?" He raised a brow.

She blinked. "Huh?" She tried to cover for the fact that she definitely wasn't paying attention to anything he might have said. She was too busy ogling his six-foot-four frame, admiring the muscles that she knew were hidden beneath his slacks. "I'm sorry, can you repeat that?"

"I had no idea you'd be in Cali." His gaze traveled slowly over every inch of her, almost like he was undressing her in his mind.

"She's staying here, too," Max said, a wide, sneaky grin on her face.

"Um," Skye croaked. Taking a deep breath, she told him she was there for work. "And I'm late for a meeting," she added. Another elevator opened, but her feet felt bolted to the floor. "I should probably get that."

He stopped her with a gentle hand on her arm. "I think we have unfinished business. I let you run the other night, but I need five minutes of your time."

Oh my. So many things could happen in five minutes. In college, they'd perfected the five-minute afternoon romp in between classes. She felt a blush creep up her neck, and fought the urge to fan herself. Instead, she tugged at her collar.

"You can run afterwards if you need to," he continued with a wicked smirk. "If you want to."

That last sentence nearly did her in, made her want to invite him up to her room right then and there. But, um . . . Max. And Paige. And every damn thing else. Sasha's words replayed in her head. *Try not to think too much. Just feel it. Just do.*

"I'm going to grab a seat for breakfast," Max said, pointing toward the hotel restaurant. After another hug, Max hurried off.

Skye swallowed. Hard. The choice seemed easy enough. Work? Or possibilities? The answer should be work. She had bills to pay, she had a job to do. She came here for a reason.

Biting down on her bottom lip, she hummed. "Can we compromise?" she said finally. "How about three minutes? Because I really have to get to this meeting."

As if the universe seemed to sense the prospect of peace in her heart and mind, her phone buzzed. Shoulders slumped, she shot him an apologetic look before taking the call. After promising Paige's manager she'd be there in a few minutes, she ended the call.

Glancing up at Garrett, she smiled. "I'm sorry, I really have to go. I'm not doing this on purpose, but there's a fire and I need to put it out."

He nodded. "I understand. Maybe we can meet later, for a five-minute drink? A shot?"

The elevator opened once again and this time she stepped toward it, intent on getting on. But before she did, she turned to him. "Okay. Call me."

"One more thing," he said, inching closer to her.

Wrapping his arm around her waist, he pulled her to him and kissed her. The kiss wasn't simple either. It was loaded—with heat that melted her from within, with questions that needed to be answered, with promises that had yet to be made. It was more than attraction, more than this moment. It was everything.

She relished in the feel of his body against her, his tongue stroking hers, driving her crazy with need for him. *Oh, how I missed this.*

Garrett nipped at the corners of her mouth, licked her bottom lip and seared her with one last lingering kiss to her mouth. When he pulled back, Skye bit back a groan. Because she wanted to go with him, she wanted to cleave to him.

He brushed his thumb down her cheek and smiled. "Now we're even."

Skye stumbled back, tripping over nothing. Embarrassed, she braced herself on the wall and walked into the waiting elevator. She spared a quick glance at him over her shoulder, just in time to see the smirk on his beautiful and talented mouth.

The doors closed and she slumped against the elevator wall. At this rate, she might not make it out of Cali without having a conversation with Garrett—or an orgasm. And she actually looked forward to either or both of them.

Garrett stared at Julius, certain the disgust he felt was shining through the cool, calm demeanor he tried to show at work. The director had thrown a temper tantrum, kicking every person out of his suite before trashing it.

Scattered glass, tipped furniture, and tossed cushions surrounded him. Julius paced the room like a caged animal, while barking orders over the telephone to someone. Garrett hoped that person was an agent or a manager, someone that could come in and handle the man pretending he wanted his marriage to survive this latest scandal. Because Garrett didn't have to know Julius to know it was an act. The writing on the wall was clear, and had been obvious since the beginning of the ill-fated relationship. Various reporters and vloggers had covered Julius's wayward track record from the time Julius and Paige were spotted on their first date to the high-priced wedding to now.

The latest news of a love child and the possible existence of even more children from various starlets in the industry didn't shock Garrett. It only confirmed what he'd thought all along. The jury was still out on whether the director had actually committed a crime. But Julius Reeves *was* a perverted, sorry-ass muthafucka who only cared about himself.

The remnants of a coffee mug rolled toward him and he picked it up and set it on the table. Standing, he crossed to the other side of the room and poured himself a drink. The movie premier would start in a matter of hours and there was work to do.

"I've contacted Heather Franklin's people." Garrett took a sip of his cognac. "Her publicist agreed to meet with us."

Drinking on the job was a first for him, but it had been a hell of a day. And it had started so promising. The surprise run-in with Skye and the promise of five uninterrupted minutes with her had made his morning. The way Max's eyes lit up when she'd shared bits of their conversation had sealed his good mood.

Then, he'd arrived at Julius's hotel suite and was hit with new allegations of misconduct, new mistresses, and new damning evidence of wrongdoing. He'd spent the last several hours working with Julius's personal PR team to infuse positive press into the sea of negative publicity surrounding them. He'd reviewed contracts and nondisclosure agreements while making calls to several affected parties to try and set up meetings.

"I need to see Paige," Julius said. "I have to see her. I don't give a damn about Heather. I care about my wife."

Bullshit. "I understand that, but Heather is part of this film, too. Her presence tonight is bound to kick up more dirt."

"I don't care," Julius repeated. "I need my wife."

Garrett had already tried to contact Paige, but he'd had no luck reaching her agent. *Maybe* . . . Nixing the idea to call Skye because he suspected her presence in the hotel had something to do with Paige, he dialed Andrew again. This time he picked up.

"What's up, Garrett?"

"Nothing much, man. It's been a minute."

"Yeah, work keeps me busy."

"Same here." Garrett eyed Julius out of the corner of his eye. "Listen, I have a situation. Could use your assistance."

"What can I do for you?"

"I've been hired to represent Julius Reeves."

Silence.

"Can you help set up a meeting with Paige? So they can talk." Garrett waited another moment before adding, "You and I both know what will happen when they have to sit on that panel after the premier. If the press senses any unease, they'll pounce."

"The man doesn't deserve any time with Paige. Have you seen the latest?"

Garrett shot Julius another glare. Unfortunately, the director was too busy tossing back drinks to see it. "I have."

"Why should I convince Paige to meet with him?"

"Because we need to strategize. Whatever they decide to do after the premier and subsequent events surrounding the film is their business. But we need to contain this for the good of the film."

Drew muttered a curse. "I'm on my way to her now. I'll be in touch."

"Thanks, man."

Julius approached him, nearly empty glass in hand. "What happened?"

"Here's what's going to happen. If Paige agrees to meet with you, you're going to have to nip this anger in the bud. If Paige agrees to meet with you, you're going to give her control over the specifics. When to meet, where to meet, and what to discuss should be decided by her. You can't afford to piss her off."

Julius nodded. "Fine."

Garrett spent the next twenty minutes getting Julius ready to meet the press, coaching him on what to say and what to steer clear of in interviews.

"Is there anything else I should know?" Garrett asked. "Something that you haven't told me?"

Julius shook his head rapidly, his gaze shifting everywhere except where it needed to be. Looking at Garrett. "No, that's it. The other stuff, the babies and shit . . . that's a lie. There are no kids, no other women."

Garrett raised a brow. "None?"

Julius sighed. "None that have come out in the press," he clarified.

"How many?"

"Does it matter?" Julius walked away and poured himself another glass of cognac. "Just know that they won't say anything."

Garrett clapped his hands together. "Okay, let's start again. Just so you know, I don't really care about you as a person, meaning I'm not here to judge you and I don't have to like you. But if I'm going to do the job you hired me to do, I need to know what can potentially prevent me from doing that."

"She's not going to say anything," Julius insisted. "And it's over anyway. I ended it last year, before I got married."

"And there is no truth to the rumors of babies?" Garrett asked again. "Not even a possibility?"

Shaking his head, Julius set his empty glass down. "No."

Fuckin' liar. Garrett had learned how to spot a liar a mile away, just being Geraldine's son. His mother had lied from sunup to sundown about the tiniest things. She'd lied about his father, about Max's father, about the blue in the sky, about where babies came from. Any and everything she could have lied about, she did. The thing that often astonished him when dealing with his mother was that she believed her own lies. Even when called on it, she'd dig in and defend the lie. And there was no doubt in his mind, Julius was cut from the same lying cloth. Which also led him to believe he wouldn't be representing him much longer.

Instead of responding to Julius, Garrett walked away and gathered his things. He needed a break.

"I need to step out," Garrett said. "I'll call you if I hear from Paige's team."

Without another word, Garrett left, letting the door slam behind him.

Chapter Six

When Skye arrived at Paige's suite several hours earlier, she'd been met with silence. Despite the people in the room, there was no noise, no movement. Paige's assistant sat at the conference table working quietly. The makeup artist reorganized brushes and mirrors without a word. Everyone in the room was somber, taking their cues from the woman they worked for. That had continued for the last few hours.

If Skye needed to get on a call, she stepped outside. Andrew had done the same, exiting countless times to take care of business. She'd moved in silence, completing much of her work on her phone so the tap of her fingers on the keyboard didn't disrupt the manufactured peace Paige had insisted on.

She couldn't blame the actress. The hits kept coming, from different news sources. All of them pushing the knife of betrayal further into Paige's back. One vlogger broke the rumors of the love child, then all of them followed in quick succession, each story getting more and more outrageous.

Paige had sat there the entire time she'd been in the suite, reading the articles and listening to the podcasts on her headphones. Many times over the course of the afternoon, Skye wanted to talk to her, to ask her how she was doing. Even if the answer seemed obvious, it always helped *her* to know that someone cared, that someone genuinely wanted to know how *she* felt.

"Skye?" Paige's soft voice jolted her out of her thoughts.

Standing, Skye approached her. "Yes?"

"Thank you for coming to L.A. on such short notice. I really appreciate you."

Paige's reputation as a humble, kind actress had kept her relevant in the industry and a darling with her fans. Although Skye didn't know Paige well, she hated that the other woman had been treated so callously by someone who'd vowed to love and honor her through sickness and in health.

"Anything I can do to help you, I'm here," Skye said. "Do you need anything?"

"My husband had an affair with my publicist."

Skye schooled her features, tried not to snarl or cuss that asshole to hell and back. "Oh?"

"And I fired her."

All the pieces of the puzzle started to click. The "whys" and the "hows" made sense now. Paige needed Pure Talent's PR team because she no longer had her own. Because the person she'd hired to represent her, to help her, had betrayed her in the worst way.

"It was before we got married," Paige continued, picking at one of her fingernails. "But I just found out last week."

Whether it happened before or after made no difference to Skye. It still reeked of duplicity. Especially since Paige's ex-publicist had been married for the past eight years, and had recently given birth to a son.

Paige shifted in her seat, tucking her long legs under

her bottom. "And I can't understand why I'm unable to get over this."

Because you married a punk-ass muthafucka who can't keep his dick in his pants? Because there's all kinds of proof that he's never been faithful to you? Skye bit down on her bottom lip. She was there to do a job, to keep Paige's reputation intact.

"Would you be able to forgive?" Paige asked.

Hell. No. Skye shook her head. "I don't think so."

Peering up at her through thick lashes, Paige raised a questioning brow.

Sighing, Skye said, "I know the pain you're feeling, because I've been there. And I couldn't forgive him. I didn't want to forget the way he hurt me."

After Garrett, Skye had dated several men. But when she'd met Broderick Hall, she considered herself done with the dating apps and hookups. She fell hard and fast for the professional football player—or so she thought. And when he'd proposed, she'd accepted.

For months, she'd planned her wedding, oblivious to the warning signs. And there had been many. The late nights, the lies, the whispers, flew right over her head. She happily ignored even her own gut because she'd become so invested in the ceremony and reception.

The truth, though, caught her attention in a spectacular way, right before she walked down the aisle. The woman, the stylist she'd hired to dress the groomsmen, had given him special attention in the dressing room at the church. And she'd seen everything. She'd watched in horror through the cracked door. What happened next almost landed her in a jail cell, if not for X.

"How did you walk away?" Paige asked, pulling Skye out of the memory.

"I just did. But it wasn't easy."

Even now, Skye still felt the sting of his deception, of all her dreams going up in smoke. Every morning, she stared at the remnants of her criminal act in the mirror, the scar under her chin from her attempt to vandalize Broderick's prized '69 Shelby Boss Mustang. She remembered the anger that had flooded her on that warm June afternoon, and she hated him for taking her there. But mostly, she hated the fool she'd been for that man. That was the one and only time she'd ever lost control that way. *Never again.*

Paige's gaze darted around the room. Sighing heavily, she said, "I'm ready to talk to Julius."

"Are you sure you want to do this?" Skye kneeled in front of Paige, who was seated in a large recliner, and squeezed her hand. "Because you don't have to see him right now, you don't have to talk to him. Not if it's going to make you feel worse."

The actress met her gaze. "What am I supposed to do? I can't hide in here forever." Her eyes welled up with fresh tears. "He's my husband. We work together. There's an event today."

Skye dropped her gaze. She wanted to argue with her, she wanted to fix it. Even if that meant whisking Paige away for the night, premier be damned. "Okay, whatever you want."

Paige grabbed Skye's arm. "I'm sorry you experienced this pain. I wouldn't wish it on anyone."

Nodding, Skye placed a hand on top of Paige's. "It gets better."

"The baby," Paige said. "I need to be sure it's not his baby. Can you find out more about it?"

"I'll make a few calls." Skye gestured to Andrew,

who exited the suite, presumably to contact Julius for a meeting.

Half an hour later, there was a knock on the door.

"Are you ready?" Andrew asked, walking to the door.

Paige nodded. "Let him in." Once the door was opened, Julius shoved his way past Andrew and made a beeline for Paige. She held up a hand. "Stop."

Skye tried to keep her eyes on Paige and Julius, but when Garrett stepped into the suite, she lost her ability to see anyone else. With wide eyes, she sucked in a deep breath. "Garrett?"

His gaze landed on her and he smiled. "Skye."

Unfortunately, Skye seemed to be the only one surprised by this turn of events. She stalked over to him. "What are you doing here?" she whisper-yelled.

"I'm with my client," he explained.

Skye glanced at Julius, then back at Garrett. "Wow. I would have never guessed."

"Honestly, me neither."

As much as she wanted to delve into his cryptic response, now was not the time. She steeled herself, switched back to business mode. Clearing her throat, Skye pivoted on her heel and approached Paige, who'd been eyeing Julius skeptically. "Julius?"

After a moment, the director looked at her. "Yes?"

"I want to start by asking you to please respect Paige's space, and listen to what she has to say before you jump in."

Garrett stood to the side of the stage, waiting for the cast panel to start. The movie premier had gone off without a hitch the night before, with Julius and Paige presenting a united front to their adoring fans and the swarming paparazzi. While they'd walked the red carpet, he'd worked behind the scenes to manage the press line, instructing all entertainment news correspondents and reporters to stick to the matter at hand—the movie.

For the most part, members of the press had respected the occasion and steered clear of unfavorable questions about personal troubles. But he'd stepped in a few times to move the couple along when some sneaky person snuck in an inappropriate comment.

Off to his right, Skye worked her magic, looking absolutely stunning in a cream jacket and black capris. Her long hair was pulled back into a sleek bun. Last night, he'd watched her handle her job with ease, offering strong support to Paige while simultaneously shielding the actress from everything that could hurt her.

Garrett didn't have his five minutes with Skye last night, but he planned to get them soon. After the premier, he'd returned to the hotel and spent the rest of his evening with Max. But today . . . he planned to make it happen.

The panel moderator stepped onto the stage and announced the cast, one by one. Julius joined them on the stage as well. The roaring applause echoed in the space as a video trailer of the movie played on the huge screen.

Garrett approached Skye. "Hey."

She turned. He half expected her to ignore him or offer a terse greeting, but she simply smiled and said, "Hey."

He eyed Julius and Paige, seated next to one another on stage. "So far, so good."

Nodding, she agreed. "Right? I was prepared for anything last night. Thankfully, I didn't have to kill anyone."

He chuckled. "Hopefully, we'll have the same luck today."

She glanced at him. "I'm trying to figure out how you're representing Julius. He's so guilty."

Garrett shrugged. Personally, he didn't care for the director. But he'd agreed to do the job because he thought it would be a challenge, an opportunity for him to tackle his own biases. "I have my doubts about him, but I'm not here to deliver a verdict. I *am* surprised Paige agreed to give him another chance, though."

"She loves him," Skye said. "She wants her marriage to work. Can't say I agree with her, but I'm here to do a job."

"Any luck talking to Heather's camp?" he asked.

While the young costar had walked the red carpet last night, she'd stayed far away from Paige and Julius. She also hadn't shown up for the cast panel that morning.

Skye pulled out her phone. "I actually talked to her this morning when I suggested she not attend the panel."

"That was you?"

"Yep," she said. "But it didn't take much convincing. She didn't want to be here."

"I can't blame her." The woman had been vilified in the press, and limiting her appearances would help the young actress in the long run.

"I don't think the baby is his, though," Skye admitted. "I think there's some foolery going on."

"Care to share?"

"Nope."

Smirking, he shook his head. "Had to try." A fan asked a question about the film's theme. "What did you think of the movie?"

Once again, Skye smiled. After all these years, her smile still had the power to knock him off his square. "I thought it was cute." She giggled. "But it's not *Star Wars*."

Garrett laughed. "It definitely wasn't that."

Before he'd met Skye, Garrett had seen most of the *Star Wars* movies. But he'd never called himself a hardcore fan. Sure, he'd enjoyed the action and adventure, but he didn't spend time thinking about the story once the movie was over. But Skye was a superfan of the original trilogy and the subsequent movies. She'd devoted hours to the movies, the comics, the books, and had even gone to several conventions. His attitude toward the science fiction series changed when he'd experienced it with her. After she'd dragged him to a marathon on campus one night, he'd walked away with a new appreciation for the series—and her.

"What can I say?" she said. "The Force has always intrigued me."

And she had always intrigued him. "I saw the last movie at the theater with Max." They'd seen it shortly after it released, and he'd thought of Skye the entire time. He always did when he watched one of those movies.

"It was well done." She grinned, her brown eyes gleaming as they always did when she talked about Luke, Leia, and the Force. "But you know I had some questions. So many WTF moments that kind of left me a little frustrated. At the same time, I couldn't be mad because this story has given me so much. When it was over, I cried." She giggled. "Because I didn't want it to be over, yet I knew it should be over."

As she talked, he thought about the last several years. Even though they'd seen each other at various events, he hadn't been this close to her since they'd broken up. The kisses were one thing, but to actually have a conversation with her was . . . priceless. Things had shifted, and he welcomed that change.

When he'd moved back to Atlanta, he'd hoped they could be like this, that they could get back a piece of their friendship. Now that he'd gotten a taste of how good they still were with each other, he wanted to push the fragile boundaries of the past to carve out a new future. Because he'd missed her. He'd dreamed of her voice, her smell, the way her eyes sparkled in dim lighting, the way she talked with her hands. He wanted more.

"Wait a minute," she said.

He blinked. "Huh?"

"I'm sorry, I just totally went off on a tangent. You probably didn't ask me that so I could go on and on about *Star Wars*."

That was exactly why he'd asked her. "No, I wanted to hear your thoughts about it. Maybe you can give me a five-minute review tonight?" Garrett was determined to get his time with her. They needed to talk.

Skye raised a brow. "Smooth."

He shrugged. "I thought so."

"You think you're slick, too. You know it'll take longer than five minutes to tell you all of my thoughts about the last Skywalker film and the future of the franchise." She made a wild hand gesture. "Despite all that annoyed me, that was a huge event."

"I agree with you," he said.

He wondered who'd gone with her to see the movie. *Did she have a date?* Because he was sure she'd been there opening day. He was certain she'd purchased her tickets months ahead, too. And he might be willing to make a bet that she took her light saber or her trusty Darth Vader–mask keychain with her.

"Well, I have several calls to make."

Nodding, he said, "Me too."

"I should probably get to it." Skye gave him one last smile before she walked away.

Garrett busied himself returning emails and working on contracts as the panel continued. Once he heard the announcer ask for final questions, he closed his laptop and packed up.

Skye stood near the refreshments table, her eyes focused on her cell phone and her fingers tapping furiously on the screen. He inched closer to her, hoping to get a few more minutes with her before Paige and Julius emerged and she left.

Garrett stopped at the table, picked up a bottle of water and a cookie. This time, she approached him.

"Tell me something," she said.

Turning to her, he motioned her to go ahead and talk. "What's up?"

"If you thought Julius was guilty, how would you handle that?"

Loaded question, loaded answer. "Why do you ask?"

She shrugged. "Did you know Heather's publicist is Paige's ex-publicist?"

Garrett wondered where she was going with this line of questions. "I did. Is there something I should know about Catherine Davis?"

He'd known Catherine for years, through his work with her clients. She'd always seemed competent, definitely someone who knew the business well.

Skye observed him over her glasses. She only wore them to read or work, and he'd always thought they were adorable in a naughty teacher way. "I'm going to need you to make sure Julius stays away from Paige tonight."

Frowning, he asked, "What happened?"

Skye dropped her gaze to her phone, pushed a button and held it up to him. He read the headline, and sighed. Apparently, Julius had been busier than he'd admitted to Garrett. It wasn't a surprise, but this latest revelation didn't bode well for the director.

He met Skye's gaze. "That's . . . interesting."

"You're not surprised."

Shaking his head, he shrugged. "Not at all."

The audience erupted in wild applause, signaling the end of the panel, and soon the cast members entered the backstage area.

Skye looked at him. "You got me?"

Garrett assumed she was referring to her earlier request to keep Julius away from Paige. "I got you."

"Thanks." She smoothed a hand over her hair. "I'll talk to you later."

"Five minutes?"

She smirked. "Garrett, do you really want only five minutes with me?"

Another trick question. The answer was no, he wanted way more than a few minutes with her. "I'll take what you give me."

Their eyes locked again and this time he was sure she understood exactly what he'd meant. Skye exhaled, and averted her gaze. "Garrett, I—"

"You bastard!"

Both of their heads snapped around just in time to see Paige deck Julius, sending him crashing into a row of chairs.

"Shit," Skye murmured, before taking off toward the melee and quickly whisking Paige away.

Garrett shook his head as disgust rolled through him. Not only did he have to handle the potential media circus surrounding his client and the latest headline, but he was pretty sure his five-minute opportunity had just slipped through his fingers. *Damn, Julius.*

Chapter Seven

"Maker's rocks, please." Skye smiled at the bartender as she took a seat in one of the leather bar seats.

After hours of damage control—not-so-veiled threats to reporters, calls to X and Uncle Jax letting them know everything would be fine, rescheduling appearances, and holding Kleenex for the distraught and heartbroken Paige—Skye was tired. And she needed a drink. Two drinks.

It had taken a while, but she'd finally felt comfortable enough to leave Paige's suite. She'd attempted to go to her own room, to sleep or even watch television. Instead of snoozing, she'd paced the floor like a caged animal. Instead of relaxing, she'd worked herself up into a slight state of panic, ticking off everything she'd done and could have done differently. It was one thing to be overwhelmed by work. Normally, she thrived under pressure. But today . . . today had been a different beast. Not only did she have to contend with Paige and her troubles, she had the added complication of working so close to Garrett.

Every second near him rendered her a little more open and a little less guarded. And she couldn't afford to let his charm, his smile, his eyes seep into her brain. What the hell was that intimate conversation about *Star Wars*? She was supposed to be working, not talking movies. And definitely not melting from the heat of his body near hers. If Skye hadn't been staring at Garrett eating cookies and drinking bottles of water, she could have prevented Paige from looking at her phone on her way off the stage. She would have stopped her client from losing all of her composure in front of countless people.

Maybe if she'd been focused on her job, she would have seen the headline earlier. The headline that had effectively ruined any chance of reconciliation between the married couple. JULIUS REEVES'S SECRET RELATIONSHIP WITH WIFE'S PUBLICIST REVEALED. The subtitle merely pushed the final nail into the coffin. DNA TEST PROVES POPULAR DIRECTOR FATHERED CATHERINE DAVIS'S CHILD.

The bartender ventured back over to her, drink in hand. He set it in front of her with a smile. "Will you be dining with us this evening?"

She tilted her head. He was cute—a little young, a little too short, and maybe too clean-cut, but . . . attractive. "What do you recommend?" she asked.

The bartender gave her a brief overview of the menu, pointing to several of his favorites. Finally, she settled on a burger with a large side of truffle fries.

"I think you'll like it," the bartender Jensen added, with a wide grin and a sexy wink.

"I hope so." She smirked. "If not, I will find you."

He leaned in. "I hope so," he said, his voice low.

Skye eyed the man, wondering if she could really go there. He was employed, which was half the battle. Hot face and body. But . . . *Who am I kidding?* She wasn't really attracted to the bartender. For years, she hadn't felt even a spark for any man. Nothing more than a fleeting look here or there. Nothing that prompted her to approach anyone. No one who made her want to get her groove on.

"Hello, Skye."

Her gaze slid over to Garrett, who'd just stepped up to the bar. *I take that back.* There was only one man that made her want to give in to her inhibitions, and he was standing next to her. The smell that was distinctly Garrett wrapped around her, squeezing her softly and filling her nose with hints of lavender and melon, black pepper and almonds. Male. He smelled masculine and sexy and delicious. *Damn, he smelled like heaven.* Closing her eyes, she exhaled slowly.

"Mind if I join you?" he asked. His voice was a low rumble that shot straight to her core and spread outward, turning her liquid.

Speechless, she motioned for him to sit. Because she couldn't think of a response other than a grunt or a whimper or a purr. She bit down on her bottom lip.

Garrett placed his order with the bartender. "How's Paige?"

How many drinks do I need to stop overthinking and start doing what I want? Skye took a sip of her drink. "How do you think?" she managed to say, glancing at his profile before tearing her gaze away. "She's upset. Hurt."

Jensen arrived with Garrett's drink and walked away without another word. Garrett tapped the bar top before he took a sip of his drink. "I don't doubt it." He leaned closer and Skye held her breath. "This won't go away, though."

Tell me about it. Distracting herself, focusing on her job, never seemed to work when she was sitting so close to him. Because all she could think about was him, when she knew she should be thinking about work. Only she knew he wasn't talking about the attraction building between them, threatening to zap her of her common sense and any shred of dignity she had. *He* was actually focused on his job. And she was focused on the way he licked his bottom lip before he took another sip of his drink.

Skye finished her whiskey in one long gulp, ignoring the slow burn down her throat. Whiskey was supposed to be savored, not gulped. She ordered another when Jensen strolled back over her way.

"You know that, right?" Garrett continued, oblivious to her inner turmoil.

"Of course," she murmured.

"We need to work together on this."

Skye was in trouble—trouble. She'd hoped to avoid this type of *alone* situation while she was there. Five minutes was one thing, but multiple interactions were . . . trouble. At the same time, she didn't want to discount him.

With a heavy sigh, she turned to him. "Garrett, my main concern is Paige. She doesn't want to see Julius, and I'm not going to suggest it to her if she's uncomfortable."

"I understand that, but she has an interest in this movie, too."

Skye thanked Jensen when he set another drink in front of her. Garrett was right. Paige did have a huge interest in the movie. The actress had a starring role as the heroine of the steamy romance, and she was also one of the producers of the project. Paige had been involved from the beginning, personally contacting the author of the book that was adapted for the film and convincing Uncle Jax to back the project. The movie had amazing buzz surrounding it, with early viewers and critics raving about Paige's portrayal of a woman torn between two very different brothers. Skye would hate for anything to dampen the public's enthusiasm.

"Fine, I can admit when you're right," she said.

"Really?" He quirked a brow, in that sexy Garrett way that used to—*still did*—drive her insane. "That's new."

Skye bit back a smile. Nudging him lightly, she told him, "Don't get used to it."

He lifted his hands up. "Okay, okay."

"Seriously, though. Paige has as much, if not more, on the line as Julius. I'm willing to work together, to coordinate, just through this release. After that, I make no promises."

"That's fair." He held out his hand. "Deal."

The whiskey she'd imbibed moments earlier had now settled low in her belly, increasing her internal temperature from warm to hot as hell. *Or is it him?* Skye eyed his outstretched hand, then finally slipped hers into his. "Deal."

Two hours and two more drinks later, Skye and Garrett were seated at a corner booth, near a huge window.

Skye laughed, shoving Garrett playfully. "Stop it!"

"I'm telling you, Yoda and Yaddle got busy and created Baby Yoda!"

"I'm not even going there with you," Skye said. "I will say that Baby Yoda is such a cutie-pie. I want one."

Garrett choked on his drink. "Cute? He's a little rodent."

"Blasphemy! He's a Jedi Master!"

"Original Yoda was a Jedi Master. We don't know what this baby thing is."

Skye hadn't laughed so much in a long time. After

she'd agreed to work with Garrett, they'd asked to be seated at a table so they could talk. The business part of their conversation had been a no-brainer, because they'd always worked well together. A bulleted list, a timeline of events, and a comprehensive plan of action going forward had been quickly finalized. After she'd typed out everything on her laptop, she'd sent him a copy via email and they were all set. Then the conversation had veered to one of her favorite subjects—*Star Wars.*

For the first time in weeks, Skye felt relaxed . . . happy. She giggled. "Whatever. You always did make fun of my Yoda love."

"Yoda is cool." He stretched his arm over the back of the circular booth. "Admittedly, I have to catch up on the new show, so I can learn all about it."

He talked about something important, something about the new *Star Wars* show. But Skye didn't hear a word he'd said. For some reason, she couldn't concentrate. Not with him leaning the way he was, not with his arm behind her. Close to her, touching her. He was warm and she was . . . blazing like an inferno.

Suddenly, she didn't want to talk about *Star Wars*, she didn't want to discuss Paige or Julius. No, she wanted to climb on his lap, rock into him, sooth the ache that seemed to be ever present when he was around.

"Skye?" Garrett frowned, meeting her gaze with his concerned one.

She blinked. "Huh?"

"Are you okay?"

She swallowed past the big-ass lump that had lodged itself in her throat. Knowing what to do in crisis situations was her specialty. But she was at a loss, torn between confessing her dilemma and deflecting. In the end, she decided to deflect.

"Garrett, I'm sorry," she blurted out.

His smile fell. Shifting away from her, stealing his warmth from her, he let out a slow breath. "Sorry? About what?"

"I'm such an asshole," she admitted. "I should have never treated you so badly. You didn't deserve it."

Garrett finished his drink, sat for a moment before asking, "Why did you?"

She shrugged. "I don't know. Well, I do know. I mean, I think I know." She rolled her eyes, annoyed with her own unorganized thoughts. "What I'm trying to say is"—she took a deep breath—"I know our breakup wasn't your fault. But I didn't count on it being so painful to just see you."

"But you moved on, you fell in love after me. You were engaged."

"Whoop-de-fucking-do," she muttered.

Garrett barked out a laugh. "Did you just say what I think you said?"

She waved a dismissive hand toward him. "Never mind." Averting her gaze, she toyed with her next words.

Garrett reached out and tipped her chin up. "What is it?"

"It's nothing. You're right. I moved on. It's not rational. I just couldn't seem to help myself."

"And now?"

"I don't want to be angry anymore." She let out a slow breath. "I want to be happy. And I realized that I can't be happy carrying so much anger."

"At me?"

"No. It was never you. It's all me."

Garrett studied her for a moment. And Skye melted

under the weight of his stare. What was he thinking? What was he going to do? Finally, he shifted, inching closer to her. "Thanks for apologizing." He rested a hand on top of hers and squeezed. "I'm glad we're able to talk about this."

Skye tore her gaze away from their hands. But she couldn't speak. She'd already made one huge step toward her healing tonight. Well, she'd made several just by talking to him, engaging with him.

"You kissed me," he whispered.

Her eyes flashed to his and her mouth fell open. Snapping it closed, she said, "You kissed me, too."

"Want to tell me why?"

"If you tell me why."

He chuckled. "You're not going to make this easy, are you?"

"That would be a no."

"Okay, then." His tongue darted out and he moistened his lips. And she followed the motion like a hawk would its prey. "I kissed you because I could think of nothing but your lips against mine, your tongue stroking mine."

Oh. My. God.

"I kissed you because you opened up a box on New Year's Eve. A box that I thought might be permanently locked."

Did he want to do it again? Because . . . *damn it.* She wanted to kiss him.

Garrett eased a little closer. So close their knees bumped under the table. Too fucking close for her to think coherently. His gaze dropped to her mouth. "I kissed you because your lips are so perfect, so ready to be kissed."

Oh shit. Now I'm wet.

"I want to kiss you again. I want to kiss you so long and

so hard and so deep that you forget about the past and the future."

His intense gaze served its purpose—to make Skye extremely nervous, somewhat uncomfortable, and horny as hell.

"Garrett," she moaned. "You can't—"

He placed his forefinger over her mouth. "Don't." Garrett leaned in and brushed his lips over her cheek. But that one cheek kiss felt more sensual, more potent than anything she'd felt in years.

Skye clenched her hands into fists, willing herself not to touch him. Because if she touched him, it was a wrap.

Garrett pulled back, pinned her with his heated stare. Those brown eyes that always seemed to see something deep within her, something that she'd tried to hide from everyone else. Those same brown eyes that lulled her into a heightened sense of arousal.

He smirked. "Your turn."

Life hadn't been easy for Garrett. He'd learned to move in silence, show little emotion, and never let sentiment stop progress. Growing up, he'd felt like he was in perpetual darkness, burdened by a scheming mother who hadn't shown him much love. For a long time, he thought he was cursed, doomed to never feel love or be loved unconditionally.

When Max was born, he'd been filled with the enduring and protective love a brother had for his little sister. And when he'd gone off to college, he'd opened himself up to genuine friendship, brotherhood—with X and with his fraternity brothers. But when he'd met Skye, she'd transformed him, introduced him to soul snatching, unconditional romantic love.

The idea that he could love someone so completely, in a way that made him a better man, had changed him. It was a selfless kind of love. He respected her, protected her, loved every piece of her.

When they broke up, it felt like he'd died, like a part of him had withered away into nothingness. Since then, he'd chased that feeling, knowing he'd probably never experience it again. Because the women he'd dated weren't Skye. They didn't have her smile, her sense of humor, her intelligence. They weren't her.

Now he was face-to-face with the woman who'd given him a glimpse of how perfect true love could be. Their five-minute drink had turned into hours of conversation. She'd actually apologized to him for treating him like he didn't matter, like *they* didn't mean anything to each other. And Garrett didn't want to walk away from the chance to recapture what he thought was lost to him. He didn't want to.

That's why he'd taken his shot, figured he'd appeal to the attraction sparking between them. That's why he'd told her the truth of what that kiss had done for him. Because he wanted more, he wanted her.

It had been a few minutes since he'd hit her with his feelings. In that time, she'd stared at him. She didn't speak, she didn't smile. She'd just stared, her eyes wide, her lips parted. She was so beautiful, so perfect. He couldn't help himself. He had to touch her.

"Skye," he whispered, brushing his fingers over her cheek. Her eyes fluttered closed. "Open your eyes."

Her brown eyes popped open.

He smiled. "Your turn," he repeated, fighting against

the overwhelming urge to pull her closer, to kiss her, to do more than kiss her.

"My turn?" she breathed.

Nodding, he tucked a strand of her hair behind her ear. "Yes, Skye."

Skye bit down on her lip, then released it. "Homework."

Frowning, he asked, "Homework?" Garrett struggled to put the pieces together. *Are we still talking about the same thing?*

"You asked why I kissed you. Homework."

"Like an assignment?"

"Exactly."

Garrett scratched the back of his neck. "From who?"

She shot him a wobbly smile. "My therapist."

"Oh, okay." He nodded—and smiled. Because that's what people did when they didn't really understand but wanted to come off like they got it. "Your therapist told you to kiss me?"

"Yes."

Garrett didn't know whether to be offended or grateful. He'd never heard of that type of homework assignment before. Then again, he'd never actually gone to therapy himself.

She squeezed his arm. "Well, no. It's not like that."

"What is it?"

"I'm seeing a counselor. We were talking about me and my penchant for overthinking everything. I feel stuck because I waste so much time obsessing about stuff. It's something I want to work on because I don't want to do that anymore."

"Okay."

"So, she gave the task of not overthinking the one thing

I always overthink," Skye continued. "You're *that* thing for me. I came to the New Year's Eve party with every intention of following her instructions. And I kissed you. Because that's what I wanted to do."

Smiling, he contemplated the soft confession. He hadn't expected that answer, and admittedly, still had questions. At the same time, he wanted to send her therapist a thank-you note for assigning good homework. Shit, he wanted to know what the next assignment would be.

"Garrett, I hope you don't think this was some sort of joke. It wasn't."

"No, I don't think that. I do have a question."

"What is it?"

"Why do you overthink me?" he asked.

Skye shrugged, pulling at her sleeve. "I don't know. I just do."

Garrett wanted to ask her more, push deeper. But he could sense it wasn't the right time or place to delve more into this. He didn't want to mess up the goodwill they'd just built. The fact that she'd thought of him, that he was on her mind, was enough for him. They could work on the rest later.

Glancing at his watch, he said, "It's getting late. I'll walk you to your room."

They left the lounge and headed to her room. On the way, they talked about polite, easy things like the weather and gardening. Skye had always wanted her own garden, and he was glad to hear that she'd realized that dream.

"I'm going to get some of those tomatoes, right?" he asked as they approached her door.

"Sure, I'll package them up real nice for you." She

pulled out her keycard. "Thanks for walking me back to my room. But you didn't have to."

He inched closer. "Yes, I did."

Skye's gaze dropped to his mouth. "You always were a gentleman."

"I'm not feeling like one right now," he murmured.

"Why?" She leaned back against the door. "What do you want to do?"

Garrett traced her bottom lip with his thumb, brushed her jawline with his fingers, enjoying her quick intake of breath. "This."

He pulled her to him, crashing his lips on hers. Garrett wanted to possess her, brand her as his with every nip, every lick. Her low moan spurred him on, egged him to keep going. But he reluctantly pulled back, resting his forehead on hers.

"Skye?"

"Yes," she breathed.

He ran a finger over her earlobe. "You never have to overthink anything when it comes to me. You know me."

"I do know you."

Unable to stop himself, he took her mouth in another kiss. Resting his hand against her chest, he reveled in the feel of her heartbeat against his palm, the way it beat in time with his. Every part of him wanted to wrap himself around her, sink inside her.

"Are you overthinking it now?" he asked.

She gripped his collar in her hands "Hm . . . Maybe." She giggled. "Okay, no. I'm not." Skye brushed her lips over his chin, his cheeks, and finally his mouth. "Come in."

"If I come in, I'm not leaving anytime soon."

Raising a brow, she whispered, “I don’t have a problem with that.”

Shit. He closed his eyes, took a deep breath. “We probably shouldn’t. Not tonight.” He kissed her forehead, inhaled the sweet scent of her shampoo. “I better go.” Pulling back, he took in her swollen mouth, her hooded gaze.

She grinned up at him. “Okay, if you insist.”

“I’ll talk to you tomorrow.”

Skye nodded, turning and unlocking her door. She turned back. “Have a good night, Garrett.”

A moment later, she was gone, safely inside her room. Away from his hands, his lips, his desire. As much as he wanted to do more, though, he knew she wasn’t ready to cross the line. And if he was being honest with himself, he wasn’t either.

Chapter Eight

"She's a beauty, man." Garrett picked up his goddaughter, Mari, and kissed her brow. The baby gifted him with a delighted grin.

"Thanks, bruh." Patrick smiled, the love he felt for his daughter evident. "She looks like me."

Garrett snorted. "Keep telling yourself that." He brushed his finger down Mari's nose. "She looks like one of her parents, but it's not you."

"Ah, you got jokes."

Garrett never left L.A. without seeing his friend, his fraternity brother. Patrick Harrison had been on the West Coast for several years, leaving his home state of Georgia for the hills of California. When Garrett told Patrick he was in town, they'd agreed to meet for breakfast at the hotel before he took Max to Universal Studios.

Garrett and Patrick met at Morehouse, during his second year when he'd decided he wanted to join a fraternity. Patrick was a fourth-year student at the time. Meeting new people had never been easy for Garrett, probably because of his childhood and the simple fact that most people had disappointed him in some way. Aside from his friendship with X, he'd been a loner on campus, preferring to study alone or chill by himself. But Patrick had proven to be a true friend.

They'd seen each other through good and hard times, celebrating unbelievable wins and mourning unimaginable losses. Through the loss of parents and siblings, girlfriends and dogs, they'd supported each other. He'd shared things with Patrick that he hadn't told another living person, and never doubted his boy would take those secrets to his grave. When he'd decided to pledge his fraternity, it was Patrick who'd sponsored his bid and helped him through the initiation process. It was also Patrick who'd given him rent and grocery money when he'd fallen on hard times. Not a loan, but a gift. Garrett had never forgotten that.

"I can't believe I'm someone's dad," Patrick mused.

Garrett puffed out his cheeks and made a face at the squirming nine-month-old. "I can't believe it either. Sometimes God does have a sense of humor. Hope you're prayed up for her dating years."

Patrick groaned, pulling a cloth diaper out of the backpack and handing it to Garrett. "Man, sometimes I stare at her and hope she doesn't meet someone like me."

Laughing, Garrett cradled the baby in his arms and rocked her, accepting the bottle his friend held out to him. "Tell me about it." He teased the little doll in his arms a bit before letting her finally latch on to the bottle. "Hard to believe you're the same person who took three different women to the scholarship ball."

Patrick had been the ladies' man of their fraternity. It wasn't uncommon for him to juggle multiple women at one time, sometimes in the same twenty-four-hour period.

"Yeah, that was some shit right there." Patrick fist bumped Garrett. "As much as I enjoyed my time on campus, though, I can't say that I miss it."

Garrett eyed his friend. "Not even a little?"

Shaking his head, Patrick waited until the waitress set down a large glass of orange juice in front of him. "Not at all."

A few minutes later, they were eating.

"You can put her down, man," Patrick said, motioning to Mari, who was happily gumming her fist.

"She's good. I can do two things at once."

"What's been going on?" Patrick cut up his pancakes in neat squares, then poured syrup over each square. Garrett never understood why his friend felt compelled to spend so much time preparing his food before he ate it. In college, they used to joke that everyone would be done eating before Patrick even took a bite.

Garrett chuckled, shaking his head. He'd finished his eggs and Patrick was still setting up his plate.

Patrick glanced up at him and paused, fork midair. "What?"

"Nothing, bruh," he grumbled. "I guess it makes sense that you're even slower in your old age."

Glaring at him, Patrick waved a dismissive hand. "Shut the hell up. If I'm old, you're old."

"I'm not the one knocking on forty."

"You're not that far behind me," Patrick retorted. "You know, if you would have told me you were coming sooner, I could have put a few slabs on the grill or something. You haven't seen the new house yet."

Garrett hadn't seen Patrick since the christening several months ago. And even then, he was in and out the same day because of a work conflict. "Look at you, family man. New house, new baby. I have to say I'm proud of you. But I don't want none of those burnt ribs you swear taste gourmet."

Patrick pointed at him. “Don’t play me. I’ve improved tenfold since I left Atlanta.”

Chuckling, Garrett shook his head. “Whatever you say. I might have to ask Ebony to confirm that before I taste anything you cook.”

Everyone had been rendered speechless when Patrick sent out the word that he’d met the future Mrs. Harrison. All the way up until the wedding, there had been a secret bet that his friend wouldn’t make it down the aisle. Garrett was ashamed to say he’d wagered on the runaway-groom scenario. Imagine his surprise when Patrick not only showed up for the wedding, but had recited heartfelt, emotional vows to his wife. And five years later, Patrick had never given any indication that he’d regretted the decision to marry. In fact, the two seemed more in love than they had been that hot August day.

Garrett told Patrick his reasons for the impromptu work trip, leaving out much of the details. The only reason he’d shared his client’s name was because it wasn’t a secret anymore. After the melee at the cast panel, Garrett had to address the press himself when a snapshot of Julius crashing into the row of chairs was leaked to the press. Thankfully, no photographer had actually caught Paige delivering the blow. That would have ramped up the coverage even more.

“I’m surprised you took the case,” Patrick said.

Garrett had asked himself the same question many times since that weird-ass meeting in Atlanta. So much so that he’d almost quit at least two times since he’d arrived in Los Angeles. It wasn’t like he needed the money. He didn’t even need the contacts or the publicity for his firm. Steele Crisis Management had amassed a slew of corporate and celebrity clientele who paid him very well for his services.

Shrugging, he peeked at his goddaughter, who'd fallen asleep in his arms. He smiled down at her, ran a finger over her chubby cheeks. "I took the case to challenge myself. I knew that asshole was full of shit from the beginning, but I didn't want to let my judgment cloud my objective review of the case. Remember I did that with Matthew?"

"I remember," Patrick said.

"And look what happened."

"I also remember that being one of your first cases," his friend continued. "Since then, you've represented countless individuals. Man, you should never discount your gut. It's done you a lot of good in your life."

Garrett couldn't argue with that logic. His gut had prevented him from a lot of calamity, especially when his mother was involved. He was also smart enough to know that his mother and her lack of good qualities had impacted his ability to deal with people who reminded him of her. Matthew and Julius definitely had Geraldine-esque qualities. While Matthew was innocent, Julius seemed guilty as hell.

"True." Garrett sighed. "I just shouldn't have done it. But I can't say that I regret it now, though."

Patrick raised a questioning brow. "Care to elaborate?"

"Would you believe Skye represents Julius's wife, Paige?"

"Skye Palmer?"

Garrett nodded slowly. "The one and only."

His friend leaned forward. "How is that?"

Visions of her lips on his, her body pressed against his, floated through his mind. After he'd left her last night, he'd had to take a long, cold shower. It hadn't helped. And he'd been forced to take matters into his own *hands*.

"Actually"—he bit down on a piece of bacon—"it's pretty good."

Patrick smirked. "I take it you're no longer on the receiving end of her ire?"

"Something like that." The baby whined a little and he shifted her to his other arm. She finally settled down. "But I'm wondering how things will be when we get back to Atlanta."

"Do you think she'll change? The Skye I remember isn't fake like that."

Although he wouldn't say Skye and Patrick were close friends, they'd traveled in the same circles for years in Atlanta. "True."

"The question is how does this new Skye development impact your life? Are you thinking of a reconnect?"

Garrett thought about the question. Reconnecting with Skye had the potential to tilt his life on its axis. As much as he wanted her, as often as he'd dreamed of being with her again, he couldn't be sure if he was walking a tightrope over grainy cement. The first breakup had left him a shattered mess. And he'd had to pick up the pieces, one jagged edge at a time, in order to be the big brother Max needed.

Of course, he was in a better position now, but did he want to just hand over his heart to her again? Because that's what any interaction beyond polite conversation would lead to. He wasn't stupid. He knew what was up. Starting anything with her, even under the guise of just sex, would set off a chain reaction that could destroy him or restore him. The latter would be great, but the former . . . could he take the chance?

"Bruh, listen," Patrick said. "You're not the same person you were when your mom died. Both of you were young, there was the added emotional aspect of your mother leaving this earth and you stepping up to raise your sister. If you're thinking of all the reasons why it didn't last, don't. Maybe this is a chance to make it right?"

Garrett stared down at Mari. She was so innocent, so unaware of life's challenges. He hoped she never felt the sting of abandonment or heartbreak, but knew he couldn't guarantee that would never happen.

Sighing, he looked at Patrick. "I don't know."

"But you'll try anyway," his friend said. "It's not in you to not at least try. The problem will be convincing her."

Garrett snickered. "That's the truth."

"Uncle Patty!" Max walked over to them and hugged Patrick. She plopped into an empty chair and stole one of Garrett's strips of bacon. "I'm sorry I couldn't join you. I'm in L.A., and I have to dress L.A."

Patrick smiled at Max. "Look at you. Becoming an adult and all. I remember when you ran around with braids and braces."

Max ducked her head. "Don't remind me of my awkward days." She slid Garrett's plate away from him and spread grape jelly over a piece of toast. "Hope you didn't still want this." She grinned and bit into the bread.

"If I did, would it matter to you?" Garrett asked. "You could have texted and asked me to order you something."

"I could have." She nodded. "But I forgot."

Patrick barked out a laugh. The baby stretched in Garrett's arms and her eyes popped open. He lifted her in his arms and peered into her eyes. He nuzzled her belly, making a growling sound. Mari squealed in delight. He continued to do that while Patrick quizzed Max about school.

When they finished eating, Max stole Mari from Garrett and broke out into a jazzy "Itsy Bitsy Spider" rendition. Mari ate up the attention. Once they settled the bill, they exited the restaurant and headed toward the door.

"It was good to see you, bruh." Patrick gave Garrett a man-hug. "Next time, you have to come on out to the house. Ebony would love to see you both."

Max cooed at the baby, placing tiny kisses on Mari's plump cheeks. "She's so adorable."

Garrett reached out, Mari held up her hands, and he scooped her up. "Yes, she is."

Max leaned forward and kissed Mari's palm. "G, you look very comfortable with the baby. Just sayin'. Right, Uncle Patty?"

Patrick lifted Mari out of Garrett's arms. "I was thinking the same thing." He put Mari's little jacket on her. "And he's getting old, so it's time to start thinking about potential baby mommas."

Max laughed. "Right? I've been trying to tell him."

Garrett shook his head. "Nah, that's a long way off." He paused when he spotted Skye walking into the restaurant. He briefly wondered what it would be like to have Skye as the mother of his child, seeing her belly full with his child. Would their baby have her eyes? Shaking his mind free, he tore his gaze from the entrance of the restaurant, where she'd disappeared.

"No babies in my immediate future," he mumbled.

Garrett had just graduated from five minutes to several kisses. Getting Skye to agree to a date was his next challenge. *And I'm definitely up for it.*

* * *

Skye had dragged herself out of the bed, showered, dressed, and made a beeline for the restaurant. Today, she'd planned to lay low, catch up on her other work, and relax while Paige took a day to herself.

She sniffed the blueberry muffin in one hand and then took a whiff of the coffee in the other. *Heaven.*

"Skye Light!"

Skye froze and turned just in time to see Max waving at her from the other side of the lobby. She waved as she rounded the corner toward her. But she wasn't alone. Standing next to her, looking like a beautiful, chiseled masterpiece in dark jeans and a long-sleeved shirt, was Garrett.

His eyes locked on hers. Even from that distance, his gaze unnerved her. Flustered, she nearly took an L in the hallway. Thankfully, she'd remained upright. But her coffee . . . It wasn't as lucky as it slipped from her grasp and splattered on the floor. Shit.

She bent low and tried to wipe up the spill with those small napkins she'd grabbed. Stupid cocktail napkins served no other purpose but to look cute on a cake table at a wedding or a kid's birthday party. Then, as if her heart hadn't just cracked into two at the loss of her cup of coffee, her muffin tumbled out of her other hand and rolled to a stop at a pair of crisp Nike Air Force 1s.

Then Garrett was staring at her with those dark pools of liquid chocolate he called eyes. And he didn't come alone, he'd brought big napkins, the ones that did a job well. Smiling, he handed her a few and helped her sop up the mess.

Once they finished, he stood and helped her up. With a smirk, he said, "I'm sorry about your muffin—and the coffee."

Skye let out a shaky breath. "Thanks. I really wanted that muffin." And the coffee.

"I'll get you another one," he rasped. She slowly realized that his voice had the same effect the coffee would have. Warm and delicious.

Her gaze dropped to his lips. "You don't have to."

"What if I want to?"

Eventually, it registered to her that they were having entirely too obvious eye sex in the middle of the hotel lobby. So she averted her gaze and pretended to straighten her . . . Hell, she didn't have anything to straighten except for her wayward thoughts. *Good luck with that.*

"Skye Palmer," another male voice called to her.

Turning, she squinted her eyes at the dark-skinned man walking toward her with a cutie-pie baby in his arms. "Patrick Harrison?" She hugged him. "How the hell are you?"

He grinned. "I'm good. How are you? You still look the same. Gorgeous as always."

She smoothed a hand over her hair. Once again, she'd been caught on a less than stellar hair day. But at least she'd managed to run a comb through her curls. She slid another gaze over to Garrett, who was watching her intently, deliberately. *It's hot in here.*

"Thanks, Patrick." She smiled at the baby, who was playing peek-a-boo with Max. "And who is this?"

"This is Mari."

Skye picked up the little girl's hand. "Hi, Mari. You're such a little cutie-pie." Baby Mari looked down at her and giggled before dropping her head on Patrick's shoulder. "And she's so happy."

Unable to help herself, she tickled the baby's tummy. Skye loved kids and had once announced she'd have no less than four. A wave of sadness threatened to dampen her mood and she willed it away.

"How is Ebony?" she asked.

"She's good. I was just telling Garrett that the next time he's in town, he should come over. That invitation applies to you, as well. Ebony would be excited to see you."

"I would love that. Tell her I said hello."

"I will. Listen, I better get out of here. I have some work to do myself."

Patrick gave Garrett one of those secret handshakes she'd always wondered about, kissed Max on the forehead, and waved at Skye before heading out.

"Wow, Patrick Panty-Man Harrison is a dad?" Skye shot Garrett an astonished look. "Who would have thought?"

Garrett laughed. "I just teased him about that today."

"His daughter is beautiful, with those puffy cheeks." She moved a strand of hair from her face and peered up at him. The damn hair fell back, and he tucked it behind her ear. "Thanks."

"So, we're going to Universal Studios," Max said, a sneaky grin on her face. "Want to come?"

Garrett nodded. "Yeah, if you're not doing anything. Join us."

She really could use a few hours out of the hotel, to take in the sun and do something fun. *Hey, that rhymed.* "Sure," she said.

"Sweet!" Max said.

Skye looked down at her outfit. The jeans were okay, but

the silk blouse and boots would not work at an amusement park. "I should probably change."

Smirking, Garrett said, "I agree. Do that, and I'll get you a new coffee and a fresh blueberry muffin."

"Okay." She couldn't stop her excitement from bubbling up. "Oh, and I take it—"

"Two creams, four equals," he interrupted.

"Yes," she whispered.

"And I'll make sure I grab the muffin with the most blueberries."

She covered her growing smile. Garrett did know her. He'd remembered how she took her coffee and how she liked her muffins. Every nerve ending in her body tingled with adoration for the man in front of her, the same man that she'd always known. "Thanks."

"Hurry," he said. "No overthinking."

She gave him a mock salute. "I'll be right back."

Skye rushed toward the bay of elevators, peeking back one time to find him watching her. She breezed into an open elevator and leaned back against the wall. It felt like they were speeding to a familiar destination she wasn't quite ready to visit. But damn it, she was going to enjoy the ride.

Chapter Nine

"Oh my God, that was so much fun!" Skye bumped into Garrett as they walked the CityWalk at Universal Studios Hollywood. Max walked ahead of them, yapping on her phone, video chatting her boyfriend. "Thanks for inviting me. I needed this."

Garrett smiled down at her. "Thanks for coming."

"And thanks for this." She held up the magic wand he'd purchased for her. She swirled it in front of his face. "I love it."

They'd spent the last few hours at The Wizarding World of Harry Potter, riding the attractions and visiting the shops. Skye loved *Harry Potter,* almost as much as *Star Wars*. Her love for Harry, Hermione, Ron Weasley, and Dumbledore was one of the reasons Max had taken to her so fast when she was dating Garrett. They'd bonded over their mutual love for the series. And when they'd stepped into Ollivanders, Skye couldn't wait to add the wand to her collection. But before she could purchase it herself, Garrett slid in with his credit card and a wicked grin.

"I'm glad you love it," he told her.

She pointed the tip at him again. "Should I cast a spell on you?"

Skye couldn't be sure, but she could have sworn he muttered, "You already have."

"What did you say?"

He shook his head. "Nothing. I'm surprised you've never been here."

Skye had visited Universal Studios several times, as a kid and as an adult. She'd been on studio tours, visited the various lands, and eaten all the good food. But she'd never ventured into Harry Potter world until today.

"Actually, I am, too," she said.

"You were singlehandedly responsible for Max's love of reading. I should probably thank you for that."

Skye stared at Max, who was talking animatedly, arms wild, eyes wide. The smile on her face was as beautiful as the sun. "It's not hard to talk about books. Especially books that take you to another world and let you fight dragons and cast spells."

"You still read a book a week?" he asked.

Nodding, Skye said, "Yes. Even if it's short story or a novella, I finish a book every week."

"Max does the same thing," he told her.

Skye stopped in her tracks. Turning to him, she asked, "Really?" She didn't know why, but that revelation made her want to cry. Because she had left a lasting impression on Max, because she'd given her something that mattered. Something besides the heartbreak of loss.

"Yeah. When we broke up, she would announce each new book to me before she read it and then she'd tell me all about it when she was done."

Skye gripped her throat. "That's . . ." she croaked. "Thanks for telling me that."

"It's just one of the things that you did for us. It made life a little brighter for her, gave her something to focus on."

Nodding, Skye smiled. "I checked on her."

"I know."

"You did a great job with her. She's happy, healthy, and so hilarious."

"I know," he repeated. "She's proof that people aren't what they've been through."

"So are you."

As good as it felt to talk to him, to be honest with him about things that she never thought she'd be able to say, Skye didn't want to put a permanent damper on the light mood. So she decided to change the subject. She tapped both of his shoulders with her wand. "Thanks again. You're pretty awesome for this."

"You're pretty amazing yourself."

They restarted their slow stroll. There were no words, just comfortable silence as they headed toward the Uber entrance. She stared at the wand, traced the detail. "You're going to spoil me," she admitted softly.

He laughed. "Really?"

"Yes, you bought me a wand, after you picked the best blueberry muffin and made sure I had my coffee fix." It had been years since a man had spoiled her, made her feel special and treasured. Garrett had never judged her little quirks, her nerdy collections and her sci-fi obsession. Instead, he'd embraced them, he'd learned about them, and encouraged her to follow her heart. If she wasn't careful, she might want to keep him.

"How about you let me take you to dinner?" he asked.

"Dinner?" She gave him a sidelong glance. "As in a date?"

"Yes."

Was it possible to feel so many conflicting emotions at

once? One or two, sure. Three or four, maybe. But all of them? At any given moment, she teetered between adoration and insecurity, amusement and conflict, nostalgia and nervousness, excitement and fear, desire and doubt. But the best part? For the first time in years, anger wasn't part of the equation. When she looked at him, she didn't feel mad at him—or herself.

Now, she felt extreme gratitude for this perfect moment. The mild weather and the good company had rejuvenated her spirit and refilled her hope. She knew that if she'd slept with Garrett last night, that act would have ruined everything. There wouldn't have been delicious blueberry muffins, Harry Potter and the Forbidden Journey, or Pink's hot dogs and bottled Dr Pepper.

Did she really want to risk this slice of heaven to jump on the ride with him again? Did she want to immerse herself into someone that could hurt her? With his kind eyes and loving ways, there was no doubt in her mind he could destroy her. A couple of hot kisses was one thing. Dates and after-dates were another.

Skye bit down on her lip. "Um, I—"

He tapped her nose, effectively stopping her impending babble. "Don't answer that right now. And don't overthink it. We're good. This is good."

She searched his eyes, looking for the truth in his words. It was there, shining back at her. He'd never lied to her. When he said they were good, he meant it. Her hesitation served as stark reminder that she just wasn't ready. And she appreciated that he understood that.

"We could grab a bite to eat together tonight," he suggested. "No dates. No promises."

"I wish I could," she said. "But I promised my parents I'd have dinner with them. Mom's cooking."

He groaned. "Is she making adobo?"

Adobo was a Philippine dish that her mother had perfected. Made with tender pieces of chicken, pork, or seafood, marinated in garlic, soy sauce, and vinegar, Skye had eaten more than her fair share throughout the years. Unfortunately, her attempts to mimic the dish had been less than delicious, leaving her longing for her mother's home cooking.

"I hope so," she said.

"Bring me some."

"I promise."

Max walked over to them and grabbed Garrett's hand. "We have to stop in that shop over there. I need ice cream."

Garrett glanced at her as his sister led him away. Once again, Skye was struck by her overwhelming emotions. And once again, Skye couldn't help but be happy that none of those were anger.

"Nay!" Skye shouted the Tagalog word for mother as she walked through her parents' house. The smell of vinegar and garlic filled the air and she hummed in delight. *Adobo*. "Nay!" Kicking her shoes off, she set her purse on the sofa and headed into the kitchen.

Her mother stood at the stove, stirring the food in a huge pot. Her oversized sweatpants swaying as she moved. Skye noted the light brown highlights in her mother's hair and the new cut to just below her ears. Country music played on the small radio she kept in the kitchen.

For a brief moment, Skye was transported into this

same kitchen twenty years ago. She remembered similar scenes of her mother teaching her how to chop vegetables while Kenny Rogers played in the background. She recalled learning how to bake cookies and fry fish. A small smile touched her lips.

She approached her mother slowly, wrapped her arms around her from behind, then kissed her on the cheek. "Hi, Ma!"

Marisol jumped and whirled around. "Ami!" she shouted, her heavy accent warm and familiar. She cradled her daughter's face. "Let me look at you, girl."

Skye smiled as her mother examined her. "Ma, you just saw me a couple months ago."

"Oh my God, you look skinny. I told you to learn how to cook."

Giggling, Skye picked up a piece of broccoli from a bowl on the table and bit into it. "I'm eating. A lot."

"You're not eating good stuff. Eat healthy stuff, not junk food."

"Okay."

"And wear other colors. You're too pretty to always wear dark colors."

Skye shrugged. "They're jeans. At least I don't have on black."

With a wave of her hand, her mother turned back to her pot. "I have new clothes for you. Me and your *tatay* went shopping in Paris on our vacation and I bought you plenty of colorful outfits."

"Ma, you don't have to buy me clothes. I do shop for myself."

"Not like I shop for you," Marisol argued. "*Sige na*. Go. In your room. Try them on."

It was like she was sixteen again. Always sixteen,

fighting with her mother about her choice to wear black bras instead of nude bras, or a sky-blue blouse instead of a navy-blue one. No matter how many times they'd argued about her supposed lack of fashion sense, her mother never stopped trying to dress her. It had been an ongoing conversation for them every visit. As a result, Skye had a closet full of clothes she'd never wear. Unbeknownst to her mother, she'd donated quite a few outfits to homeless shelters, too.

Even though Marisol denied it, Skye wondered if it upset her mother that she didn't follow in her footsteps at Marisol P Fashions. While Skye loved fashion, had even been to several fashion weeks in NYC and Milan, she hated the fashion business. The time she'd spent interning for her mother paled in comparison to the rush she'd felt when her father used to bring her to the Pure Talent offices.

Skye would follow Uncle Jax around, barking orders in her head and coming up with plans to help clients in trouble. Once her uncle realized her penchant for public relations, he'd cultivated it and helped her get experience she wouldn't have had if her uncle wasn't the owner of one of the best talent agencies in the country.

As she strolled through the house, she noted the new paint on the walls and the updated furniture. Her parents had recently remodeled the house, prior to their big move back to Cali. Skye liked the décor. Tan, bronze, and cream with bursts of color to add flavor. Her mother was definitely a master at setting a vibe. The house was big, but it felt homey, comfortable. And that had everything to do with her mother's interest in textiles and feng shui.

The office door was ajar, so she stood at the threshold

and peeked in. Her father sat at his desk, his head down as he scribbled on a piece of paper.

"Hi, Daddy!" She entered the office and walked over to him, embracing him and kissing him on the cheek.

"Baby girl." Her father smiled. "I've been waiting on you."

She grinned. "I'm here." Skye studied her father. At sixty-five, he was still handsome, debonair. His brown skin was smooth, the salt-and-pepper hair on his head and face was neat and trimmed. "You look handsome. Are you hitting the gym?"

Jacob grinned. "Your mother convinced me to join. We go three days a week."

She leaned against the desk, folded her arms. "How are you feeling?"

A couple months ago, he'd given them all a scare when they thought he was having a heart attack. Fortunately, it was acute angina and not an active cardiac event. He'd also been diagnosed with high blood pressure. Since then, they'd been trying out different meds to control it. But Skye had been scared out of her mind with the thought that he could be seriously sick. Although he wasn't her biological father, he'd adopted her at a young age, and she couldn't love him more. He'd never treated her like she was anything but *his* child.

"I'm good, baby girl. I've never felt better."

She knew from her mother that he'd changed his diet, added in more green vegetables and less Almond Joy candy bars. "I'm glad."

"What's going on? Jax told me you were stepping into Carmen's role for a bit. How do you feel about that?"

"I thought it was what I wanted, but I'm not so sure."

He studied her silently. "That's a surprise."

"Not really." It felt good to talk to her father. They'd always had the type of relationship where he encouraged her to tell him the truth, to tell him whatever she was thinking.

"Why do you say that? This is something you've wanted for years."

Skye had wanted a lot of things for years. She'd had a plan for her life. By thirty-three, she should have had a husband and kids, a dog, and a picket fence. But that wasn't her reality. And she didn't know if that dream would ever be realized. She thought of Garrett, but then shook her mind free of the burst of hope that settled into her heart when she thought of him.

Sighing, she said, "I've been feeling like I'm not fulfilled. Initially, I thought it was because of Carmen, because she kept me on a tight leash, micromanaged my work. But now . . ."

Skye couldn't put her finger on it. The only thing she knew for certain was that she wanted more. She wanted to feel like she was pursing her passion, not just doing a job. She wanted to do the type of work that would make her feel accomplished, that would have an impact.

"I guess I'm just going through something," she continued. "I'm sure it will pass." Well, she hoped it would pass, because she was tired of thinking about it all the time. It was just another thing to obsess about, to overthink.

Her father stood and hugged her again. Kissing her brow, he squeezed her shoulders. "You'll figure it out. You always do." Marisol's loud call echoed through the house and her dad winked. "Time to eat."

After dinner, her mother set a banana pudding on the table. When Marisol married Jacob, she'd learned to make several of his favorites. Not only was she a master at

Philippine cuisine, but she could throw down on the soul food. It was normal for her to make fried chicken and black-eyed peas, egg rolls and *pancit* for dinner. Her parents had managed to blend their cultures seamlessly, and Skye loved it. She loved them.

Skye scooped up a mound of banana pudding and tasted it. "This is so good."

"I found you a date," her mother announced.

The spoon in her hand crashed to the table and flipped over onto the floor. Skye scrambled to pick it up. The last time her mother had hooked her up, she'd had to send a 911 text to Duke asking him to come in for the save. She didn't particularly want to experience that again.

Skye cleared her throat. "Nay, I don't need a date." And she didn't want a date, not with the son of her mother's friend.

"A friend of mine, her son is moving to Atlanta. I told him you lived there and could show him around. He's a nice man, bae. The VP of finance for a pharmaceutical firm. Lots of money."

Skye glanced at her father, who was quietly chuckling. Meeting her mother's gaze again, she repeated, "I don't need a date. I'm perfectly fine."

"Me and your dad are getting older. We want you to be happy and settled. You're living in Atlanta. We don't see you. I'd feel better if you had a man."

Skye rested her elbows on the table and massaged her temples. "I have friends. Uncle Jax, Aunt Ana, X, Zara, and Duke all live near me in Atlanta. I'm not alone. I have support. And when I need to see you, I can easily hop on a plane. Don't worry about me."

"Marisol, come on," her father interrupted. "Let the girl

find her own date. She's a grown woman, with her own home and a successful career."

"Work isn't everything, love." Her mother stood and picked up an empty dish. "I'd like a little grandkid."

Without another word, Marisol stalked off into the kitchen muttering about babies and weddings. Skye smiled at her dad and mouthed "thank you" before dipping her spoon into her pudding. Going on a date with some stiff finance guy wasn't her idea of fun. But the simple fact that her mother had brought up the D word made her rethink her earlier decision to turn down Garrett's invitation to dinner. Maybe it wasn't a bad thing after all. Because going on a date with tall, dark, and handsome Garrett was a whole different story, one that she thought she might want to take a chance and write.

Chapter Ten

"I want to make sure I'm available for the meeting." Garrett opened his calendar. "Schedule it for two weeks. I can be in Houston then," he told Tara.

A soft knock on his door drew his attention away from his computer. Standing, he walked to the door, giving Tara a few notes on another case file.

"Okay, I'll be in touch." Ending the call, he opened the door, surprised to see Skye standing there. "Hey."

She held out a plastic container and smiled. "Hi, I brought you some adobo and rice." She pulled a small bowl out of her bag. "Oh, and a small helping of banana pudding."

Garrett grabbed both containers and opened them, taking a whiff of the meal. "Smells good."

"I figured you'd want to eat it as soon as possible." She leaned against the door, stared at him with those big, beautiful brown eyes.

"Come in," he said.

"Where's Max?"

"She's in her room. Apparently, she's too old to share this big-ass suite with me."

Skye twisted the strap of her purse and blew an errant piece of hair from her face. “I should probably go. I have a lot of work to do.”

“Come on,” he prodded.

She bit down on her bottom lip. And he bit back a groan because she was stunning. They’d spent hours together today, and he still wanted more of her. Her dark brown hair was down, the waves wild and free. She still had on the ripped jeans she’d worn to the theme park, but she’d changed her shirt. Instead of the white T-shirt, she had on a black blouse.

He held up the containers. “You know you want to watch me devour this adobo.”

With a sigh, she nodded. “Okay, I’ll come in for a minute.” She entered the room. “Maybe I’ll just steal a piece of that chicken from you.”

Several minutes later, they sat at the table, sharing the adobo and rice and playing Speed with a deck of cards Max had brought with them.

“Shit!” she shouted when he blocked her ace of spades. “You’ve always cheated at this game.”

“Impossible,” he teased. “You’re just slow.”

They raced to the finish line, each of them frantically laying their cards on the growing pile. When he went out first, he did a fist pump.

She stood, tossing her cards on the table and kicking at the air. “Ugh! You won again. I quit.”

“You never were a gracious loser.”

She smacked his shoulder. “Shut up. It’s your hands. They’re too big.”

“What does that have to do with anything?” he asked incredulously.

“A lot,” she argued.

"Make that make sense."

She laughed. "No. I don't have to explain myself to you."

Chuckling, he bit in to a piece of chicken. "This is better than I remembered."

Skye took a sip of wine from the glass he'd poured and leaned back in her chair. "I can't believe you haven't had this in ten years."

"Why can't you believe that?"

"I don't know. My mom isn't the only person who knows how to make it." She took a piece of chicken and popped it in her mouth.

"I know, but I haven't met anyone who can make this dish."

She observed him quietly. "How are you, Garrett?"

The question caught him off guard. "I'm fine. Why?"

"Are you dating?"

"Do you think I'd be dating someone and kissing you the way I did?"

Her mouth lifted in a half smile. "I guess not. I asked how you were because I haven't in a long time. And I'm curious."

Now it was his turn to study her. Back in the day, he could sense her thoughts without her speaking a word. Time had passed, though. They didn't know each other the same anymore. But that didn't stop him from wishing he could read her mind.

"What do you want to know?" he asked.

"I just want to know if you're good."

"I'm good."

She flashed a soft smile. "I have a confession to make."

Curious, he leaned forward. "Are you going to tell me that you want me?"

There was one thing that hadn't changed, and that was the look in her eyes when she wanted him to touch her, to kiss her. She had tells, quirks that had always given him a clue. Like the way she tucked her hair behind her ear, shifted in her chair. Or the way her gaze flickered from his eyes to his mouth. And the way her breathing slowed when their knees bumped under the table.

"Do you need me to?" she asked.

Garrett shook his head. "No."

Without another word, he pulled her onto his lap and into a kiss. His heartbeat pounded in his ears as their mouths got reacquainted, licking and biting and sucking. He dipped his tongue into her mouth, loving the way she moaned, the way she rocked into him.

Her hands slipped under his shirt, brushing her fingers over his skin. Pulling her closer, against his erection, he pushed into her. Her sharp gasp egged him on, made him want to strip her bare right there and slide into her sweet heat.

"Oh God," she gasped. "Garrett."

Ten years. He hadn't heard her whisper his name like that in ten years. The sound of her voice, the feel of her skin against his fingertips, the taste of her . . . *Damn.*

She dug her fingernails into his scalp, kissing him with a passion that he felt in every bone, every muscle, every nerve ending in his body. If he didn't stop, there would be no turning back. Yet, as much as he wanted this, he knew they had to stop. Because he was sure she'd regret it in the morning. And he needed to wait until he could trust that she wouldn't, that she was ready for everything a night together would entail.

So he had to press pause. Reluctantly, he pulled back,

sucking on her bottom lip one more time before breaking the kiss. She kissed him again, though, pulling him back to her, letting him explore her mouth leisurely.

With a groan, he pulled back again, swallowing hard. “Skye,” he whispered. “We shouldn’t do this.”

She leaned back, a pout on her swollen mouth. He brushed her bottom lip with his thumb, placed a gentle kiss there.

“I want to, but it’s not the right time,” he said.

Her shoulders fell and he knew she understood. Slowly, she climbed off of his lap and returned to her seat, finishing off the wine in her glass. She glanced at him, a dazed look in her eyes. “I . . .” She closed her eyes and released a deep breath. “I should probably go.”

He grabbed her hand. “Skye, you don’t have to go.”

She stood. “No, I should. Because you’re right. It wouldn’t be good if we did what I want to do.”

Caressing her face, he ran his thumb across her cheek. “What I want to do, too.”

Leaning into his hand, she said, “Just so you know, I won’t act like this didn’t happen.”

Relief surged through him, nearly stealing his breath. Even if he hadn’t admitted it to himself, he’d wondered if things would go back to the status quo once they made it back to Atlanta. Nodding, he said, “Good.”

“That’s not to say it’ll happen again. I think we can both agree there are a lot of things that have happened between us. Emotions are high right now. I would hate to do something we’d regret in the morning.”

The way she’d articulated his own thoughts reinforced the decision to pull back, to give it more time. “I agree.”

“I don’t regret this, though. I missed talking to you,

laughing with you. I missed the easy way we were with each other. This felt good to me." She stood and picked up her purse. "All of it."

He walked her to the door. "Skye?"

She didn't turn around, but she didn't make a move to open the door.

Leaning into her, he inhaled her hair, brushed his lips over her ear. "Let's not let this be it," he whispered. Grabbing her hand, he linked their fingers. When she didn't immediately pull away, he continued. "Don't overthink it. You know me."

A soft sigh escaped her mouth, and he knew she understood him.

"I want to deal with this," he said. "I want to explore whatever this is, whether it ends with you in my arms or not. Because I missed you, too. I missed this. So much."

Skye dropped her head, but still wouldn't turn around so he could see her face, search her eyes. But he wouldn't push her. He never did.

"Okay," she whispered. "I'll talk to you later." She opened the door. "Bye, Garrett." Then she walked out.

Garrett closed the door. They hadn't made any promises, they hadn't voiced any expectations. Tonight, they'd crossed a line. Yes, she'd run out, but this time, he felt certain this wasn't the end.

"What's up, man?" Garrett gave X dap and slid onto a seat at the high-top table.

"Shit." X took a sip of his beer. "When did you get back?"

After he placed his drink order, Garrett answered, "Last night."

The rest of his time in L.A. had been spent with Julius, strategizing on ways to mitigate the director's mounting troubles. He hadn't seen Skye since their Universal outing, but they'd spoken several times, usually about work, sometimes about random stuff, but never about them.

"I had to get Max off to school," Garrett continued.

"Did you drive her back?"

"Yeah." The early morning drive had been pretty uneventful. She'd spent most of the time alternating between telling him off-the-wall things and texting her friends. But having the extra time with her was a good thing. "Met the boyfriend," he grumbled.

X frowned. "Boyfriend? When did that happen?"

The waitress returned with a bottle of Modelo, and they ordered dinner. "I'm trying to figure it out. Every time I see her, I think about the little girl who had tea parties with fake tea and dry-ass desserts from her Easy-Bake oven."

"Bruh, I remember that damn oven." X laughed. "The first time I went to Houston with you, she made those chocolate chip cookies. She was so happy, but they were hard as hell. We had to just eat them."

"Right." Garrett sighed. "But she's a brilliant cook now and a grown woman."

The compulsion to pummel the little punk that called himself her boyfriend had hit Garrett hard. The young student was nice enough, respectful. As far as Garrett was concerned, though, the boy would never be good enough for Max. The realization that he'd pretty much turned into every cliché he'd seen or watched on television had struck him. When did he become that father who never wanted to watch his baby girl grow up?

Over the years, he'd always told himself that he would be the big brother Max needed, that he would support her life choices, that he wouldn't be a dominating force in her life. After all, he wasn't her father, he was her brother. But when he'd dropped her off, when he'd hugged her, when he'd watched her kiss her boyfriend and walk into her apartment without turning back . . . his heart hurt like he was giving her away at her wedding.

"You're having a hard time with this," X said. "I don't blame you."

"I do." Garrett shrugged. "When did I become that guy?"

"When you left your life to be there for her, when you became a father."

"I'm not her father," Garrett murmured.

"You definitely are. You're the man who took care of her, made sure she had everything she needed. You're her dad."

"I'm her brother."

"Shit, you're her brother-dad, then."

Garrett chuckled. "That's dumb as hell."

"It's semantics, brotha attorney." The waitress came back a while later with their dinner. "Anyway, Skye said you two ran into each other."

Ran into each other. That's . . . simple. Garrett couldn't deny the turn of phrase bothered him, because their interaction was anything but simple. Having drinks, kisses, buying wands and blueberry muffins . . . flirting. There was nothing simple about California.

He glanced up to find X studying him thoughtfully, a slight frown on his face. "What?" he asked.

His friend raised a brow. "You good?"

"Yeah." He bit into a chicken wing.

"She also said you are representing Julius Reeves?"

Garrett gave X a little rundown of how that came to be. "He's an asshole."

An asshole who was now being investigated by Los Angeles and Atlanta police departments for improper conduct. It was only a matter of time before the first criminal charges were filed, followed by the civil suits. Garrett had fought with himself the entire drive home from Alabama about his own involvement. But he didn't want to walk away just yet, not while Skye was involved. He felt like he needed to be there, to keep an eye on things. Especially since Julius had never even tried to hide his disdain for Skye.

"Regret you took the case?" X asked.

"No comment."

"I'll take that as a yes. So why not just end your association with him?"

Garrett trusted X, but he didn't particularly want to talk about Skye and the progress he thought he'd made with her in California. "I'm giving it a little more time."

"Okay. Skye also told me you two talked."

Garrett paused, then set his beer bottle down. She hadn't whittled down their interaction to just running into each other, after all. "Did she tell you what we talked about?"

"No. I don't need to know." That was one thing he'd appreciated about X. His friend stayed in his lane at all times. "That's your business. But there's a lot you don't know about those years you two weren't together."

Before he moved back to Atlanta, he and X had seen each other numerous times each year. He'd always asked about Skye, but it was more surface questions like how she was doing or was she happy. Garrett had read about her engagement to Broderick Hall and, of course, he'd known about their breakup. But he'd never asked X about it.

The mention of things he didn't know about Skye made him want to know more now. He got the gist that X alluded to something unpleasant, something that had contributed to her need for therapy. One day, he hoped they would be at the place where she could share those things with him.

"And I know there are things that she doesn't know about your time away from her," X continued.

Garrett nodded. He'd gone through some shit he'd like to put behind him, had some relationships he'd like to forget.

"You're my brother, man," X said. "I've never interfered with you and Skye. I'll just tell you like I told her . . . be careful with each other. There's a lot of pain and past there."

"I hear you." Garrett ate another wing. "What you got up in the next few days?" he asked, changing the subject.

"Headed to Ann Arbor," X told him. "Zara wants to check out a college basketball player, one who might be thinking of entering the NBA draft this year. And we have to go to a baby shower."

Chuckling, he said, "Wow. You at a baby shower. Who's having a baby?"

"Duke's sister, Bliss," X said. "She's due next month."

"Right." Garrett remembered Duke mentioning becoming an uncle. "I was wondering where Duke was."

"Yeah, he's hanging out with his family."

"That's cool. It's a lot of them." Duke had seven siblings, and all of them were close. Garrett couldn't even imagine having that much family.

"When we get back, Zara wants to have dinner and a game night at the house."

"Cool. Just let me know when. Did you set a date?"

"No." X told Garrett about the wedding-planning book Rissa bought Zara and how Zara had started using it as a laptop desk. "And she threw out all the hotel brochures last night."

Laughing, Garrett said, "So I take it your bride-to-be really isn't feeling the whole wedding thing."

"Man, I don't know what we're going to do. At this point, I don't even care. I just want to be with her. That's what matters to me."

Garrett grinned at his friend, happy that X had finally found happiness with Zara. The two had been close friends for a long time, living in neighboring homes for much of their childhood. Things changed when she moved to Atlanta to work for Pure Talent as a sports agent. Next thing Garrett knew, Zara and X had fallen in love while sneaking around with each other.

"I get it." Garrett finished his beer. "If you decide to elope, just warn me. I don't want to be around when your mother finds out."

X barked out a laugh. "Shit, I wouldn't want to tell Mom. She'd kill me."

Garrett's phone buzzed. He picked it up and read the new text message from Julius. Groaning, he typed back a response. "Shit," he grumbled.

"What the hell happened?" X asked.

"I have to go." Garrett stood. "You'll read about it soon enough."

"Alright. I'll get the bill. Let me know if you need anything, bruh."

"I'm good. Keep me posted on dinner."

Garrett rushed out of the bar. He opened the messenger app and typed a text to Skye: Charges filed against Julius. Warn Paige.

Her response came back right away: Shit. Ok. Maybe I should cast a spell on him and send him to a barren land.

Smiling, he typed: Be my guest. I'll be in touch.

The little bubbles jumped on his screen, then stopped. Then started again. Finally, he received the response: Soon, I hope.

Garrett reread the text twice. If she wanted to talk to him soon, he'd make sure he did just that.

Chapter Eleven

"Hello, Skye," Sasha said, a soft smile on her face.

Skye set her tablet on the table and peered at the screen, grateful that Sasha had agreed to pencil her in today for a video session. She'd flown to Ann Arbor for a baby shower, and was driving herself crazy with her scattered thoughts about Garrett, about her life. "Thanks for seeing me."

"How are you?"

Now that she was talking to Sasha, she didn't really know what she wanted to say. She'd had a plan, to tell her about Garrett and L.A., but she couldn't find the words. Probably because she didn't really know what was going on, or if it was even a good idea to try and figure it out.

Skye sighed. "Remember we talked about me over-thinking things?"

"I do."

"It started when I was a kid, when my dad wanted to adopt me."

As a child, Skye had struggled with the knowledge that she'd never get to know her biological father. He'd died when she was a baby. What she knew about him always made her feel like she was missing something by not getting the chance to meet him. He was a veteran, a member of the United States Marine Corps, an activist. He'd volunteered at homeless shelters, served positions in the local NAACP, and even played the organ at a local church. By all accounts, he was a wonderful man. And he didn't die at war or in the line of duty doing his job as a police officer. He passed away because he had cancer, a rare form of leukemia.

Her mother made sure she knew what an honorable man her biological father was, gave her pictures, letters, jewelry . . . everything material that he'd owned. But it still didn't fill the empty part of her that didn't know what it was like to be held by him.

"My dad, the man who raised me . . . I love him so much." Skye blinked, surprised at the sting of tears filling her eyes. "I do. He never made me feel like I wasn't his. So I don't feel I lacked for anything in life. Still, there's a part of me that feels like I don't belong. Sometimes I feel a little empty, like there is a void that can never be filled. Does that make any sense?"

"It does. And it's quite normal, Skye."

Closing her eyes, she took a deep breath. "When it was time to finalize the adoption, my dad asked me if I wanted to take his name." Skye remembered the day vividly, the summer breeze on her skin, the warm sun shining on her, the smell of her dad's cologne as he presented her with a necklace. He'd asked her if she had any second thoughts about the adoption. "I told him I couldn't wait for the adoption to be final. But I also told him that I didn't want to change my last name. Because I felt like I wanted to honor my biological father."

Sasha shifted, but didn't speak.

"He said he understood," Skye continued. "And I know he did, because he never brought it up again."

"That's a good thing, Skye."

Skye nodded rapidly. "Yes, it is. My dad is a good man, the best."

"So what's the problem?"

"My mother ended up having two miscarriages, and as a result, he never had his own biological child. He doesn't have anyone to carry on his name." She felt the familiar burn in her throat, the one signaling a stupid ugly cry. Pausing, she gave herself a few seconds to pull herself together. "My last name is Palmer, not Starks. I've always wondered if I hurt his feelings by not taking his name. Just like I've always wondered if I hurt my mom by not designing clothes. Just like I've always wondered if Garrett could ever truly forgive me for leaving him when he needed me the most."

Breaking up with him the way she did had haunted her. And now that they were getting closer, she wondered if there could ever be a second chance for them because of it. It wasn't wise to fall hard when there were so many variables, so many ways it could all blow up.

"Skye, those thoughts make you human." Sasha smiled. "You're not perfect. From what you've told me, you took great care explaining your position with your dad. I'm sure you probably did the same thing with your mother."

And she had. She's taken her mother out to dinner during her senior year in high school, gave her a glass dolphin figurine, and thanked her for being a wonderful mother to her. Then she'd broken the news that she didn't want to design clothes, that she didn't want to take over Marisol P Fashions.

"In the short time I've been seeing you," Sasha continued, "I feel confident in saying that you don't make decisions lightly."

"I try not to. But it always feels like I make the wrong choices. I gave up my virginity because my high school boyfriend pressured me, even though I knew I wasn't ready. Then he went and blabbed about it to everyone. After Garrett, I fell in love with an asshole who hurt me to my core. And embarrassed me publicly. Those are just the relationship decisions."

"What about Garrett? You don't think you made a good decision with him?"

Skye had fallen in love with Garrett during *The Empire Strikes Back*. He was everything that she'd dreamed of. And he'd never treated her like an afterthought, like arm candy, or with anything less than respect.

"Garrett was nothing like those others."

"So you didn't make a bad decision when you gave him your heart," Sasha said. "Give yourself credit for that."

But Skye had made the bad decision to leave him, to let him go. She'd made the biggest mistake of her life ten years ago.

"I have to ask you a question about Garrett," Sasha said. "Do you think that he doesn't know that you don't make decisions lightly, that you think about things before you do them?"

"No, he knows that about me."

"Okay. Why wouldn't he forgive you for doing what you thought was best at the time?"

"Because I didn't talk to him. I just broke up with him. He doesn't know how I came up with the decision."

"How about you tell him?"

Skye wiped a tear from her cheek. In her heart, she knew they needed to have the conversation. But she didn't want to burst the bubble they'd been in, the baby steps and big steps they'd taken. "I feel like we're walking a tightrope right now, that anything can happen to knock us off and destroy the progress we've made."

"Tell me more about this progress."

Skye gave Sasha a rundown of everything that had happened in L.A., from the kiss at the elevator to adobo and cards. "I want him. More than that, I miss his friendship. I don't know that it's right to try to recapture what we lost. Because if it doesn't work, where does that leave us? Not talking again? Walking through life, going to all the same functions, and not acknowledging each other?" She groaned. "Why did I have to kiss him?"

"There's nothing wrong with following your heart. I tasked you with not overthinking something that you wanted to do. It's very telling that your way of completing this task was to kiss Garrett."

"There's so much past between us."

"Does it feel like that past is insurmountable when you're with him?"

"No," Skye admitted.

On the contrary, it felt pretty damn good to be with him. They hadn't seen each other in a week, but they'd talked several times. And not just about Julius and Paige's drama. They'd chatted about her job, his job, the new Marvel movies, cold cuts. She'd told him about Carmen and he'd shared some of his practice woes with her. Last night, she'd fallen asleep on the phone with him, which prompted her call to Sasha that morning.

Skye tapped her fingers together. "I just need to know if I'm doing the right thing. Can you just tell me?"

"That's not for me to say," Sasha said. "It's something you have to decide yourself."

Skye shook her hands in midair. "I know I'm supposed to do the work. I'm committed to doing the work. But I just need someone to tell me that it's okay to explore this."

"Do you want to explore it?"

Rolling her eyes, she grumbled a curse. "I don't know . . . yes. I want something. But I need to be sure it's not just sex. Garrett is very attractive. His voice, his body, his face . . . he's hot. What if I'm just horny?"

Sasha laughed. It was the first time she'd done that. "I'm sorry, Skye. Is there something wrong with being horny?"

"Yes! Because I can't afford to just sex Garrett."

"You're assuming it would be just sex."

"If it's not, then that's huge." Skye bit her thumbnail. "Does that mean we're going to be in a relationship again? How would that work? What if it doesn't work? What if we're not as compatible as we were?"

"Skye, you're doing it again. Overthinking it."

"Which is why I called you!" It had been a long time since she'd had sex with anyone, let alone someone she felt a strong connection with.

"Okay, how about you just take this one step at time? Stop looking ahead."

"Is that your way of telling me to just do it?"

"No. I'm telling you to just feel. If that means you decide to have sex with Garrett, that's okay."

It sounded like permission to Skye. "Just do it?"

"Yes. I want you to practice self-care. Please make an effort not to spend so much time thinking of what can go wrong in any given situation. It's not healthy. Your father loves you. Your biological father loved you. Your mother loves you. And you actually did have a great relationship with Garrett. The breakup doesn't change that. Those are all good things. Focus on that. And do you."

"Thanks, Sasha. I have to get out of here. I'll be back in Atlanta in a couple days. I'll email you."

"Sounds good. Take care, Skye."

"You too."

A few hours later, Skye was eating cake and laughing with her friends at Duke's parents' home. The baby shower was an intimate affair. Only close family and friends had been invited. Although the sun was shining, she wouldn't dare step foot outside on the gorgeous patio. It was cold as hell in Michigan. So cold she'd made an impromptu stop at Target to buy a heavier coat.

Zara slid a huge wedding-planner book over to her. "Take this. X's mom just gave it to me. As if I need another damn book."

"Irritated much?" Skye sipped her mimosa.

"Hell, yeah. I'm telling you, this wedding is going to kill me."

"Oh hush," Zara's sister Rissa said. "You'll be just fine. Look at me."

Rissa was marrying Los Angeles city councilman Urick Roberts in June. Skye was one of the bridesmaids, and had helped with the planning. The two families wanted a grand affair, and Skye was here for it. She loved party planning.

Zara rolled her eyes at her sister. "Whatever."

"What's the hesitation?" Skye asked, licking butter-cream icing off of her fork.

"This baby," Zara mumbled.

Skye dropped the fork. "What?"

"Are you . . . ?" Rissa stood. "Zara!"

Zara gripped her sister's arms. "Sit your ass down,

Rissa," she ordered through clenched teeth. Skye laughed when Rissa sat down on her chair, hard. "I haven't told anyone else yet."

"I hope you told X," Skye whispered.

"Of course, he knows," Zara confirmed. "I just wanted to wait until after the first trimester to say anything."

"When are you due?" Rissa asked.

"July twenty-third. We had a particularly freaky Halloween."

Skye giggled. "It was probably that damn leather and lace you wore to the Halloween party."

Suddenly, the knowledge that her friend was having a baby made Skye feel emotional. She glanced over at Rissa, who was dabbing at her own eyes.

"Aw, hell," Zara grumbled. "You guys . . . stop crying. I'm the one that should be crying."

Skye's chin trembled. "My Z-Ra is having a little baby."

A hint of a smile spread across Zara's face. "I know."

"I'm going to be an aunt," Rissa said.

"Me too," Skye cried.

A moment later, all of them were crying and hugging. Pulling back, Skye said, "So you know I'm not letting you walk down the aisle with a belly full of baby. That's a wrap."

Rissa giggled. "Can you imagine the pictures?" She gasped. "Wait. This means you're going to be huge at my wedding."

Skye winced. "Right. We may have to rethink your dress."

"And it's going to be hot as hell in June and I'm due in July," Zara said. "How about I just sit this one out?"

"Are you crazy?" Rissa hissed. "You're my sister."

Finishing her mimosa, Skye said, "She's right, Z-Ra. You're the maid of honor."

"The maid of honor who can't even drink a damn mimosa," Zara added. "I'm going to be miserable and sober at the bachelorette party. That's no fun."

"Okay, let's think about this." Rissa leaned forward. "I'm willing to give you a pass for the bachelorette party. But you better have your round stomach at that damn church on time."

Skye nodded. "Right. We'll have to rethink your bridesmaid dress, though."

"And color," Zara said. "I refuse to wear peach and look like a peach."

Laughing, Skye shook her head. "You're crazy."

"Back to this wedding." Zara took a long gulp from a bottle of water. "I think we're going to just have a small ceremony." She swallowed visibly. "Next month."

"Next month!" Skye and Rissa shouted simultaneously.

"Shh." Zara scanned the room. "Be quiet. Either next month or early March."

"You really are crazy," Skye said. "I can't pull something together in a month. Not with Carmen on medical and Paige's marriage blowing up."

"She's right," Rissa agreed. "That's impossible."

"It's not if we keep it simple," Zara said. "I don't need all the bells and whistles. I don't need a huge ceremony. I just want to marry the man I love and live happily ever after."

"Oh God." Skye snatched a tissue from a holder on the table. "The tears. I probably look like a raccoon."

"You're beautiful, Skye." Zara grinned. "I want both of you to stand up with me as my maids of honor. X is going to speak with Garrett and Duke. We'll be having dinner at our house to discuss the whole thing."

Skye sniffed. "Okay, I'm here for whatever you need."

"Just get me to the altar. That's what I want."

Skye and Rissa ticked off a couple of ideas for locations and scheduled a call in a couple of days. Reaching out, Skye took Zara's hand in hers. "You know I got you."

"I know," Zara said. "Now. What's going on with you and Garrett?"

Skye blinked. "Huh?"

"About time you asked the damn question," Rissa said. "I've been waiting for this, woo chile."

"Really?" Skye shook her head. "You've been waiting for this, Rissa?"

"Well, you did text us about drinks and Universal," Zara said with a shrug. "We got questions."

Giggling, Skye said, "Questions that won't get answered today."

"Did you at least give him some?" Rissa asked.

Skye smacked Rissa's leg lightly. "No. And if I did, I wouldn't tell y'all."

"Oh hell no." Zara sliced a hand in the air. "When X was giving me the flux, I seem to remember plenty of jokes coming from you, Skye. Turnabout is fair play."

"Whatever." Skye waved a dismissive hand toward her bestie. "We just talked. There's really nothing to tell."

Rissa elbowed Zara, then asked, "So you don't want to have sex?"

"I'm not answering that." Skye finished her cake and mimosa. "Besides, we just started talking. Don't you think it's too soon to be intimate?"

They both said no at the same time, then gave each other a high five.

"Shit, sex is good," Rissa said. "I love it."

Skye knew that. She didn't need the reminder. "Good for you."

Zara shifted in her seat. "What Rissa is trying to say is"—Zara gave Rissa a sidelong glance—"we know you're overthinking shit again. Don't."

Skye pondered Zara's words as the topic switched to food and babies. It seemed like the universe was giving her signs that it was okay to get busy. First, Sasha. Now, Rissa and Zara. So maybe it was time to listen.

"I'll have two scoops of cappuccino chocolate chip." Skye tapped the glass in front of her choice, then glanced at Garrett. "Which one are you going to try?"

He studied the selections, torn between old-fashioned vanilla and butter pecan. "I'll take two scoops of vanilla."

The lady behind the counter walked away to start their order.

He smiled down at her. "I can't believe you talked me into this."

Garrett never skipped lunch. It was one of the most important meals of the day for him. Yet, Skye had managed to convince him to forgo tacos for ice cream.

"Aw, live a little. You won't regret this." Her eyes widened when the lady handed her the cone, and she immediately sampled the sweet treat. Moaning, she nodded. "This is so good."

They'd met at the Pure Talent offices to discuss the Reeves fallout. As usual, they'd worked fast and efficiently, which left some time to for ice cream before her afternoon staff meeting.

Garrett paid for both cones and they walked out of the parlor and headed toward a small park across the street. He spotted an empty bench and they took a seat.

"It feels so good out here." Skye crossed her legs, drawing his attention to her high heels. Damn. She was so damn sexy all the time. He was addicted to her smile, her scent, her hair. But it was her shoes that always made him stop and stare. Because he loved the way her legs looked in them.

"I'm thinking we should have the meeting in the Pure Talent building," Skye said. "I just think Paige would feel more comfortable there."

Paige had agreed to have a conversation with Julius, but Garrett wasn't confident the marriage could be saved at that point. The embattled director had been indicted on several charges of sexual harassment in Atlanta and was set to appear in court next week.

Skye was firmly in the "Julius ain't shit" camp and he couldn't blame her. The media was having a field day, but ticket sales hadn't suffered due to the breaking news. In fact, they'd increased. Probably *because* of the latest headlines and the simple fact that people thrived on drama nowadays.

"That's fine with me," he said.

"Even though it won't change anything. I spoke to her last night and she's not talking reconciliation anymore."

Again, Garrett didn't blame the actress. The marriage vows were to love your spouse through sickness and health, until death. But adultery, lies, and criminal actions were deal breakers for most people. “I’ll meet with him tomorrow. We can coordinate schedules later.”

“Thanks.” She grinned at him and his pulse raced. *So beautiful.*

“How was Michigan?”

Skye had returned to Atlanta a couple days ago. It had been almost two weeks since he’d seen her. “It was fun. I got to catch up with my favorites. By the way, have you talked to X?”

His friend had called him yesterday, but he hadn’t had a chance to return his call. “Not yet. Is everything okay?”

The corner of her mouth quirked up. “Everything’s good.” Her eyes sparkled with amusement, and he wondered if she knew something he didn’t.

“What’s going on, Skye?” he asked. “You know something, don’t you?”

She shrugged. “No. I’m just happy for them.”

“Did they set a date or something?”

“Something,” she said simply. Turning to him, she beamed. “But I may need your assistance to help with the wedding.”

“You want me to help you plan a wedding?”

“Not plan, but assist.”

He studied her with narrowed eyes. “Alright, spill it. What’s going on?”

Batting her lashes, she said, “I’m not saying anything else. After you talk to X, call me.”

Garrett leaned back and finished his ice cream. “Fine, I’ll call him today.”

“I was thinking, though.”

He hoped she was thinking about him as much as he’d been thinking about her. Things had changed for the better between them, and he wanted to keep moving forward in a positive direction.

"We haven't really talked about stuff," she continued. "Maybe it's time that we do?"

"What are we talking about?" he asked.

She searched his eyes. "Whatever is happening between us."

Leaning in, he smiled. "What do you think is happening between us?"

"Something good."

"Does this mean you'll let me take you out to dinner?"

Shooting him a lopsided grin, she said, "What if I cook for you?"

"You want to cook for me?" He raised a questioning brow.

The Skye he remembered hated everything to do with cooking. And she used to avoid it at all costs.

"Hey, I've got skills in the kitchen now." She bit into her cone. "I even bake cakes from scratch."

"Wow, now I have to see this."

"Do you have to travel this week?" she asked, finishing her ice cream.

He nodded. "I have to go to Houston Sunday."

"And we have dinner at X and Zara's Saturday. How about Friday night at my place?"

"That's fine."

"I'll bake you a German chocolate cake."

Garrett was pleasantly surprised she'd remembered his favorite cake. "You remembered," he said.

She averted her gaze. "I remember everything," she whispered.

He leaned closer, until the tips of their noses were touching. When she made no move to put distance between them, he brushed his lips over hers softly. He licked her lips, tasting the mixture of chocolate and coffee on them. But he made no move to deepen the kiss. "Me too," he murmured against her mouth.

Skye touched his face, brushed the tips of her fingers over his cheek, down his jawline. They stayed like that for a moment, not kissing, just sitting in each other's space, staring at each other.

"Okay, it's a date," she said.

He inhaled her skin, nuzzled his nose against her jaw, before placing a soft kiss there. "It's a date."

Briefly, Garrett wondered if going to her house was a good idea. It was one thing to take her out in public. But being alone with her, at her place, where there were several hard and soft surfaces, might be the tipping point for him. Right now, they were moving at a slow and cautious pace. Were they ready to increase the speed to fast and furious?

Chapter Twelve

A knock on his office door drew Garrett from the case file on his desk. “Come in.”

Tara poked her head in. “You have a visitor.”

Frowning, he glanced at his watch. “Who is it?”

His assistant looked nervous, uncomfortable. “It’s Julius Reeves,” she said, her voice shaky. “I told him you were busy, but he insisted.”

Garrett stood and approached Tara. “Is that all he did?”

Tara was the first person he’d hired when he started his practice. She’d worked for him in Houston and had proved herself invaluable to his business. When he’d decided to move to Atlanta, he offered her a chance to come with him, which she’d politely declined initially. He’d been in Atlanta for two months, struggling with an inept assistant, when she’d contacted him and asked if the offer was still on the table.

They weren’t just employer-employee, they were friends. He’d gone to her wedding and he’d helped her through her divorce. And he’d been an honorary “uncle” and mentor to her teenage son. To see her flustered and nervous made him want to know why.

"Tara," he prodded. When she met his gaze again, he asked, "What's wrong?"

She sucked in a deep breath and waved a hand at him. "It's nothing. But . . ."

"Listen, if he said something to you, or did something, you need to tell me."

"He didn't," she said, shaking her head. "It's just, he gives me the creeps. That's all."

Garrett studied his assistant, noting the slight tremor in her hands when she touched her face. "Are you sure?"

She nodded. "I am."

He didn't believe her. Sighing, he told her he'd handle Julius. She slipped out of his office, and he walked to the lobby. Julius sat, one leg crossed over his knee, typing on his phone.

"Julius," Garrett greeted. This time, he didn't reach out to shake his hand. "What can I do for you?"

"Where's your lovely assistant?" Julius asked, looking around, presumably for Tara.

"Gone," Garrett said simply.

"I wanted to thank her for her help."

Garrett clenched his teeth. "What can I do for you?" he repeated.

"I need to discuss the meeting with Paige. Can we talk in your office?"

"No." Garrett had almost told Julius to talk to another crisis manager. But he felt like he'd be leaving Skye in the lurch by doing so. They'd spent a significant amount of time, over the last few days, strategizing their next steps. He didn't know how long he would last, though.

Julius stepped back. "Excuse me?"

"I'm busy. How about we schedule a call Monday?"

"Do you treat all of your clients this way?" the director

asked incredulously. "Maybe I should start looking for someone else, someone who makes time for my case."

"If that's what you feel the need to do." Garrett slipped his hands in his pockets. "But as I said, I'm extremely busy."

It wasn't a lie. He'd been holed up in the office all day, managing his increasingly heavy workload. If business continued to pick up, he'd have to consider hiring another associate. His current associate, Marq, had been a great addition to the practice.

"Feel free to give me a call and we can set up time to talk," Garrett continued. "I understand you're a busy man, but I have other paying clients that are just as important."

Julius stomped to the door. "Fine, I'll come back Monday."

Garrett didn't want him to know he'd be out of town, so he said, "Don't. If you want to meet in person, I'll be happy to schedule some time on my calendar. In the meantime, I'd appreciate it if you didn't just drop by unannounced."

The director eyed him, but didn't argue. "I'll have my assistant call to make an appointment."

"Thank you. Enjoy your weekend."

When Julius left, Tara stepped out in the lobby area. "I'm sorry, Garrett."

"Don't apologize. Are you going to tell me what happened?"

She smiled sadly. "Nothing happened. I told you, he just gave me the creeps."

It wasn't like Tara to lie to him, so he had no choice but to take her word for it. But he knew that he wouldn't be representing Julius Reeves much longer. "Okay, I won't push, Tara. If he made you uncomfortable in any way, I will kick his ass right before I walk away from the case."

Tara laughed. "Oh, please." The nervousness had left her voice. "He's a paying client."

"I don't care."

"I care. Besides, if it wasn't for him, you wouldn't be going to Skye's for dinner tonight." She waggled her eyebrows. "By the way, I stopped at the grocery store and grabbed what you asked for."

Garrett had shared his plans with Tara over lunch. "Thanks. Appreciate it."

"Interesting gift, though." She arched a brow. "Let me know how it goes over."

He chuckled. "I will."

"It's in the refrigerator." She walked to her desk. "You might want to head out and get ready for tonight. For some reason, I think things are about to change for you."

"I'll leave when you do," he said. "We'll walk out together."

"Oh boy," she murmured. "Are we going to do this from now on?"

"Until you tell me the truth," he countered. "Give me a minute to pack up."

Later, he knocked on Skye's door, suddenly nervous about where the night would lead. Tara's words echoed in his head. Yet, things had already changed. And he hoped the positive changes kept coming.

The door swung open and Skye stood there, a smile on her face. He swallowed hard. It was almost like she'd bathed in sunlight, the way her skinned glowed. Maybe her smile *was* the sun, shining on him.

"Hey, Garrett." Her chest was heaving, like she'd been running. "Come in." She pulled him inside. "I'm just finishing up dinner."

The first thing he noticed—aside from sway of her hips

and the curve of her ass in those jeans she wore—was the smell of spices, onion, and soy sauce mixed with the soft hint of apples and rum. Then he noticed the vibrant décor, the warm grays, soft blues, and art on the walls.

He followed her into the kitchen. "How long have you been here?" The fact that he had to ask her that didn't sit well with him. He'd been in Atlanta for a while and this was the first time he'd been to her townhome.

"A couple of years," she replied. "I bought it after I broke up with Broderick."

"It's nice." He walked over to the stove, where she stood. Peering into the wok, he groaned. "You're making *pancit*?"

She grinned. "I know you love it, so I figured I'd make it for you."

The noodle dish had been his first introduction to Philippine cuisine. When he'd tried it at one of their family functions, he'd almost eaten himself into a coma, it was so good. The combination of chicken, shrimp, vegetables and noodles was addictive.

"Smells good."

She opened a drawer, pulled out a fork, and scooped out some noodles. Holding it up to his lips, she said, "Taste it."

Opening his mouth, he let her slide the fork inside, never breaking eye contact with her. It was better than he remembered. Back then, Skye wouldn't make it herself, choosing to get it from her mother. But he was glad to see she'd mastered it. "So good."

"Thanks. Have a seat. Can I get you anything to drink?"

He slid onto a bar stool by the island and set his gift on the countertop. "Water is fine for now."

Glancing at him over her shoulder, she asked, "Sure? I have wine, cognac, or soda."

"What are you drinking?"

She tipped her head toward the glass of red wine sitting near the stove. "It's a cabernet, which I know you don't like."

Smiling, he asked for the cognac. "Neat."

"I know how you like it." Skye pulled a balloon glass from her cabinet and filled it with his drink.

Several minutes later, they were seated at her dining table. Skye had outdone herself on the meal, serving *pancit*, sautéed green beans, and baked chicken. She'd also made *lumpia*, or Filipino fried spring rolls.

As usual, he'd eaten too much food. "Thanks for this." He leaned back in his seat.

She bit into a spring roll. "You're welcome. Over the years, I've grown to like cooking. And I've really tried to pick up some of my mother's recipes. She's getting older, and I'd like to be able to cook for her and my dad someday."

"How are your parents?" he asked.

Her eyes lit up the way they always did when she talked about her mom and dad. "Good. I miss them being close. But they're happy back in Cali."

"Well, you do have support here in town. So that's a good thing."

Coming from a small family, Garrett appreciated the close-knit circle Skye and X had. The Starks family wasn't big, but they had a core group of friends that had become family, like the Reids and the Youngs. And they'd invited him in from the moment they'd met him, offering him the same support they'd given each other. Even after he'd broken up with Skye, that hadn't changed.

"I know." Skye finished her wine. "I'm grateful for my peeps."

They talked briefly about Julius's visit to the office, but he didn't want to delve into it too much. This night was about them, not work. "I've made a decision to end my association with him after our next meeting with them."

She nodded. "Good. I'm surprised you lasted this long. He's such an asshole."

"Anyway, enough about him." He set his napkin on the table. "I brought dessert." A little while after he'd arrived, he asked if he could put his gift in the refrigerator. When she stood to retrieve it, he held his hand out. "I can get it."

She plopped back down. "Hey, I'm supposed to be the hostess here."

"And you've hosted me. My turn." He winked. A few minutes later, he walked back over to the table with the bag. "Open it."

Eyeing him skeptically, she picked up the bag, opened it, and looked inside. She gasped and closed it quickly. "You didn't."

He barked out a laugh. "I sure did."

She cracked up, pulling out the bag of sugar snap peas. "You're hilarious. And you remembered." Whenever they went to the movies, she'd always bring those peas and munch on them instead of popcorn, because she hated it. "Oh my God. Garrett, you . . . I don't even know what to say."

"You've already said enough."

She opened the bag and bit into one. "I still love these things."

"Some things never change."

Standing, she rounded the table. "I'm going to tear these bad boys up." She bent down and kissed him. "Thank you."

The air changed around them as she stood before him, eyes locked on his. He pulled her onto his lap. "Skye, I think—"

Skye placed a finger on his mouth. "Let's not think, Garrett. Not right now."

Raising a brow, he asked, "What do you want to do?"

She searched his face, dragging her thumb over his bottom lip. Leaning in, she brushed her lips against his, so soft he might have dreamed it. Skye kissed her way over his jawline to his ear, and whispered, "You."

You. Skye had just laid all of her cards on the table. But she couldn't care. She *didn't* care. She just wanted him.

Having him at her place, in her safe space, felt all too right to be wrong. There was no awkwardness, no tension. She didn't think about everything that could go wrong, she didn't tick off the many reasons they shouldn't go there. Instead, she'd concentrated on how she felt when he was near. *Alive. Calm. Hot and horny.*

Garrett had bought her peas, for goodness' sake. He'd remembered everything small yet important about her, from how she took her coffee to what she liked to snack on. He'd told her that she knew him. Which was true. But *he* knew her.

Yes, she knew they should probably talk. They'd fallen back into an easy vibe with each other, a comfortable existence. And she didn't want to go back to how it was before, because she craved the interaction. No, they didn't know what the future held. But, right now, she needed to feel like a woman, like a boss. She wanted to feel desirable, beautiful, sexy. And Garrett had always made her feel like his own personal priceless treasure.

Resting her nose against his cheek, she kissed the stubble there. His scent wrapped around her like a warm blanket. She wanted to drown in him, submerge herself in him. She brushed her fingertips over his forehead, down the bridge of his nose, over his mouth.

When she met his gaze again, she said, "I know it seems like this might be a mistake," she whispered.

He watched her intently. She swallowed, unnerved by the fire in his gaze, the hunger.

"I don't care that it is or isn't. I only know that I—" She gasped when he reached up and pulled her hair out of her bun. He swept her waves off of her shoulder, and brushed his hands down her back. A second later, her shirt was flung on the floor behind her. "Garrett, I . . ."

Whatever she was going to say died on her lips when he perched her atop the table. He unbuttoned her jeans and peeled them off. So slow, so painfully slow, she thought she'd explode from the building pressure in her core. Just from his touch. No thrusting, no kisses, no sucking, no biting, no tongues . . . just the anticipation of his hands on her skin.

Every nerve ending in her body seemed to come to life as he kissed the tops of her feet, her ankles, up her legs to her knees. And when he brushed his lips over her inner thighs, nipped at her skin, she cried out.

"Skye."

She shivered at the feel of his breath on her skin. "Yes," she breathed.

His massive hands slid up her legs, gripped her hips

and pulled her closer. "I need you to be sure this is what you want."

Peering down at him, she nodded rapidly. Because if she talked, she might just beg him to take her panties off and have her for dessert.

With an oh-so-sexy smirk on those sexy-ass lips of his, he said, "I need words, Skye."

"Shit," she murmured when his thumb slipped beneath the band of her underwear. "Um . . . Damn." She swallowed when he slid his thumb down her slit. "I'm sure," she managed to say, right before he pressed that same talented thumb on her clit. "Please."

She raked her fingers through his hair and fought the urge to pull him closer. But she didn't have to fight long, because he pushed her underwear aside, pressed his face against her, circled her clit with his tongue, and sucked the tiny bud into his mouth. And she came. Long and hard as he feasted on her, savored her. A second orgasm crested within her moments later, and she came again.

He scooped her up in his arms. "Bedroom."

Unable to speak, she pointed to the stairs.

Garrett carried her through the house and soon she was on a bed. Not her bed, though. She giggled.

"What's wrong?" he asked, pulling her panties off.

"This isn't my bedroom." She fell back on the mattress. "This is the guest room."

He laughed and scanned the room. Crawling onto the bed, he kissed her stomach, the tops of her breasts, her chin, and finally her lips. "Nice room. I'm sure your guests are very comfortable here."

She smiled at him. "I'm a good hostess."

Garrett searched her eyes. "You're so damn beautiful, Skye."

Her body seemed to bloom under his intense gaze. Biting down on her lip, she tugged his shirt up and off. She smoothed her hands over his chest, down his stomach. "You're beautiful, too." She unbuckled his belt, slid it off, and tossed it somewhere. "So hot." Skye unbuttoned his pants and dipped her hands inside to grasp his erection in her palm. Stroking him, she sank her teeth into his chin before soothing it with her tongue. "So fucking sexy."

"Fuck," he moaned, stopping her movements. "You probably should stop. It's been a while."

Laughing, she pulled his wallet out of his back pocket and held it up to him. "Condom?"

The wickedly delicious quirk of his mouth let her know he'd come prepared. "Open it and pull it out."

She did as she was told, while he took his pants and underwear off. Sheathing him, she purred when he rested his hard body on top of hers. He felt so good. And the time for talking was over.

Garrett crushed his mouth to hers as he entered her. His whispered curse signaled she felt as good to him as he did to her. They stayed like that for a moment, still. Then, the urge to move overtook her.

Slow and easy movements were soon replaced by fast and deep thrusts. When they came, they came together, with their mouths fused and their gazes locked on each other. Skye struggled to breathe as her orgasm tolled through her, snatching her soul with its intensity. She clutched at him, held him to her.

Seconds later, she fell back on the mattress. He collapsed on his back next to her. Euphoria was soon replaced by a barrage of crazy thoughts as the realization that they'd just crossed a line dawned on her. She'd opened herself up to him, she'd let him in. Not just into her body, but her mind, her heart. What does this mean? *What the hell did I just do?*

She sat up, hands braced to her chest. Looking around the room, she felt panic well up in her gut. *I have to go.* But she couldn't go. She was in her place, on her spare bed.

Then his hand was on her leg, squeezing her, offering her comfort. "Skye, it's okay."

Closing her eyes, she took in a deep breath. "Is it?" she asked, her voice sounding small and unsure even to her own ears.

His hand smoothed up her back. "Don't panic. Don't overthink this. You know me."

Skye felt the tension leave her body as his words pierced her heart. She glanced at him. "Can we do this and be okay?"

He wrapped his hand around the back of her neck and pulled her to him. Pressing his lips against hers, he kissed her until the doubt disappeared. Garrett rolled her over so that he was lying on top of her again. "Yes, we can." Then, she was lost.

Chapter Thirteen

Garrett played his hand, smirking when Duke and X grumbled a curse. "Give me my muthafuckin' money!"

"Ah, shit." X smacked his leftover cards on the table.

Garrett poured the quarters out of the "kitty" bowl into the growing pile in front of him. They'd started game night with Tonk, a card game they often played. So far, Garrett had been the big winner, and while they were only playing for quarters, he reveled in defeating his friends.

"Man, let's play some spades," X said.

"Nah, bruh." Duke opened a bottle of beer. "Not happening. You and Zara are sore winners."

Garrett laughed. "Right."

"Man, shut the hell up," Duke told Garrett. "You ain't shit either."

Zara entered the man cave, a bowl of potato chips in one hand and a small container of French onion dip in the other. Skye followed with more beer. The two ladies sat on the leather sofa. Garrett tried not to stare, but he lost that battle.

Tonight she was dressed comfortably in joggers and a white tee. Her hair was once again styled in a high bun with loose tendrils framing her face. Casual and sexy. His favorite look on her.

After last night, after waking her up with an orgasm and a cup of coffee, he'd gone home and immediately regretted the decision to not talk to her about what had happened. They'd been so wrapped up in each other, so filled with desire, he didn't want to ruin anything they'd shared with his thoughts. So instead he'd pretended he was good with wherever this went. Even though there was no way he'd be content to be her friend with benefits. He wanted more. And he needed her to know that.

Vaguely, he heard someone say "Bruh." But he didn't look to see if they were talking to him. He couldn't take his eyes off of Skye. She laughed, her head falling back as delight lit up her face.

"Brotha Garrett."

He blinked, and turned to find X and Duke staring at him. "What?"

Duke smirked. "Shit, man, why don't you just go sit with her?"

"Shut the hell up," Garrett grumbled. He picked up the deck of cards and shuffled them.

"I'm just sayin'," Duke added. "That shit was obvious as hell."

X nodded. "Very."

"I know you're not talking shit, bruh," Garrett said. "Not after Donutgate."

Duke barked out a laugh and gave Garrett a fist pound. "Right. Still funny as hell almost a year later."

X glared at them. "And I don't regret that shit either."

Garrett guzzled down the rest of his beer. "You shouldn't. You're marrying her."

"And she's going to be the mother of my kid."

Pausing, Garrett glanced up at X. "You're talking about kids already?"

"Yeah, we are," X replied.

"Man, can you set the damn date first?" Duke cut the deck. "And preferably not in the summer. One wedding is enough."

"Too late," X said.

"For the wedding not being in the summer?" Garrett asked, while he passed out the cards.

"No. The summer would be too late to have the wedding because my kid will be here in July."

Garrett frowned. "Your kid?"

"Our kid," X said. "Mine and Zara's."

"Bruh." Duke dropped his cards on the table. "Stop playin'."

Xavier shrugged. "I'm serious."

All three of them stood. Duke congratulated X first with a hug and Garrett followed suit. Zara and Skye joined them, and Garrett embraced the future mother and wife. His brother was going to be a father. He couldn't be happier for them.

"So, I'm glad he finally said something," Zara said, bumping her hip into X. "I've been waiting for him to break the news."

"I had to be creative." X rubbed Zara's belly and kissed her nose. "I wanted it to have maximum impact."

Garrett met Skye's gaze, noted the amusement in her eyes. He pointed at her. "You knew."

She grabbed his finger and pulled him to her. "I did."

Tapping her nose, he said, "I knew you were holding back."

Grinning, she shrugged. "I felt it would be better coming from him."

Garrett glanced at Duke and X to find them eyeing him curiously. But he couldn't care less. It felt good to actually have a conversation with her in front of people, which didn't consist of polite or not-so-polite small talk. He'd half expected her to pretend they hadn't spent the night wrapped around each other, but he was pleasantly surprised when she'd greeted him with a hug *and* a kiss earlier. It didn't even matter that it was a quick brush of her lips against his cheek.

"And Zara threatened me with having to come into the birthing room if I spilled," Skye added.

Zara giggled. "You're still coming into the birthing room."

"No, I'm not." Skye batted her eyelashes at her friend.

"Yes, you are," Zara sang, in a dramatic high note.

"Never." Skye mimicked her friend's tone. "You'll be just fine with X, your mom, and Rissa's bossy ass. I'll be waiting to meet my little cousin-slash-niece-slash-godbaby when she's clean and has on one of those cute hats and a onesie." She bent down and talked to Zara's belly. "And I can't wait to kiss those cheeks."

"Move," Zara said, feigning annoyance. "You can't talk to the baby if you don't want to see the main event."

"Oh, please, Z-Ra." Skye waved her hand. "I love you."

Zara cracked up. "I love you, too. But you get on my nerves."

Garrett watched Zara and Skye retreat to the sofa, and sat back down at the table. Picking up his cards, he asked, "Whose turn?"

"Yours," Duke said. "Brotha Obvious."

X snickered and gave Duke a pound. "Obvious as hell."

Garrett pulled a card from the deck and spread with a run of clubs. "How about y'all just concentrate on not losing your damn money."

After game night, he drove Skye home and walked her to the door. She grinned up at him. "Want to come in?"

He wrapped his arms around her waist, pulling her closer. Leaning down, he nibbled her neck before placing a kiss on her mouth. "If you want me to."

"I wouldn't ask if I didn't want you to."

He raised a brow. "If I come in, I'm *coming in* everywhere. Is that what you want?"

"Again, I wouldn't ask if I didn't want you to."

Seconds later, they were stumbling into the house, clinging to each other, removing clothes, kissing, and biting and licking. They didn't make it to the bedroom this time. Instead, she shoved him onto the sofa and straddled his lap.

He slid a hand up her back, wrapped it around her neck and held her to him as he devoured her mouth. Garrett wanted to consume her, make her remember everything that was good about them, everything that made them perfect together.

He teased her nipples with his thumb before he pulled one into his mouth, sucking it until she shuddered against him.

"Yes," she whispered, holding him to her.

Parting her slick folds with his finger, he slipped a finger inside her heat, then another. He pumped slowly while she rode his hand. Suddenly, he needed to taste her. Pulling his finger out, he flipped her on her back.

She yelped. "Garrett," she squealed. "You're so wrong for that."

"Quiet," he said, pressing his face into her core. He inhaled her scent. She was so wet for him, so sexy, so responsive. He could do this every single day—forever—and never be satisfied. He would never get enough of her. Spreading her, he circled her clit with his tongue and slid his fingers into her again. He worked her with his tongue, reveling in her taste and the feel of her against his tongue. Skye came on a tortured sigh, calling his name over and over again.

He went back in for more, but she closed her legs, trapping his head between her thighs. Chuckling, he said, "Skye." He tickled her legs. "You have to let me go."

"No," she murmured. "You're killing me."

She caressed his face, and pulled him to her. He traced her lips with his finger, completely aware of where his finger had been. Unfazed, she kissed him.

"You are so damn hot," she whispered between lingering kisses. "But . . ." She slid onto the floor, between his legs. "It's my turn."

She gripped his dick in her palm, and licked him from the base to the tip. *Shit.* He swept her hair out of her face. He wanted to watch. She was glorious, those full lips around him, those brown eyes on him. When she sucked him into her mouth, the ability to think evaporated under her skilled tongue, her warm mouth.

Skye hummed as she worked him, winding him up like a doll. She was too good, too freakin' sexy. And he was close. So close. But he didn't want to come like this. He wanted to be inside her.

"Skye," he groaned. "Come here."

Dazed, she released him and glanced up at him. "I'm not done."

"Yes, you are." He picked her up and perched her on his lap. "I want inside you. Now."

With a wicked smirk, she lowered herself on him. It didn't take long for them to come together again, each of them gasping the other's name as pleasure took over.

Skye collapsed on his chest, burrowed into him. He wrapped his arms around her, brushed his hands over her back.

"I'm thirsty, but I don't want to move," she said.

He chuckled, smacking her ass lightly. "I feel you."

She sat up and smiled. "Want a bottle of water?"

"I'll have that"—he brushed a finger over a nipple—"and another helping of you."

Standing up, she stretched, unashamed at her nakedness. "I think that can be arranged."

Later, they lay facing each other. They'd finally made it to her bedroom, but he didn't take the time to look around. He was too engrossed, too captivated by her.

"I'm so sleepy," she said, closing her eyes.

"Me too. But I can't fall asleep."

She frowned. "Why?"

He sighed. "Because I have to say something to you. I need another five-minute talk . . . about what we just did." He felt her tense and start to pull away, but he held her there with a hand against her back.

"Sex?"

"Yeah, that. But I need you to know that it wasn't just sex."

* * *

Skye blinked, Garrett's words registering in her brain. Not just sex? *What is it?* The urge to pull away from him surged within her.

He touched her face, traced the line of her jaw. "Don't bolt on me. It's okay, Skye."

But was it really okay? They'd just spent two nights making love without a care in the world. Talking seemed like the logical next step. So why did the prospect make her stomach clench? *Because I want it to be more than sex.* And that scared her.

"It's okay, Skye," he repeated. "You know me."

Skye loved and hated that he could read her so well. On the other side of that, he knew that his touch, his voice calmed her.

"If this isn't just sex for you, what is it?" she asked.

"Us."

She closed her eyes and let out a breath she didn't realize she'd been holding. "Us? There's so much that's happened, Garrett. So much hurt."

"I know." The ghost of a smile touched his lips. "Which is why we need this five-minute conversation."

She giggled. "Okay. So talk."

"I'm not interested in a friends-with-benefits situation, Skye. I'm a grown-ass man. I have a career that I love. I have a home. Now, I want a home life."

His words filled a space in her that hadn't been filled in . . . ever.

"I want to spend time with you," he continued. "I want to spoil you. I want to wake up with you in the morning and fall asleep with you at night."

"What exactly are you asking?" she said. "Are you telling me you want to be in a relationship with me? After everything that we've been through, after the years of not talking? Do you really think it would work?"

"I don't know, Skye. Yes, a lot has changed. But this . . ." He placed his hand over her heart. "This hasn't changed."

"But it has. You don't know everything that I've been through, Garrett. I'm not the same woman you knew."

"So, we take it slow, get to know each other as we are now. Date."

"Does this mean that my five-date rule applies?" she asked.

Skye didn't have a rule. She didn't actually believe in setting rules within a relationship. Zara had done it with X and it had backfired when she fell in love with him. Then, her bestie was so stuck in the rules, she couldn't tell him. With their history, Skye didn't want to do that with Garrett.

He barked out a laugh. "I think we've passed that part of the journey."

Garrett had a way of putting her at ease, making her feel safe. But he didn't know everything. "What if you don't like the new me?"

"I already do." He ran his thumb down her chin and she fought to keep her eyes open. "The best parts of you haven't changed. You're still a woman who is strong in her convictions, committed to her work, and devoted to her family. The rest is just a small part of you, a chapter in your story."

This man. Skye wanted to take the leap. Because he was so good, to her and for her. He understood her. The simple act of relating her journey to a story, knowing how important reading was to her, made her swoon. But still . . .

"I treated you so badly." Her throat burned as shame

rolled through her. "You didn't deserve it." She'd basically made him the villain in their story. She'd acted like he had meant nothing to her. And even though she knew she was wrong, she was stubborn, and she'd continually made the same mistake. If she could even call it a mistake, because it was a choice. It was a choice to act like he'd hurt her, when she knew that she'd hurt him.

"And you apologized. I accepted."

"Do you really?"

He kissed her nose, then her cheeks. "Yes."

"But if we are going to talk, we should talk about everything, right?"

He laced his hands through her hair, calming her nerves. "In due time." Garrett chuckled. "We don't have to discuss everything today."

She grabbed his hand, kissed each of his knuckles. "So . . . slow? We take it slow."

"As slow as you need it to be."

Skye bit down on her lip. "What if this doesn't work?"

Garrett kissed her brow. "Let's not think about that. If we're going to do this, then we need to just do it without worrying about the future."

"We just got to this place. If this doesn't work, where does that leave us?"

"Friends."

"Are you sure?" she asked.

As usual, her mind ran rampant with thoughts of worst-case scenarios. Maybe instead of just walking past each other at an event, they would end up cursing each other out every chance they got? Maybe they wouldn't even be able to look at each other without wanting to cry or throw shit?

"Listen, Skye." He pinned her with an intense gaze.

"You mean too much to me to go another decade without talking to you or laughing with you or eating with you. Just being together. We're both adults. We're going into this with eyes wide open. If this doesn't work, it will be okay. *We'll* be okay. What did I tell you? You. Know. Me. I wouldn't tell you a lie."

Skye traced his cheek with her thumbs, brushed her lips against his, before deepening it. And as they made love to each other, she knew she made the right decision. Because she *did* know him. And she knew he meant what he said.

Chapter Fourteen

Garrett met Skye's gaze from across the conference room. His flight had landed an hour before the meeting at Pure Talent, so he hadn't had time to talk to her before they started. They hadn't seen each other in over a week, and even though they'd talked every day while he was in Houston, he missed her. That simple fact prompted him to come to a very sobering conclusion. They'd talked about taking it slow, but his heart had already started speeding to the finish line.

Julius's ranting drew his attention away from Skye's eyes, her skin, her legs in that skirt. He probably should be focused on his job, but again, he couldn't seem to concentrate on anything else but Skye.

They'd already been at it for half an hour, trying to get the couple on the same page with regards to the movie—and the pending divorce announcement. But Julius had nixed every single idea, and spent the majority of the meeting acting like a little—

"Garrett?" Skye said.

He glanced up at Skye. "Yes."

"I've prepared a joint statement for the media regarding

the divorce once the complaint is filed. Can you please review and get back to me with changes? I've sent it to your email."

Garrett nodded. "I can do that."

"Is there a reason why I can't write my own statement?" Julius asked. "I'm the one who knows the truth. Everything else is a lie."

Skye pursed her lips. "Mr. Reeves, it's best for both of you if we coordinate on this announcement."

"I don't care," Julius said. "I'll write a statement."

Garrett shot his client a sidelong glance. He wondered who came up with the bright idea to try and bring Paige and Julius together to discuss their ongoing saga. Halfway through the meeting, he'd realized there was no point in trying to reason with Julius.

The man had already been indicted on several charges, yet he'd refused to admit to any wrongdoing. Everything was everybody else's fault. The baby he had with Catherine wasn't his fault. The accusations were lies. The media was tearing his marriage apart.

Garrett had even prepped Julius before the meeting today, but the director had his own agenda. When they'd arrived earlier, Julius had immediately tried to convince Paige to give him another chance. That didn't work. Then the asshole tried to appeal to his wife's heart by crying fake tears and dropping to his knees to beg her to listen to him. That didn't work. Next, Julius switched up to anger, railing against all the forces that had tried to keep them apart with lies. That didn't work either.

"You know what?" Julius blurted out. "You have no one to blame but yourself, Paige. If you'd been a little more loving, maybe I wouldn't have sought affection from someone else."

It was the first time Julius had admitted to any wrongdoing, but it was wrapped in a cloak of blame. And that tactic *did* work, just not in the way the perverted director probably hoped. Because Andrew jumped up and stopped Paige's fist from connecting with Julius's jaw in the nick of time.

"I fuckin' hate you!" Paige screamed. "I want you out of my life, you lying bastard. Go to hell." Then she stormed out of the room, with Andrew on her heels.

Up until that point, the actress had done a good job of maintaining her composure during the meeting, through the lies, through the tears, through the incessant yelling. When she'd responded, she always spoke in a calm, even tone. No shouting. No crying. No emotion. Not many people could have done the same in her situation.

Paige had also handled everything with grace in the media, in every appearance to promote the movie. Which was no small feat since their marriage had been thrown up, twisted around, and dissected for all the world to see over the last several weeks. Garrett guessed that had a lot to do with Skye, who'd been relentless in her role as Paige's publicist.

Julius paced the room like a caged animal, grumbling curses, flinging accusations. Garrett was ready to end this so he could take Skye home, strip her bare, and make love to her on any available surface.

"Alright." Skye leaned back in her chair and crossed her legs. "I understand that you're upset, Julius. But this isn't accomplishing anything. The divorce filing is pretty much a done deal. Paige agreed to meet with you today to discuss the best way to handle that in the news. How you feel or don't feel about her and your marriage doesn't matter at this point. If you're not going to talk to her like you have some sense, then we're done here."

Julius whirled around, teeth bared. "Who the hell do you think you are?"

Garrett knew Skye could take care of herself, but that didn't stop him from wanting to step in.

"Oh, that's easy. I'm Skye Palmer." She stood. "Maybe you should remember that the next time you walk into Pure Talent and act like a toddler throwing a temper tantrum. This is a place of business. We're here to do a job. Let's get to it, or you can get the hell out."

"I don't give a damn who your uncle is," Julius sneered. "I will ruin you."

"Take your best shot," Skye said, leaning forward and planting both hands on the table. "But understand this, once you take yours, I'll take mine."

"Listen, you little bitch," Julius roared. "I—"

Standing, Garrett blocked the director when he looked like he was going to charge at Skye. "I wouldn't do that if I were you," he growled. "Back the hell up. Now."

He was past the point of professional. Rage, blinding and hot, filled him to the brim. It took all of his willpower to not choke Julius. Garrett had held his tongue when Julius lashed out at Paige, because Andrew had been there to defend his own client. But what he wasn't going to do was let that puny, punk-ass fool get anywhere near Skye.

The director stepped back, a deep frown on his face. His fists were clenched at his sides like he wanted to hit him.

I wish that muthafucka would.

Skye squeezed his arm, and Garrett wondered when

she'd crossed the room to him. "It's okay," she whispered. "We're good."

"What the hell is your problem, Garrett?" Julius roared, nearly tipping over a chair. "You work for me."

Not for much longer. "Maybe so, but if you think I'm going to stand here and continue to let you intimidate this woman in my presence, you're mistaken."

"That woman—" Julius pointed at Skye—"disrespected me. Don't think for one minute that I don't know who convinced Paige to go through with this."

"How about you take responsibility for your own actions?" Skye said.

"How about you shut the hell up?" Julius snapped.

Garrett looked over at Skye. "Can you give us a moment?" he asked her.

Her gaze flitted from him to Julius and back to him. "Are you sure?"

"Yes. I'll let you know when we're ready to proceed."

Once Skye left the room, Garrett turned to Julius. "I'm sure you're used to people doing your bidding. But I'm not one of them. It's time you find someone else to represent you. I'm done, effective immediately."

"We signed a contract," Julius said.

"A contract that you apparently didn't read, because I don't need your permission." Garrett had built in several clauses to protect himself in cases such as this.

Julius snickered. "It's just as well. You've done a piss-poor job anyway. When I'm done with you, you won't have a practice."

"I wouldn't bet on it." Garrett shrugged.

"You don't know who you're fucking with."

"Neither do you."

"And that Skye Palmer? Not even Jax Starks will be able to help her salvage her reputation once I'm through with her."

"Don't even think about it," Garrett said, ice in his tone. "Trust me, you don't want to go there. I'm not one to be underestimated."

"Is that a threat?"

Shaking his head, Garrett said, "Not at all. I promise you, you don't want to take me there. You're not the only person who knows the truth." It wouldn't take much to nail Julius to the wall. The asshole was as guilty as he was pompous. "Yours is the only character in question right now."

"Well, then, it's time you leave."

Garrett knew Julius was full of shit. All that false bravado, all that talk never amounted to anything. "I'll leave when you do. And, make no mistake, if I hear that you've done anything to hurt Paige or Skye, you will not like my response."

Julius stormed out of the room seconds later without another word, leaving Garrett alone. He placed a call to Xavier to let him know about the confrontation and subsequent threats against Skye. His friend immediately jumped into action, notifying security and ensuring Julius would no longer be allowed in the building. Opening his laptop, Garrett replied to several emails. He'd just sent an email to Tara to handle the case closeout when Skye entered the conference room again.

She glanced around. Frowning, she approached him. "Hey?" she asked. "Where's your client?"

Garrett leaned back in his chair. "Hopefully, on his way to jail."

She laughed. "Funny." Running her fingers through his hair, she asked, "You quit, didn't you?"

"It was time." Taking her other hand, he kissed the inside of her wrist. She smelled like vanilla and oranges. He nipped the skin there, then soothed it with his tongue. "I'm sorry to leave you in the lurch. You'll probably have to work with another crisis manager, one that will do whatever he asks."

"I'll be just fine." She leaned against the table and tilted her head, studying him. "Are *you*?"

Pulling her back to him, he slid his hands up her legs, wrapped his arms around her waist and squeezed her. Burying his face in her stomach, he held on to her for a moment, savoring the contact. "I'm good."

She stroked his hair. "Julius is an asshole. Paige is done talking, so I'm going to act accordingly to distance her from his issues. We'll be rolling out a new plan in the next few days, before she starts shooting her next movie."

"Does this mean you're going back to L.A.?"

Since the couple had separated, Paige had moved to California from Atlanta, where the two had made a home. He guessed that Skye would probably be traveling to L.A. often until this whole thing blew over.

"Maybe. Right now, it's going to be hard to do that. My boss is still on leave and there are things that need to be done here. I'm hoping Paige can find a new PR firm to represent her so we can kind of step back a little."

He peered up at her. "Are you okay with that? Because you seem to love this type of work."

"No, I don't have a problem with her hiring a new PR agency. Pure Talent doesn't have the manpower to give each of our clients such personal attention. For someone like Paige, she needs a dedicated publicist."

"I get it. I just think you thrive when you're working with her." He'd seen the sparkle in her eyes on several occasions since they'd started working together. Even if she wouldn't admit it, he knew she wanted to do more of that type of work.

"Maybe," she said.

He stood finally and planted a kiss on her mouth. With his thumb, he parted her lips and dipped his tongue inside. The purr that escaped her mouth went straight to his groin. And to show her, he pulled her closer. "Dinner tonight?"

Her mouth curved into a beautiful smile. "What time should I be ready?"

"Seven." He kissed her again and started to pack up his briefcase. "I'll be on time."

Skye walked into her office and took a seat at her desk. Since she'd stepped in for Carmen, she'd worked long hours to clear her boss's desk. Most nights, she'd stayed up until the wee hours of the morning getting her own work done, because she'd spent the day doing everything else.

Burying her face in her hands, she closed her eyes and took a deep breath. It was still early, and she had so much to do. After that stupid-ass meeting, she had agreed to more work. She wanted to help Paige, she wanted to see the actress happy and whole. And while she hadn't specifically encouraged her to go through with the divorce, she couldn't deny she was happy when Paige had told her the news.

The woman had suffered enough in the short-lived

marriage. From the beginning, rumors had swirled that Julius was a low-down, dirty-ass dog. And Paige was a beautiful, kind woman. She didn't deserve the trouble.

A knock at the door pulled her from her reverie. "Come in."

Paige poked her head into the office.

Skye stood. "Hi." Smoothing a hand over her skirt, she rounded the desk. "I thought you were gone."

"I came back. To talk to you."

Skye motioned for Paige to take a seat on the sofa in her office. "Okay." She took a seat on an adjacent chair. "What's up?"

Paige let out a weary sigh. The last few weeks had taken a toll on the gorgeous actress. Her once bright eyes were dead, sad. Her big hair was pulled back into a harsh bun. And her skin seemed pale, like she was sick or getting over a bug.

Skye reached out and squeezed the other woman's hand. "It's okay. Do you want something to drink?" She kept her small refrigerator stocked with water, juice, and a bottle of tequila for emergencies. "Need a shot?"

Paige let out a strained laugh. "No, I'm good. I wanted you to know that I am so grateful for you, for your support."

"No need to thank me."

"I know it's your job, but you've gone above and beyond what the agency would normally do."

"Don't worry about it. That's what we're here for, to support you."

"I'm going to meet with a publicist in the morning, but I wanted to ask if you wouldn't mind staying on for a few months. Just until the divorce announcement and the remaining movie appearances are done. And through the award-show season."

"Sure thing."

Paige closed her eyes and let out a slow breath. "When I got married, I thought we would be the exception to the rule. The fact that we aren't just hurts."

Skye knew the pain well. "I know. But the good news is you're still young. Julius Reeves isn't the end-all-be-all. You can do much better than his sorry . . ." She cleared her throat, remembering Paige was still a client and she was at work. Earlier, she'd lost her composure a little bit, but she wouldn't make the same mistake now.

"You can say it. He's a sorry-ass muthafucka."

Grinning, Skye said, "I wasn't going to add that *muthafucka* on the end of it. But it fits."

They both laughed.

"Skye?" Paige said.

"Yes?"

"Have you ever considered going out on your own?"

Skye blinked. "What? On my own, as in business?"

"Exactly. You're good at this. I imagine you have rules to follow being an employee of the agency, so you can't flex your muscles as much as you could if you worked for yourself."

Skye pondered Paige's words, noting the similarities in this conversation and the one she'd just had with Garrett. "Thanks for saying that, but I'm not looking to leave Pure Talent."

"Is it because of your uncle?"

Uncle Jax would never want Skye to stay if she wasn't happy. He'd always encouraged her to do what was in her heart. She shook her head. "No, not really."

"So you like your job?"

There was that question again. And Skye couldn't seem to find a consistent answer.

"I love my job," she chirped. And sometimes it was true.

She worked entire days, planning and attending events, contacting reporters, negotiating for press time, and generally putting out fires. Yet, she felt like she was phoning it in, doing what was needed, but never feeling satisfied that she'd done anything worthwhile. Skye had spoken to Sasha about it, but they hadn't broached the subject again in any other session. Maybe it's time to do that.

"At any rate"—Paige stood—"I hope you'll consider that you have so much more to offer. And if I know Jax Starks, he would agree. I don't think it's a coincidence that he picked you to work with me."

Skye frowned. She'd always assumed X had been instrumental in ensuring she took over for Carmen in the interim. Because they'd talked often about her job and her goals. It would be just like him to advocate for her to take on this task. *What if he hadn't?*

Standing, Skye smiled. "Whatever you say, Paige." She walked her to the door. "Are you flying back to L.A. tonight?"

Paige nodded. "In a few hours. No offense, but I don't like Atlanta. I miss the beach."

"I do, too, sometimes."

"Well, if you ever decide to leave the agency, there will always be a job for you with me. Come to the beach."

Moving back to L.A. hadn't crossed her mind. She'd grown up there, spent a lot of time in Cali. But she'd never considered a cross-country move. Her life was in Atlanta. Her friends, her job . . . Garrett.

Sucking in a deep breath, she said, "I'll visit you."

Paige nodded. "We'll talk soon?"

"Definitely. I'll call you tomorrow with some ideas."

"Perfect."

After Paige left, Skye made her way up to the executive floor and straight to X's office. His assistant gave her the go-ahead, and she marched right in. X sat at his desk, his eyes narrowed in concentration.

"Hey, cousin." Skye took a seat in one of the chairs across from the desk. "Got a minute?"

He nodded, while he tapped away at the keyboard. When he was done, he glanced up at her and grinned. "Always."

"I had an interesting meeting today."

"The one with that punk-ass Julius Reeves?"

She smirked. "What did you hear?"

X leaned back in his chair. "Enough."

Curious, she asked, "What? Do you have cameras in the conference rooms?"

He shook his head. "Nah, Garrett filled me in."

"Ah, that makes sense."

"Is that why you want to talk? Believe me, when Garrett told me that fool threatened you, I was ready to find him and hem him up myself."

Skye laughed softly. "You're reformed, cousin. I wouldn't want you to revert back to your old ways."

X's quick temper was legendary among their family and friends. Growing up, her cousin had no trouble finding a fight. Which was why she suspected he liked the game of football. Last year, his anger had almost landed him in jail and Pure Talent in court. But Zara had been a calming influence on him. And he'd evolved since they'd become involved.

He snorted. "Ha, that's what you think. I don't have a

problem coming out of retirement to kick his ass. And I'd do it with a smile on my face so the paparazzi could get a flattering pic."

Cracking up, she shook her head. "You're a nut."

"Anyway, what's going on with you?"

The conversation with Paige kept replaying in her head and she had to ask him one burning question. "When you asked me to take over for Carmen while she was on leave, was that your idea?"

"Hm . . ." He glanced up at the ceiling, seemingly to think of the sequence of events. "Carmen called Dad and told him about her leave. He wanted you to handle Paige. Then I suggested you step into the role on an interim basis."

Skye sucked in a deep breath. Paige was right. Uncle Jax had been in the midst of this, pulling the strings. Now she had to find out why. "So, Uncle Jax wanted me to personally handle Paige?"

X nodded. "Yes. That conversation happened between him and Carmen. He brought it to me later."

"Oh." She swallowed hard. "That's . . . enlightening."

"Why?" he asked. "You don't like the job?"

It was a question, but for some reason, she suspected her cousin already knew the answer. Nodding, she said, "Sure."

"That doesn't sound convincing."

"I'm not trying to convince you."

"Then stop lying."

Skye dropped her head. "I don't know, X. I just want more. I don't want to seem ungrateful, because Uncle Jax has been wonderful to me, supportive, encouraging. But I feel like I'm missing something."

"Personal?"

She smiled. "I'm not talking to you about Garrett."

He barked out a laugh. "Not yet, anyway."

Rolling her eyes, she continued. "Whatever. I'm talking about my career. I can't put my finger on it. But I'll figure it out soon."

"Now, that I'm certain of." He stood and walked around the desk. She walked into his open arms. "I know you'll get to the bottom of your feelings."

She pulled back, eyeing him. "You're so sure."

"I'm sure of you. Listen, you're capable of anything. A leader. Whatever you decide to do, I've got your back. How many times do I have to keep telling you this?"

"Forever."

"Done deal."

She smiled. "Thanks, X. I appreciate you."

"Any time. And when you're ready to talk about Garrett, I'll be here for that, too."

Shoving him away playfully, she stuck out her tongue and made her way to the door. "Be quiet. Let me be great and handle my own grown woman's business. Bye, X."

"Be good, Skye," he yelled after her. Duke had told her the same thing on New Year's Eve. She hadn't followed his directions then, and she definitely wouldn't follow X's now.

Chapter Fifteen

"How are things going?" Sasha asked.

Skye thought about the seemingly simple question. On the surface, one might think she was doing great. Over the last few weeks, she'd continued to rock out her job and had continued to see Garrett. But her mind continued to be a building storm of turmoil. Because the more she worked, the more she knew Paige and Garrett had been right.

As much as she'd thought she wanted to run the publicity department at Pure Talent, she knew now that having the title wasn't her endgame.

"Things are going okay," she answered honestly.

"Tell me more about that." Sasha sipped something from her mug, and Skye wondered briefly if she was a tea or coffee person.

Focus. Skye didn't know where to start, so she decided to start with what she thought had been the good parts of her past few weeks. Smiling, she said, "X and Zara are getting married and having a baby."

Sasha smiled. "That's nice."

"It is." She relaxed in the chair. "They've set a date. March third."

Her therapist's eyes widened. "That's soon."

Skye explained the reasons why they'd decided to do it quickly. "I don't blame them. She doesn't want to be big pregnant and walking down the aisle, and they both want to be married before the little cutie is born."

"Makes sense. So tell me what you've done to help them. Because I know you've been supporting them."

"Anything less than excellent is not acceptable for two of the most important people in my life. And a wedding—this wedding—will be a grand occasion."

Skye had taken over the planning of her best friend and her cousin's nuptials. Zara had initially wanted to marry on a remote island somewhere, but had recently settled on Hawaii for their destination.

In short order, Skye had secured the wedding venue, Haiku Mill. She was currently working with their in-house coordination team to finalize the details. She'd also confirmed the guest accommodations. Just that morning, she'd picked up the hand-drawn invitations she'd ordered, and planned to mail them once she left her appointment. Zara preferred an intimate wedding, so they'd kept the guest list fairly small. Only family and close friends would attend.

Skye gave a brief history of the relationship between hers, Zara's, and Duke's families. "We all grew up together, not technically family, but *family*. Does that seem weird?"

"Not at all."

"Our parents are still close, and we've all maintained regular contact with each other. And this is the first time that two of the families will be joined together. That's pretty awesome."

"Sounds like it will be a beautiful and elegant ceremony and reception."

"I'm confident it will be. The closer we get to the day, the more excited I get. My Uncle Jax has a holiday party every year, but a lot of us don't make it for whatever reasons. This will be the first time, in a long time, everyone will be together."

"You're talking about the three families, the Starks, Youngs, and Reids?"

Skye nodded. "Right. Of course, the Youngs make up a huge part of the guest list, as you know." She laughed. Duke had a lot of siblings and some of them had married or were in committed relationships. "But I've personally called everyone on the guest list and I haven't had anyone tell me they couldn't make it. Which is good."

"I'm glad things are going so well on that front. Now, we haven't talked in a few weeks. But the last time we did, you mentioned your complicated feelings for Garrett."

Skye remembered that before-sex conversation. It felt like a lifetime ago. Since then, she and Garrett had spent a lot of time together. Not just having sex, but reconnecting. And she found herself looking forward to after work, because inevitably, that meant seeing him.

"How are things on that front?" Sasha asked.

Unable to hide her smile, Skye sighed. "I took your advice. We talked, and both of us admitted that we want to see where this could lead."

"And you're comfortable with that decision?"

Nodding, she said, "Actually, I am. We're both busy, but we've found ways to make it work." Their five-minute conversations had never been that short, but she loved it when he requested that exact amount of time. Because she knew she'd be treated to good food, good conversation, and good sex. Everything good about them before was ten times better now.

Last weekend, they'd made a quick trip to Alabama to see Max. The college student insisted they go out on a double date, forcing Garrett to be nice to his little sister's boyfriend. Skye had laughed every time she caught Garrett glaring at the young man who'd stolen Max's heart.

"This is good news, Skye." Sasha grinned. "You've actively gone after something that you wanted and you're able to enjoy the experience without overthinking it too much. That's progress."

"I wouldn't say I haven't been overthinking it. Because I definitely have."

Thoughts constantly invaded her brain at odd times during the day, about her relationship, about whether they could even call it a relationship, about the future, about what she would do if there was no future. So many questions, so many concerns. But she'd done her best to push through. Because being with him was so much more than any negative thought. When she was with him, she felt alive. The more time she spent with him, the more she was reminded that it had always been that way. Garrett was the first person who'd made her feel sexy, made her feel capable, made her feel loved. And she realized that time apart hadn't changed, or dampened, the love she had for him.

"Is it possible to love someone this soon?" Skye asked.

Sasha eyed her thoughtfully. "Do you think you're in love with him?"

Shrugging, Skye said, "I don't know that I ever stopping loving him." No matter how hard she'd tried, no matter what she'd told herself, Garrett was the man that she'd envisioned when she thought of her endgame. He was the man she wanted in her life. *But would he be that man?* And could she allow herself to let him?

Right now, she was all in, but she knew herself. Her best intentions were somehow never enough to sustain a relationship. What made her think this time would be different?

"Skye, I can see that you're struggling with this. And I want to caution you against skipping ahead to an uncertain future. The problem with overthinking is people tend to live their lives based on what *could* happen as opposed to enjoying what *is* happening."

Swallowing, Skye dropped her gaze, stared at her hands. "It's almost like asking someone to look forward, but don't look too hard."

"I'd like to think of it as preparing for a vacation. When you book a trip, like the one you're taking to Hawaii in a few weeks, you have to book your flight and room, make sure you have your money together, watch the weather forecast to make sure you pack the right types of clothes. You spend time ensuring you have everything you need on the trip. But when you get there, you have fun. You're not thinking about the things that can happen. You're focused on what you're doing, taking excursions, going out to eat, having a good time with your family or your loved ones. Yes, you know that something could go wrong, but you're not anticipating it."

She'd never been good at taking things as they come. Even in her job, she couldn't afford to not look at every angle at all times. "I get the analogy. At the same time, I wonder if I'm just hardwired to look for an exit plan. I do it every day in my job, and I've done it throughout my life. And when I don't do that, when I let my guard down, things tend to explode."

"Sometimes horrible things happen whether you're waiting for them or not. People break into houses that have alarms, some people develop lung cancer even if they've never smoked a cigarette a day in their life."

Skye wondered if Sasha was speaking from experience. "True."

"But you can't stay in your house forever because you're scared someone will break in. There's nothing wrong with taking a leap, putting yourself out there. Pain is a natural part of life. It hurts, but you can move past it. You *have* moved past it. You might be wary, you may be frightened, but you're still here."

After her session, Skye decided to walk back to the Pure Talent office building. It was a nice day for February, and the fresh air helped clear her mind. Sasha had given her a lot to think about.

During her first appointment, she'd mentioned she felt stuck in indecision. Which was likely the result of years of second-guessing her choices in life. She'd already made the first step, and started seeing a therapist. She'd taken other small steps, and nothing had blown up in her face. And even if it did, she couldn't say she regretted the decision to kiss Garrett on New Year's Eve. Because that one action had opened up possibilities.

She felt her phone buzz in her jacket pocket. Pulling it out, she smiled when Garrett's face flashed on the screen. "Hello," she said.

"Baby, I have a surprise for you." The low rasp of his voice always set off wild flutters in her stomach. And it didn't scare her. It felt good.

Grinning, she asked, "What is it?"

"If I tell you what it is, it won't be a surprise. Where are you?"

"Just leaving my appointment." She stopped at a hot dog vendor and ordered one. "Why?"

"Instead of going out tonight, let's eat in. My place."

"Are you cooking for me?"

He chuckled. "Yes, but I also have something for you."

"Okay. What time do you want me there?"

"Whenever you get here. I decided to work from home this afternoon."

"I'll come now," she blurted out. *What the hell am I doing?*

"This early?" He sounded skeptical. "I thought you had meetings this afternoon."

"I do. But I can push them back." Skye didn't know where this change of heart came from. In all of her career, she'd only played hooky a handful of times. It wasn't like her to even want to skip work.

"You don't have to do that," he said.

"I want to." Her answer surprised her, but it was true nonetheless. She *did* want to be with him. And she *would* change her day around to make it happen. And it wouldn't make her any less of a bad-ass boss to do so. "I'll be there within the hour."

"G, what are you doing?"

Garrett stared down at the tablet sitting on the countertop and smiled at his sister, who'd insisted on an impromptu video chat. Max was eating a bowl of chips, a curious look in her eyes. "Living my best life."

She laughed, probably because she knew he hated that popular song. "You got jokes. Are you cooking?"

Garrett placed two sweet potatoes in the Instant Pot and started the timer. "What part of *mind your business* didn't you get?"

"Come on, G. You always ask me what I'm doing, and I tell you."

It was true. She'd always been very forthcoming with him, and he felt blessed in that area. Even if she knew she'd get in trouble, she was honest. As a teenager, she didn't try to hide anything, even though he had wished she would sometimes. He had no idea how to handle girl fights and boy crushes, but she'd shared her many woes openly anyway. And he'd listened.

"That's because I'm the . . ." The word *parent* died on his lips, because he wasn't that. "I'm the boss."

"You always told me I was a boss too."

"Of your life, not mine."

If she was sitting in front of him, this would be about the time she would have tossed one of those chips at him. He laughed. "Fine, if you must know, I'm cooking dinner. For Skye."

"Yay!" his sister squealed. "I hope you're making something you can actually cook well."

"What's that supposed to mean? I can cook."

"You can, but other than hamburger pie and some other things, you've kind of fallen off since I left the house. Remember Thanksgiving dinner? You burned the macaroni and cheese and put too much pepper in the greens."

Garrett remembered that incident. But there was a very good reason he'd messed up dinner. "The football game went into overtime. I couldn't concentrate on dinner when I had money on the line."

Max shook her head. "If that's what makes you feel better. What are you making? That way, I can warn Skye to eat before she gets there."

"Be quiet. I'm making flank steak, sweet potatoes, and roasted asparagus."

"Yum. Okay, then. You have my approval to proceed."

Shaking his head, Garrett lined the asparagus on a baking sheet. "Glad you approve. Classes going okay?" He drizzled olive oil over the spears and seasoned them before sliding the pan into the oven.

Max crunched on a chip and held up one finger, signaling him to wait until she finished chewing. When she was done, she said, "I really love my Digital Logic class. My prof is kick-ass. I wish you could meet her." Max babbled on about classes and some of the campus activities she was involved in. "I've been swimming a lot more, while I look for another part-time job."

"That's good. You need to get back to it. It always relaxed you before." Once she'd graduated from high school, she'd cut back on her time in the pool and decided not to try out for the swim team. "Are you reconsidering the team?"

She shrugged. "I don't know. Maybe. I do miss it."

Maybe he was a proud . . . brother, but he'd always thought Max was good enough to swim in the Olympics. Of course, that's not what she wanted. But still . . . "Then you should definitely keep doing it."

"I will."

"Did you get my email about the wedding?"

She beamed. "Yes, and I'm excited. I might need to purchase three more bathing suits. Can't wear the same thing to the pool every day."

He chuckled. "I'll get your ticket. Are you going to be good to miss classes?" The wedding was scheduled for the week before spring break, and he'd been concerned she wouldn't be able to make it work with midterms.

"Yep. I already talked to my professors. And . . ." She

paused as if contemplating something. "I was wondering if Dame could come."

Garrett paused, salt shaker in hand. "Excuse me?"

"We were talking and he's never been to Hawaii. So I said he should come?"

"Where is he going to stay?" He raised a brow. "I hope you don't think he's staying in your room."

"G, we're both adults. You already know we're having sex. So . . ."

Garrett heard the front door open. He'd texted Skye that he'd leave the door unlocked for her. "I don't know, Max."

Skye walked into view, a plant in hand, and set it on a table near the window. Every time she came to his house, she'd brought him what she called a "man plant." So far, he had four of them.

"I'll have to check with Skye about the guest list," he lied. When she heard her name, she froze and turned to him, a questioning look in her eyes. "I'll let you know," he told Max.

He knew that Zara and X wouldn't care if Max brought a date, but he did. It was all him. When Garrett envisioned his time in Hawaii, he imagined nights wrapped around Skye and days exploring the island with Max when they weren't doing wedding stuff. The fact that she wanted to invite a date made him sad in a way. Because it meant she was truly becoming an independent woman. She didn't need him.

Skye walked over to where he stood, leaned up on the tips of her toes and kissed him. Then she peered down at the tablet and waved. "Hi, Max."

Garrett tried to not be affected by the simple display affection, by the way she'd walked into his house as if it was hers, the way she'd placed a plant on his table and then come and greeted with him a kiss. Now she was talking to his sister about school and clothes.

He took the flank steak he'd already prepared and set it on the indoor grill he had. The ladies yapped away about skin care while he cooked.

Skye leaned over the counter. "I think a good moisturizer will help with that. What brand are you using?"

Max told her the brand and then asked her another question. It went on like that for a few minutes, with Skye giving Max advice and his sister eating it up.

Garrett observed Skye for a moment. An emergency meeting at Pure Talent had thrown a wrench in their plan to spend the afternoon together, which he understood. But he noticed that she looked tired, irritated. She was smiling and all, but it didn't reach her eyes. He wondered what had happened between the time she'd called him and her arrival.

"So what's this I hear about the guest list?" Skye asked Max.

"I told G that I want to bring Dame to the wedding. He said he had to check with you."

Garrett ignored the pointed gaze Skye sent his way and flipped the steak. Yep, she'd already figured him out.

"It's fine, Max." Skye shot him a sidelong glance. "If you want to bring your boyfriend, you can."

Max yelped. "Sweet. I'll tell him. He has his own flight money and he'll chip in on the hotel."

"He should be paying for his own trip," he grumbled.

"He will," Max said. "Thanks, Skye."

"You're welcome." Skye poured herself a glass of water. "I can't wait to see you."

"Me too. But I better let y'all go. My brother looks a little irritated."

"I'm fine," he told his sister. He wasn't. "Talk to you soon."

They ended the video chat and Skye turned to him, arms folded across her chest. "You want to tell me what that's about?"

"Nope," he said simply, transferring the steak to a serving plate.

"Really?"

"I just don't think she should get in the habit of footing some man's bill. If he wants to go, he should pay for his own."

"Oh, I agree with that." Skye wrapped her arms around him. "But I don't agree with you giving her a hard time about wanting to bring a date. She's twenty years old. She's in a relationship."

He sighed and rested his forehead against hers. "I don't like it."

"Because she's not your little sister anymore?"

He thought about that question. The more it replayed in his mind, the more it didn't ring true. Max wasn't just his little sister. She was *his* little girl. "It's kind of hard to watch her grow up, sometimes."

"It's inevitable. But let me tell you something from one daddy's little girl to another little girl's daddy . . . She'll always need you."

He pulled her closer, buried his face in her neck. "Promise?"

"I promise."

They held each other for a minute, swaying to an internal melody only they heard. Garrett knew he'd fallen in love with her. Again. If he'd ever really stopped loving her. But he wasn't sure she was ready to hear it. They'd only been seeing each other for a few weeks, but it wasn't a huge leap due to their history. Still, he wouldn't tell her. Not until the right time. Whenever that was, he didn't know. He just knew it wasn't today.

Skye tensed in his arms and pulled back. "Smell that?"

"Shit," he murmured. He'd been so engrossed in her, in the music they made together, that he'd burned the asparagus.

Turning, he opened the oven and pulled out the charred vegetable. He held it out for her to see, and she burst out into a fit a giggles. "Yikes, that's tragic."

Cursing, he dropped the pan in the sink. "Whatever you do, don't tell Max."

"Why?"

"No reason. Just don't mention it. We can have green beans instead." Garrett opened a can of green beans, poured them into a pot, and turned on the stove.

She leaned against the counter and watched him. "Okay. So where is my surprise?"

He started slicing the steak. "It's coming. It's in my bedroom."

She arched a brow. "Should I take off my clothes now or later?"

Garrett pulled her to him and trailed kisses over the line of her jaw to her ear. Sucking the lobe of her ear, he bit down. When he met her hooded gaze again, he groaned, torn between finishing dinner and making love to her right there. "Trust me, I fully intend to be inside you in a matter of hours. But my gift is not my d—"

She clamped her hand over his mouth. "Don't you dare say that. That's blasphemy. Because your dick is a gift." She sucked his bottom lip into her mouth and brushed her hand over the hard ridge of his growing erection. "It's the gift that keeps giving me delicious orgasms."

He laughed, and smacked her butt. "If you keep talking to me like that, you might be bent over this countertop taking everything I have to give."

With a wicked grin, she turned around and pushed her pants and underwear down. "I'm ready when you are."

Damn. He let his gaze rake down the arch of her back, over the curve of her ass. Decision made, he turned off the stove and unplugged the Instant Pot. "You better run."

Skye screamed and took off for the bedroom, stripping the rest of her clothes along the way. She was halfway up the stairs when he caught up to her and scooped her into his arms. He carried her the rest of the way, his mouth fused to hers.

When they entered his bedroom, he strode to the bed and dropped her on top of it. She spread out for him, her hand hitting the gift he'd left there for her.

"What's this?" She rolled over and gasped. Her eyes lit up as she grabbed the stuffed Baby Yoda and hugged it. "Aw, you bought me a Baby Yoda." She grinned. "He's so cute."

"Whatever you say," he grumbled.

It was small, but he caught the slight tremble of her chin, almost like she wanted to cry. But then it disappeared just as quickly. A second later, Baby Yoda whizzed past his head and landed on the chair in the corner.

He eyed her. "Tell me how you really feel?"

She perched her naked self up on her elbows and narrowed her eyes on him. "Baby Yoda can wait. Right now, I need you naked on this bed with me."

Garrett couldn't deny her anything. He took his clothes

off and stepped up to the bed. Gripping her legs, he pulled her to him. Without warning, he flipped her over, laughing when she yelped in surprise. She recovered quickly, getting up on her knees and bending forward.

He smacked her ass lightly. “I like this view.”

She glanced at him over her shoulder and he almost forgot to breathe. She was stunning in every way. “Don’t look too long. I need you.”

There was that word again. *Need.* She needed him, and he needed her. Not wanting to keep her waiting, he pressed himself against her entrance and slowly entered her. He leaned forward, placed a kiss over the back of her neck. “You’re killing me,” he murmured over her skin when she pushed back, pulling him in deeper.

“Good.” She straightened, craning her neck and kissing him.

He cupped a breast in one hand while the other slipped over her clit. The purr that followed settled it. This time would be hard and fast, because he was already on the verge of exploding. He’d take his time with her on round two.

“Garrett, please.” She bit down on his lip. “You can take your time later.”

And he did as he was told, making love to her until she screamed out her release. He followed shortly after, her name a tattered growl on his lips as his own climax hit him like a train.

She collapsed on to the mattress and rolled over on her back. He rested his head between her breasts to catch his breath. He felt the tips of her fingers stroking the back of his neck. Then he felt the rumble of laughter against his head.

Peering up at her, he frowned. “What’s so funny?”

“I really wanted that asparagus.”

They laughed. “I’ll buy you some for next time.”

“Garrett?” He met her waiting gaze. She traced his bottom lip with her thumb. “I’m ready for round two.”

He smirked. “That can be arranged.”

Chapter Sixteen

Garrett walked into his bathroom to find Skye brushing her teeth—with a toothbrush she'd brought to his house. And it felt like normal, like she was meant to be in his bathroom, in nothing but a pair of boy shorts and one of his T-shirts. He leaned against the door jamb and watched her.

When she finished, she met his gaze through the mirror. And once again, the smile she flashed didn't reach her eyes.

He walked into the bathroom and stood behind her. "Food will be here in forty minutes." Dinner hadn't turned out like he'd hoped, so they decided to order in. Pizza and wings. *Simple.*

"I'm starved," she said.

He swept her hair off of her neck and kissed her neck. "What's going on, baby?"

Skye shook her head, averting her gaze. "Nothing. I'm just tired."

The last several weeks, Garrett had spent time reacquainting himself with Skye. A hungry Skye was a hangry Skye. If she was bored, she got anxious or she worked. He could always tell if she was hot, because she would get cranky. She went for walks when she felt stressed out. And when she was horny . . . she found him. This wasn't tired Skye. This was thoughtful, almost sad Skye.

"I'll give you tired," he said. "You have been working long hours. But you're something else, too." He rested his chin on her shoulder. "I won't push you, but you know you can talk to me."

Skye sighed, and turned to face him. "Not in here. There's a toilet right there."

Garrett pulled her out of the bathroom and led her to the bed. She climbed onto the mattress and rolled over on her back. He joined her. They both stared up at the ceiling for a long while.

Finally, she said, "Something's missing."

He looked at her, waiting for her to continue. Because the *something* could be anything—her job, her family. *It could be us.*

"I thought I knew what I wanted." She turned onto her side, and he shifted to face her. "But after I called you today, I went back to the office to pack up my laptop and come here. My boss was in my office waiting for me."

A surge of relief washed through him. As selfish as it was, he was glad she wasn't talking about their relationship. He tucked her hair behind her ear. "Isn't she on leave?"

"Yes!" She shook her head. "She came in and just went through my desk. No respect for my privacy. When I confronted her, she blamed me for not keeping her abreast of what's been going on. Then she proceeded to tell me that she would resume her duties from home. Garrett, I almost blew up. I was so pissed. I told her to leave. I wanted to tell her to go to hell. But I didn't. I was the good, calm employee."

"That's fucked up. Did you tell Jax or X?"

"I can't do that, Garrett. When I started, I heard the whispers from people who didn't think I was qualified to do the job. I worked my ass off to prove that I was capable, that I deserved the job. Not just because I'm the niece of the CEO, but because I'm good at what I do. Now I'm respected, trusted. And I got to this level *without* running to my uncle every time someone said something I didn't like." She swallowed visibly. "I'm just not sure it's what I want anymore."

"What do you want?"

She bit down on her lip. "What if my job is not at the company I've worked so hard for?"

"Maybe it's not," he said.

"But that's crazy, right? You know . . . I had plans for Pure Talent, things I wanted to see to fruition. I never wanted to work for anyone else."

"Skye, it's okay to reevaluate." He pinned her with his gaze. "You're not stuck there."

Burrowing into him, she wrapped her arms around him. "I feel like I'm just going through the motions. And I'm not happy."

"What are you going to do about it?"

She leaned back. "I think I want to start my own company."

Garrett was proud of Skye. He'd seen her light up when dealing with Paige, and suspected she'd stumbled across her calling. "That's good, baby."

"Really?" The hope flickering in her eyes made him want to give her everything she ever wanted. "You think so?"

"I do," he told her. "I know you can do it."

She scooted off the bed and ran down the stairs. Minutes later, she came back in, a pad of paper in her hands. "Can we talk about it?"

He sat up and patted the mattress next to him. "Come on."

The pizza came a few minutes later. They ate and planned, talking about everything from scope to business name to tax status. An hour later, he'd already drafted the bones of a business plan.

She placed a hand on top of his. "Thanks for this, babe."

He winked. "Anything for you."

"Garrett! You bought me Baby Yoda! You're always spoiling me."

"It goes both ways. You brought me a plant today."

Giggling, she said, "It's a jade plant. Some people call them money trees."

Setting the pad of paper down, he pulled her onto his lap. Brushing his lips against hers, he said, "That's a plant I can get with."

When she'd brought over the first one, a bamboo palm, she'd told him that plants purify the air, protect against certain illnesses, and even boost immunity. He didn't care either way, but he *was* glad that she'd felt so at home with him.

"I hope I don't kill it."

"I told you, that's what I'm here for. I'll make sure you don't."

He brushed his thumb over the scar under Skye's chin. "Are you ever going to tell me what this is about?"

"I wondered when you would ask that question."

"So . . . ?"

While they hadn't really talked about their own past relationship, they'd shared some things about their lives over the last ten years. She'd told him about some of the men she'd dated and he'd shared his experience with Brianna. X had warned him that a lot had happened, and he wondered if the scar on her chin was connected to something she didn't want to remember.

With a heavy sigh, she picked up his hand and entwined their fingers. "X is the only person I've ever told about this. Not even Zara."

Garrett felt honored that she trusted him enough to tell him something that she'd obviously wanted to keep hidden. "What is it?" Suddenly, a sobering thought crossed his mind. And it made him want to kill someone. "Did someone hurt you?"

Her face on his cheek calmed his rising ire. "No. Well, not physically. But I was hurt."

"It's okay if you don't want to talk about this. I won't push you."

She searched his eyes. "You never do. I love that about you."

I just love you.

"Anyway, when I found out about Broderick, I kind of flipped out."

Garrett didn't know specifics, but he did know that she'd canceled her wedding. X had never given him any details, but it had to have been bad for her to walk out of the church on her wedding day. The press had speculated there was infidelity on the part of the groom, but he didn't know for sure.

"I broke the law," she grumbled.

Shocked, he asked, "You what?"

"It seems like a lifetime ago now. But I caught him cheating on me on the wedding day."

Fuckin' asshole.

"I walked out and never spoke to him again. But I did try to bust the window out of his car."

He blinked. *I wasn't expecting that.*

The corner of her mouth quirked up. "It was a bad day. And I was in my car, listening to that song by Jazmine Sullivan. Next thing I knew I was standing on the hood of his car with a sledge hammer. Don't ask me where I got it. Of course, it didn't work. So I just used the hammer to tear up the outside of the car. If I'd had a crowbar, I would have carved *fuck you* on the hood, but I didn't. It felt like I hit that car for hours, but it couldn't have been that long."

Garrett imagined Skye angry, hurt, crying. It made him want to hurt someone, namely Broderick. "How did you cut yourself?"

"I was so angry, I slipped and fell off the car, and cut my chin on a piece of metal that was in the garage. Luckily, I only ended up with this scar." She rubbed it with her forefinger. "When my chin wouldn't stop bleeding I called X and he came. He took me to the hospital to get stitches. Then he handled it."

"What did he do?"

She shrugged. "I have no idea. He wouldn't tell me."

"I'm surprised he didn't kick his ass."

"Believe me, he wanted to."

"Can't blame him," he said. "I would have had the same urge." Garrett kissed the scar. "I'm sorry you had to go through that."

She dropped her gaze. "Garrett, I really am a hot mess."

"I wouldn't call you that. You're human."

"A human wrecking ball," she muttered under her breath.

He hated to hear her talk like that about herself. Because he didn't see her that way. Skye Palmer was the sun, all light and warmth. Sometimes she blazed hot and could burn, but she was still beautiful in all her glory.

"Don't say that," he commanded softly. "We all have faults."

She snorted. "What are your faults?"

"You know better than most," he said. "For a long time, I carried so much hatred in my heart for my mother." Even now, he couldn't be sure he didn't still hate her a little, even in death. Especially because his mother had chosen to drive under the influence that night. As far as he was concerned, she didn't care about anyone but herself and her own pleasure—or pain. The fact that she had a daughter to get back home to hadn't fazed her one bit. "It colored everything I'd ever done. When I moved back to Houston, I had to kind of push past that resentment for Max. She still noticed, and we had a hard conversation. But I still struggle with forgiveness."

She eyed him warily. "You forgave me."

"Because you didn't really do anything wrong, Skye. Sometimes relationships end. Don't get me wrong, it hurt. Despite everything, I can't believe that you hurt me on purpose. It was a difficult time for both of us."

"I sort of blamed you for it," she admitted. "Our breakup."

He frowned. "Me?"

Nodding, she laid her head on his chest. "It took a long time to open up to anyone after you. Broderick was a chance for me to kind of move past that, so I took the jump. And when it ended so badly, I made it your fault. Because if we had been together, I would have never been humiliated on my wedding day. Deep down, I knew it was illogical, so then I blamed myself for blaming you." She shook her head. "Forget it, it's kind of convoluted."

"No, actually I get it. It's easier to transfer negative energy to someone else than to take that shame or blame on yourself."

"But it still was illogical."

"It is what it is." He tipped her chin up so he could peer into her eyes. "Skye, we've never talked about this, but there are a lot of things I wished I could have done differently back then. I should have recognized that you weren't ready to be someone's mother figure."

"That was only a part of it," she admitted. "Despite what you've always said about your mother and your relationship with her, I knew losing her was hard on you."

Skye wasn't wrong. Despite his relationship with his mother, and his arguments that he was fine, her death had hit him harder than he ever imagined it would. He'd struggled with this grief, while he tried to be strong for Max.

"And Max needed you," Skye continued. "She was a child who lost her parents in a horrific way. She needed her brother. After the funeral, I watched you try and figure out ways for us to be together, to see each other. I could see it was taking a toll on you."

Juggling his responsibilities with Max and his desire to be with Skye had been difficult. "It was," he said.

"I told you that I couldn't relocate my life, but that wasn't it." Skye sighed. "Your focus should have been on Max. And I felt like I'd get in the way of that. I wanted you to be able to go to Max without worrying about me. Then I saw you with your friend Brianna."

Garrett frowned. "When?"

"After we broke up, I went to Houston to try and walk

back what I'd said. But I saw you and Max and Brianna together. And I thought . . . she was what Max—and you—needed. I left that day convinced I was doing the right thing. It was confirmed when I heard you and Brianna were together."

"Not for long," he said. "It took a while to even try with her. But it wasn't right. She's happily married with kids now. Max is still close to her, too."

Skye nodded. "But you *did* try, for Max. I knew you would. I don't blame you for trying to give your sister a stable home."

This was the first time she'd given him a reason. Deep down, he'd always known it. Because he knew her. And he couldn't argue with that logic. "Max needed me."

"Exactly. But now, being here with you, I wish I had made a different decision."

Garrett wanted to tell her how he felt. He wanted to tell her that after they broke up, he couldn't sleep without her, couldn't think about anything but her eyes, her smile. But when he could finally look at a sunset without imagining her skin, when he could finally look at a cloud without seeing her face, he'd told himself he wouldn't jump back into that position anytime soon. And he hadn't. Until now.

Tapping her nose, he said, "The good news is you did make a different decision—at midnight on New Year's Day. No regrets?"

A slow smile spread over those lips. "No regrets. Garrett?"

"Huh?"

"Round three."

* * *

Skye paced the waiting area outside of Uncle Jax's office, turning her speech over in her mind. She checked her watch: 4:30. She'd purposely waited until the end of the day to schedule her meeting because she didn't want to be interrupted. She also knew it wouldn't be a long meeting because it was Valentine's Day, and her uncle always celebrated the holiday with his wife.

"Skye?" his assistant called.

She froze and turned to her. "Is he ready?"

The assistant nodded. "Go on in."

Skye tugged at her jacket and strolled into the office. "Hi, Uncle Jax."

The years had been good to him. His light skin was smooth and his salt-and-pepper beard gave him a classic look. He'd always reminded her of royalty, the way he held his head, his mannerisms. He was confident, assured, and extremely intelligent.

Her uncle stood up, his arms wide. "Skye."

She walked right into his arms and hugged him. "Welcome back."

Since X had been promoted to partner, Uncle Jax had spent more and more time out of the office, going on vacations with Aunt Ana. The two were #relationshipgoals. Long-term marriages ran in the family. Both her parents and her uncle and aunt had been married for decades and seemed more in love now than they did back in the day.

"How is Aunt Ana?" she asked, taking a seat. "I've been meaning to call her, but I've been so busy with work."

"She's good." Instead of going to his own chair, he took the seat next to her. "Going crazy over this wedding."

Skye had talked to her aunt and Zara's mother often, trying to get the wedding together. The decision to elope had put both women in a tizzy, and Skye had to calm both of them down on several occasions just to get shit done.

"I think we're on track, though. Invitations went out, responses are already coming in."

"Good. Is there anything you need from me?"

Skye told him no. "But I will need your credit card for expenses."

He chuckled. "No problem." Uncle Jax leaned back in his seat. "So, I know you're not here to talk about the wedding. To what do I owe this honor?"

She took a deep breath, held it for a few seconds, then released it. Meeting his gaze directly, she said, "I want to start my own company."

Nodding slowly, Uncle Jax studied her for a moment. He'd been in a business where the poker face ruled. It was no small feat to start a talent agency that catered to people of color, but he'd done so spectacularly, working tirelessly to make sure the agency had an impeccable reputation, a wide array of talent, and a robust investment portfolio. Because of his devotion to the company, clients and employees alike had stayed loyal to him. Ironic that she'd come to tell him she wanted to leave.

"You want to start your own PR agency?" he asked, his voice even.

Uncle Jax had taught her to never let anyone see her sweat. It was just one of the many nuggets of wisdom he'd imparted to her over the years. Every lesson, every talk had stuck with her. Even seemingly innocent conversations over chicken and waffles had been imprinted on her brain, little tips about public speaking and technical writing or looking the part and having a firm handshake. She'd learned so much from him, and she hated to leave him in the lurch. But she had to do what was best for her.

Skye nodded. "I do." She gave him a brief overview of her plans. "I'm interested in doing more to directly support clients. Working with Paige lit a fire in me, and I want to expand on that. I want to build my own empire."

Uncle Jax stared at her, a mixture of pride and awe on his face. He was proud of her. She'd seen that look before, at her ballet recitals, at her high school graduation, on her first day of work at the agency. And one thing also struck her . . . he wasn't surprised.

"Niece, I know that you've wanted to carve out your own niche here. I also know that there are some things you haven't told me about your experiences at the agency. I'm not so busy that I don't know that you've struggled."

"Why didn't you say anything?"

"Because I've known you since you were a little girl. I know how stubborn you are. I wasn't going to step in unless you asked."

She nodded. "You're right."

"I've watched you. I've seen your work, and I've known where your heart lies."

"That's why you asked me to handle Paige."

He nodded. "I figured it was time for a little push."

"Thank you," she said. "I needed that."

"I know." He patted her hand, like he'd done so many times before. "And don't think I don't know about Carmen. There are some politics involved, but she won't be here much longer."

"She really is terrible," Skye confessed. "I really tried to work with her."

"And you've done more than most would have done in that same position."

"I want you to know that I'm willing to do anything to help make the transition smoother for Pure Talent. I'll stay on until you find a suitable replacement and I'm available to consult."

"Duly noted. And just so you know, I've never been more proud of you. You've grown into a beautiful woman, with a good head on your shoulders. If you want to go out on your own, you should know I'd never stop you. In fact, I have a proposal for you."

Skye emerged from Uncle Jax's office a new woman. Instead of going to her office, she walked right out into the sun. Peering up at the sky, she took in a deep breath. *I did it.*

Pulling out her phone, she texted Garrett, letting him know she was done for the day.

His response came seconds later: I can't wait to hear all about your meeting. Stuck in the office, but I'll see you tonight.

She typed out a reply. Her finger hovered over the SEND button. Staring at the message, she reread it over and over again: I'll be there with bells on. Love you.

Skye had been so excited she'd typed it without even thinking. They'd grown so close in a short period of time. Throughout her workday, every day, she found herself thinking about how he smelled, how he felt, how he tasted. Just thinking about him now, made her want to call him to hear his voice. Hell, she wanted to jump him, let him fill her in a way only he could. She ached for him.

They'd spent all sorts of time together—food time, movie time, talking time, sexy time, and quiet time. The quiet moments between them were just as important, just as meaningful as any other. They didn't need words, they needed proximity to each other, contact. But was she ready to tell him she loved him? *Is he ready to hear it?*

Sighing, she deleted the words from the text and hit SEND. When she told him she loved him for the first time, it wouldn't be in a text message. It would be in person, so she could see his response. In the meantime, she had to get ready for her Valentine's Day surprise.

A few hours later, Skye entered Garrett's loft. She'd fallen in love with the space from the moment he'd brought her home with him. Warm neutral colors, beautiful artwork, wall-to-wall windows, comfortable brown leather furniture. It was all him. All Garrett.

She set the Macho fern she'd bought for him in the corner near the television, and turned the pot until it looked just right. Stepping back, she eyed it.

"Hey, baby."

She turned, unable to contain her joy at the sight of him. He'd changed from his normal work attire. His hair was wet, signaling he'd just got out of the shower. He wore low-riding sweats and that was it. No shirt, no shoes. Just one piece of fabric separating her from one of her favorite parts of him. *Perfect.* "Hey," she said, her voice coming out more breathy than she'd intended. "Happy Valentine's Day."

They'd decided not to celebrate the holiday with purchased gifts. The gift of time was more valuable at this stage in their relationship.

He grinned. "Happy Valentine's Day."

Skye smirked, thinking about her surprise. Instead of taking an Uber, she'd driven her own car to his place because she didn't want to take a chance that anyone would catch a glimpse of what she had in store for him.

Inching closer to him—but not too close—she said, "We're celebrating."

His gaze raked over her, starting at her feet to her face. "What are we celebrating?"

"Uncle Jax accepted my resignation and offered to invest in my company. Forty percent!" She'd expected Uncle Jax to offer to refer clients to her, rent office space, or something like that. But when he'd suggested they partner with each other, she had to pick her mouth up off the floor. "He knew! He knew I wasn't happy. And he was just waiting for me to realize it."

The corners of his mouth turned up. "I had no doubt that he would be supportive."

"He wants to set up a formal meeting, with me, him, X, and my dad." She clapped her hands together. "I can't believe it. I'm so excited."

"I'm not surprised at this outcome. I'm very happy for you."

"Thank you," she said. "If it wasn't for you, I wouldn't have been as prepared today."

"You would have."

Skye closed her eyes. He believed in her. *God, I love him*. "Still, I'm thanking you."

"You're welcome." He approached her, gripping her hips and tugging her to him. He traced her bottom lip with his tongue, before kissing her fully.

Pulling away, she stepped out of his grasp and fanned herself. "Damn."

"Skye," he said, coming toward her. "Why are you so far away from me?"

"Oh, he's going to fire Carmen's ass."

"Why do you have on a coat?"

"And I'm going to help him during the transition like we talked about."

"Okay." He stopped in front of her and unbuttoned her coat.

Maybe it was her mind playing tricks on her, or her imagination, but she could have sworn she heard a low growl burst from his throat.

She slipped out of her coat and let if fall on the floor, baring her naked body to him. "I figured it was a waste of time wearing clothes. Since I had a feeling you'd be taking them off."

They didn't make it to the bed, or even the sofa. He took her right there on the living room rug, making love to her so hard and long, she couldn't see or hear or feel anything but him. Only him. She fell over first, gasping for air as her orgasm took her over, wringing her dry. Then, he followed.

He collapsed onto his back and pulled her to him. "I think this might be the best Valentine's gift I've ever received." He kissed her brow.

She snuggled into him. "Me too." They stayed there for a while, until their breathing evened out. Then he scooped her up, carried her upstairs, and set her on the bed. He climbed onto the mattress and pulled her into his arms.

Wrapped around each other, she asked, "Can we have a five-minute talk?"

The rumble of his laughter against her body calmed her. "Uh-oh. What are we talking about?"

She perched herself up so she could look into his brown eyes. "This might seem strange or even premature, but I really love being with you."

His eyes softened. "Me too."

"I appreciate how you've always taken care of me, how you've always supported me. I don't know if I deserve it, but I'm so glad that you're you."

"Skye, you—"

She placed a finger over his lips, and he nipped the tip. "No, let me finish. I need to say this. Garrett, I've made some crazy mistakes in life. But my best mistake was kissing you at the start of the year. This time we've spent together has meant more to me than I can even articulate. And . . . *mahal kita*."

His eyes widened.

"And I just wanted you to know that." She dropped her head on his chest, but he tipped her chin up.

"I love you, too, Skye."

His words bloomed in her heart. "You do?"

"How could I not? You give me plants and naked surprises."

She pinched him. "Stop."

Brushing his lips over the inside of her wrist, he said, "I'm serious. And to show you"—he flipped her over—"round two."

Chapter Seventeen

Garrett greeted Ana with a hug. "Hi, Ana."

Ana kissed his cheek. "Garrett, it's been so long. Come on in."

He walked into the house. "Thanks for having me over for dinner."

"It's our pleasure. And a special occasion."

Jax had officially announced his retirement from Pure Talent at the end of the year. He'd stay on as the chairman of the board, but would not represent clients anymore. Ana had decided to celebrate the milestone by having one of her elaborate dinner parties.

"I can't believe he's doing it. He's still young."

"True, but he's worked hard all of his life. He's ready to rest. And I couldn't be happier. Follow me." She led him through the house.

They stopped off at the kitchen, where Zara was icing a cake. Well, it looked more like she was eating the frosting. He hugged her. "Hey, Zara."

She beamed. "What's up? Where's Skye?"

"Work."

Zara's shoulders dropped. "I feel so bad that she's doing all this work for the wedding."

Since Skye had submitted her resignation, she'd been at the office more, trying to make sure things were in order at the agency before her last day. And when she wasn't working on her succession plan, she was barking out orders to florists, event planners, and photographers. The wedding was in a week, and everyone had been running around trying to get the last-minute details together.

"You know she wouldn't have it any other way," he said.

Zara licked more frosting off of the knife. "Shit, now I have to get another one." She put it into the dishwasher and grabbed a clean one out of the drawer. She giggled to herself. "I am so greedy. If I don't stop eating, I might not fit my dress."

He chuckled, shaking his head. "I'm sure you'll be alright."

Even if she couldn't fit in her dress, she'd be alright. X would marry her if she had on yoga pants and UGGs. That's how much his best friend loved his wife-to-be. Garrett felt the same way about Skye. He just wanted to be with her, to love her.

After she'd told him of her love, they'd fallen into a routine of coupledom and it felt damn good. So good, that he had a proposal for her. Not *that* proposal, but one he thought she might accept. He'd find out tonight.

"How's Max?" Ana asked, stirring a huge pot of greens on the stove.

"She's doing well. In college kicking butt. She'll be at the wedding."

Ana pulled a prime rib roast out of the oven. "Good. I'm sure you're so proud of her."

"I definitely am."

Zara chimed in, "X told me she has a boyfriend. How's that going for you?"

Garrett had finally mellowed out about the boyfriend.

Still didn't mean he was looking forward to the interloper coming to Hawaii. "Admittedly, it was tough. But I'm okay with it."

"And work?" Ana asked. "I hear you're doing great business."

"Thanks, I appreciate that. Work is good. Just took on a new corporate client."

Last week, he'd posted a job for a new associate and had decided to move his office to a bigger location. Thanks to Jax and X, he had a lead on the building next to the Pure Talent offices.

"That's wonderful." Ana stepped over to the counter and gingerly took the knife from Zara's hand. "Step away from the cake, dear."

Zara pouted. "But it's so good."

"I know. I made it, and I'll make you a small one to have at your house next month—after the wedding."

Garrett barked out a laugh and quickly stopped when Zara glared at him. Holding up his hands in surrender, he said, "You know that was funny."

Zara shook her head. "Oh, shut up."

X strolled into the kitchen. "What's up, bruh?" They greeted each other with their signature handshake. His best friend turned his attention to Zara, who was staring at the cake longingly. "It's okay, baby. I'll cut you a big piece later."

Zara's eyes lit up. "With extra frosting?"

"You know it," X responded. "I just heard that Julius was also indicted in California."

"Yeah, I read about it today," Garrett said. He wasn't surprised. Julius was on a downward spiral. And instead of scouting movie locations, the director was looking at a jail term for his misdeeds. Studios were refusing to work with him, both his agent and publicist had resigned, and he'd been hit with more civil lawsuits. One lawsuit in particular, from Heather Franklin, was seeking damages for pain and suffering and loss of income, among other things. Apparently, Julius had leaked the rumor about her being pregnant with his baby to protect Catherine, the baby's real momma.

"He's such a jerk," Zara said. "I'm glad Paige left him."

The doorbell rang, and Ana hurried off to get it.

"You all set for the wedding?" Garrett asked Zara and X.

"Thanks to Skye," Zara chirped. "I'm telling you. She's a lifesaver."

In more ways than one. "She's neck deep in wedding."

"Garrett?" Zara leaned in. "Please, when you're in Vegas next week, don't let Duke lead you all astray. I need X to be on that plane on time."

The fellas were headed to Vegas for a one-night excursion, before hopping on a flight to Maui. The ladies were headed straight to the island. According to Skye, they had a lot to do.

Garrett snickered. "You know I got you."

"Hello." Marisol entered the kitchen and gave all of them hugs. She cradled Garrett's face in her hands. "It's been a while. You look good."

Grinning, he told her thank you. "It's good to see you."

Jacob walked in next. After he embraced everyone, he turned to Garrett. "Son, how the hell are you?"

"Good."

Ana kicked the men out of the kitchen a few minutes later, and they retreated to the media room. Jax joined them shortly after. Glasses of cognac were poured and cigars were lit as they talked about politics, sports, and the wedding.

"Make sure you put the toilet paper on the roll correctly," Jacob said. "Marisol throws a fit about that. It's over, not under."

"And never, ever tell your wife that she looks okay," Jax added. "It's a wrap from there. You might as well sleep on the couch."

They laughed heartily.

"Uncle Jake, we already live together." X sipped from his drink. "I'm good on the toilet paper."

"How about you, Garrett?" Jax asked. "How are things going with Skye?"

Jacob's eyes flashed to his. "My Skye?"

While they hadn't talked specifically about her telling her parents about them, he'd assumed she had. The fact that her dad was obviously surprised made him feel some type of way. *Is she hiding it from them on purpose?*

Nodding slowly, he said, "Yes. Your Skye."

"When did that happen?" Jacob asked.

"New Year's Eve," X offered. "I was right there when it went down. Things shifted from there."

"That daughter of mine is so busy she forgot to tell us she was seeing someone." Jacob chuckled. "So you'll have to forgive us."

Garrett frowned. "For what?"

Ana knocked on the door and poked her head in the room. "Dinner is ready."

At the dinner table, he took a seat across from X just as Skye breezed into the room. "Sorry I'm late." She went around the table greeting everyone with a hug or a kiss. And when she got to him, she winked. "Hey, baby."

Marisol hurried in carrying a huge tossed salad. "Ami, you're here."

Skye took the bowl from her mother and set it on the table. Then she gave Marisol a hug. "Nay, I missed you."

"Oh my God, let me look at you." Marisol circled Skye, straightening her already straight skirt and playing with her collar. "Black again, Ami. You should wear pink."

Skye shook her head and sat next to Garrett. "Yeah, no."

"I'm telling you, you need to wear color. Black is so dark and dreary."

"It's fine, Nay." Skye poured a full glass of water for herself. Then she glanced at him. "Want some?"

He nodded and held out his glass. "Thank you."

The doorbell rang. Ana frowned. "I'm not expecting anyone else."

"Oh boy," Jacob murmured.

Marisol perked up. "I invited someone, Ana. Hope you don't mind."

"Not at all," Ana said. "Jax, will you get the door?"

Jax stood and disappeared around the corner. Moments later, he was back. "Um . . ." He chuckled. Hell must have frozen over because this was the first time Garrett had ever seen Jax flustered.

A man stepped forward from behind him. "Hello, everyone. Robert York."

"Hi, Robert," Marisol said, a wide grin on her face. "Have a seat. Right over here." She shuffled behind them to the empty seat next to Skye.

Suddenly all the pieces clicked together, and he knew the moment they clicked for Skye, too, because she froze. "Nay? What are you . . . ?"

"Robert, I'm so glad you could come meet my daughter.

Skye, this is Robert. The man I wanted you to meet. Maybe he can be your guest to the wedding."

"What?" Skye shouted.

"Oh no," Zara whisper-yelled.

"Shit," X added.

When Garrett glanced at Ana, her mouth was wide open. And Jax . . . well, he was still shaking his head.

"Oh boy," Jacob repeated, massaging his forehead.

Skye bolted to her feet. "Nay, why would you bring someone here like this?"

"I told you I had a date for you," Marisol said.

"And I told you I don't need a date. Because I already have one. Right here." She squeezed his shoulder. "Garrett is my date."

Marisol blinked. "Oh."

"This is so embarrassing," Skye muttered. She looked at Garrett and mouthed "I'm sorry."

Jumping into action, Marisol apologized to Robert. "Maybe you should go. I'm so sorry. I'll walk you out." She nudged the clueless guy out of the dining room.

When they were gone, Skye plopped down in her chair. "What the hell just happened?"

Garrett laughed, then everyone else followed. "I guess your mother really wanted you to have a date," he said, squeezing Skye's leg.

Marisol rushed back into the room. "I'm sorry, Garrett. My daughter tells me nothing."

"That's because I was going to tell you tonight, Nay. In person."

"Oh, Ami. I'm sorry." Marisol turned to Garrett. "And you, I'm so happy. I like you better anyway."

Garrett heard a few more snickers around the table.

Glancing at Skye, he couldn't help but laugh. His girlfriend was flustered, cheeks and neck red, eyes wild. But she was stunning. And she was his.

"Hi, Daddy." Skye walked into the den where her father sat on the sofa watching television. She hugged him. "How are you?"

He squeezed her hand. "Tired. The flight in was kind of bumpy. But I'll be okay."

Once again, worry crept in. He looked like he wasn't feeling well. "Do you need anything?"

Looking up at her, he shook his head. "I'm fine, baby girl."

She sat down next to him. "You sure?"

"Yep. Interesting dinner, huh?"

Skye still couldn't believe her mother invited some stranger to the house to date her. "I can't even begin to dissect that scene."

"Never a dull evening." He glanced at her. "And Garrett . . . are you two serious?"

She wouldn't pretend she didn't have doubts—about their ability to go the distance, about their future. But she felt better than she had in years. "I think so," she said.

"Where is he?"

"Just left," she replied. "He had to get some work done tonight."

"I'm glad to see you happy," her dad said. "It's about time. How are things going with the business launch?"

Skye had talked to her father at length about her plans. He'd offered his assistance and money to help her get the business off the ground. Which was just like him. He'd always stood in the gap for her.

"I already have my first client," she told him. "Paige Mills."

When she told Paige about her decision, the actress hired her on the spot. And Uncle Jax had given his blessing to go forward even though they hadn't found hers or Carmen's replacement yet. The news that Uncle Jax had terminated Carmen had shot through the office like wildfire. Because in all of his years of business, he could count on one hand the number of times he'd had to fire someone.

"That's amazing, baby girl. She's a big name."

"And she's already referred several people to me. But I told them I wasn't accepting another client until my business is truly up and running. I'm excited, though."

The NAACP Image Awards show was taping tomorrow. Her first act as Paige's publicist consisted of flying out to L.A. to attend the event with her client. Currently, Paige was on location filming her next movie. But she'd fly into Cali for the show tomorrow as well.

Skye watched her father's eyes close. "Daddy?"

His eyes popped open, and he looked at her. "Hi."

"Hi. I have something I want to run by you."

"What is it?"

She'd thought about this for a while, but had always talked herself out of it. At her last session with Sasha, she'd told her therapist of her plans and she felt good about the direction her life had taken. "I've made a decision about something."

"Okay."

"Years ago, you asked me if I wanted to take your name."

He nodded. "I remember that."

Tilting her head, she peered into his eyes. "I said no at

the time because I wanted to honor my biological father. You said you understood, but—"

"I do understand." He patted her knee. "I've never held it against you. I know you love me."

"I do, Daddy. Which is why I've decided to change my name to Skye Palmer-Starks."

Tears filled her father's eyes. "W-what?"

"I know you never held it against me. But I did." She sucked in a deep breath. "I've thought about this for so long. I've heard all the stories about my biological father, but I don't know him. I know you. You've been there for me through everything. Never judging me, always loving me."

A tear fell out of his eyes, and she caught it with her thumb. "Baby girl, you've never had to have my name for me to consider you mine."

"Which is why I want to have your name. I want to honor my biological father, but I want to honor my real dad, too. And you're that."

He sighed, and pulled her into a hug. "You have exceeded all of my expectations. I couldn't have asked for a better daughter. I love you, baby girl."

Skye buried her face in his neck. "I love you, too, Daddy."

After spending time with her parents, Skye went to Garrett's house. When she walked in, he greeted her with a searing kiss. "Hey, baby," he said.

"Hi." She kicked her shoes off and followed him into the house. "I'm sorry I'm late. I was talking with my parents about some things."

"How did that go?" He poured her a glass of wine and handed it to her.

"I think we've come to an understanding. I'm sorry about the whole date thing."

"Don't apologize. That shit was funny."

"I'm glad you all found humor in it. I had a great talk with my dad."

After her dad had accepted that she was perfectly fine with her decision, he told her he wanted to go to the courthouse with her when she made the name change official. And they'd made plans so that he could be in town. As for her mother, they'd had a conversation as well and agreed that Marisol would stay out of her love life, and her closet.

"Name change, huh?" he asked. "That's dope. I'm sure he was ecstatic."

"He was. It was a perfect moment between us. Tears and truth."

Garrett wrapped his arms around her, and kissed her jaw. "How did your meeting with Paige go?"

Skye told him about the job offer. "The whole ride to Uncle Jax's, I wanted to pinch myself. It feels like a dream."

"That's because it is. It's your dream."

"I really love you," she breathed, kissing his nose. "You make me better."

He turned her in his arms so she faced him. "I feel the same." Garrett grabbed a small envelope that was sitting on the countertop. "I have something for you."

Frowning, she asked, "What is it?"

"Open it."

She tore the envelope open and dumped the contents in her hand. It was a key. She shot him a skeptical look. "What's this for?"

"Skye, I know it hasn't been long. We've already discussed that fact many times. But I know what I want. And she's standing here with me, looking beautiful."

She felt tension start at her toes and travel upward. *Is he going to . . . ?*

"I don't want to be with anyone else."

Panic rose, threatening to choke her. "Garrett—"

"Move in with me, baby."

Chapter Eighteen

Today was Garrett's mother's birthday. Today was also the anniversary of her death. Every year on this day he had chosen to power through. When Max was young, he'd take the day off to spend with her. The goal? To put some positivity back into the day. After Max left for college, he'd worked like it was any other day. Yet, despite his best efforts to handle client business, he felt unsettled.

A barrage of emotions sat just beneath the surface. One minute, he felt like he'd blow, the next he felt overwhelmingly sad, but mostly he was angry. Still angry after ten years. Still angry that the woman who was supposed to love him, the woman who was supposed to support him, never had. A mother should do everything in her power to make sure her kids were fine. A mother shouldn't deliberately hurt her child.

The first time she'd hit him, he was seven years old. At ten, his mother stole the money he made from washing cars in the neighborhood. When he turned sixteen, he got a job. She'd drained his bank account. He moved out on graduation day. He hated to leave his sister, but he had to get away from that house. His stepfather wasn't perfect, but he was a far better parent to Max than his mother had ever been, so Garrett had made the decision to move away for college. He'd visited as often as he could, though. Only Max. Never his mother. Never at that house.

It had taken years of diligence to clean up his credit after his mother used it to buy cars, get power turned on in his name, and other things that never seemed to help them get ahead. He'd vowed to always be a better man, better than her.

Moving back into his childhood home after his mother died had taken a toll on him. But he'd done it anyway, because Max needed the stability. Eventually, he couldn't take it anymore and they'd moved. She was better for it. So was he.

Garrett stared at the computer screen, at a contract he'd started drafting earlier. Page one. Nothing seemed to be working today. He supposed it could be because of the significance of the day, but more than likely it had nothing to do with his mother and everything to do with Skye.

He'd presented her with a key two days ago. The key didn't signify that he wanted her to move in with him. It was a symbol. Garrett didn't care if she wanted him to sell his house and move in with her or if she preferred to shop for a house together. He just wanted a commitment. He wanted to know that he had a home to go to at night. Because he'd learned a long time ago that a house didn't make a home.

Instead of telling him yes or no, she'd asked him if she could think about it. Then she'd hopped on a flight to California for work. Garrett tried not to be irritated with her. After all, he knew the demands of her job. Hell, he had his own job demands. But what did she have to think about exactly? It was either yay or nay. Move in or maintain separate homes.

Garrett couldn't deny the doubt that had crept in, slithered through him like a snake ready to sink fangs into skin. It didn't sit right with him, made him feel something he didn't want to feel about Skye. *Conflicted.*

To make matters worse, they'd barely talked since she left town. A quick text here or there, a short phone conversation before bed or in the morning. Nothing substantive, no more than a few minutes per interaction. S*he's running.* From him?

If she was indeed running from him, could he live with that? Where would that leave them? It would leave him alone, struggling to find a way to move on. The longer they continued, the harder it would be to walk away if he had to.

Sighing, he called Tara and told her was out for the rest of the day. He didn't go home, though. He went to the bar. One cognac later, he turned to the doorway just in time to see X walk in. When his friend spotted him, he headed his way.

"What's up?" X slid onto the bar stool next to him.

"Nothing," Garrett replied.

"It's noon. And you're drinking."

"Bad day."

X tapped the bar and ordered the same drink Garrett had. When the bartender set it in front of him, he said, "Today is hard, I know."

Garrett shot him a sideways glance, and snorted. "That's the understatement of the year."

"I can't imagine what you're going through, bruh. How's Max?"

The first thing Garrett had done that morning was call his sister. Surprisingly, she'd forgotten what day it was.

And he was glad. Glad that she wasn't bogged down in emotion like he was, that she was moving forward.

"She's good. Studying for her last midterm."

X didn't say anything else. They just sat there in silence, drinking. It was the gesture, the fact that X knew he didn't want to talk but still made sure he was there. Brothers.

Later, he got a text from Skye. She was back. He arrived at her place shortly after seven.

"Hi," she said, a wide grin on her face. She leaned up on the tips of her toes and kissed him. "You look sexy."

"Hey, baby."

She headed to her bedroom. An open suitcase was on the bed. He knew she was leaving for Hawaii tomorrow with Zara, but seeing her empty suitcase on the bed still jarred him for some reason. She'd had time to get off her flight, empty her suitcase, wash her clothes, and start packing again. *How long has she been home?*

She glanced back at him over her shoulder. "I missed you."

Normally her declaration would make him feel centered. But he felt anything but. Because he wasn't sure if he believed her. And that didn't bode well for them.

"Did you?" he asked.

She paused. A few seconds later, she dropped a bathing suit into the suitcase and turned to him. "What is that supposed to mean? Of course, I missed you."

"We've barely spoken since you left. I was just making sure." And now he was *that* guy. The needy man who wanted to know where his woman was every second of the day. Damn it, that wasn't him.

"Things were so hectic, babe. I only had a short amount of time to make sure Paige was settled, so I was on the go from the moment I landed. In between events, I had to keep calling the caterer and the wedding venue. There were some issues with the resort that had to get worked out."

Everything she said made sense to him. He'd fallen in love with a very busy woman, a woman that was now starting her own PR agency. Still . . . *Is she as committed to me as she is to everyone else?*

He shook his mind free from his mother. Skye and his mother were very different people. His mother had never been committed to him. But Skye had loved him, she'd taken care of him . . . *until she didn't.*

"Garrett." She approached him. "I feel like you're upset with me. And I know why."

He raised a brow, not even bothering to deny he *was* in fact upset with her. "Do you now?"

"You asked me a very important question and I tabled the discussion. I thought about what you asked and I just . . ." She sighed, fidgeting. "I don't think it's a good idea right now."

Garrett felt dread in his gut. Did he really put himself out there with her again for her to overthink her way to destroying them?

"Does that include us?" he asked.

She frowned. "No. God, no. You have to admit we both have a lot going on. I'm trying to get my business off the ground. While I was in L.A., I set up several meetings with potential clients. There's a lot to think about. If I decide I want my home base to be in Atlanta and my biggest clients are in L.A., I—"

"Okay," he interrupted. "I understand."

She let out a heavy sigh as her shoulders sagged. "I'm so glad you understand."

"What I understand is you're still not ready for us.

We want different things here. And I don't know that I have it in me to wait around for you to leave me again."

She blinked, stumbling back a few steps. "Wait." She held a hand out. "What? When did this become about me leaving you?"

"I don't know, Skye. It sounds like you're heading to the conclusion that you want to move to Los Angeles."

"Garrett, no. That's not what I'm saying."

"It sounds like it to me. I'm just coming to my own conclusion. You left me when I needed you the most, and I'm not interested in letting that happen again."

"That's not what I did," she argued. "I didn't leave you. We broke up. Two different things. You said it yourself, it was no one's fault. I let you go so you could take care of your sister."

"And I was thinking it would have been so much easier if you'd been there." He didn't mean to say that. Garrett knew it wasn't her responsibility to take care of his sister, to uproot her life to be with them. But he was angry.

Tears filled her brown eyes and he wanted to kick himself for lashing out. But he couldn't afford to have his heart broken again. He'd already had too much of that in his life.

They stood in silence, staring at each other.

Skye wiped a tear from her cheek. "Okay. I knew you felt that way. I knew you hadn't really forgiven me."

He dropped his head. "I don't want to do this, Skye. I have to go."

"No!" She grabbed his arm. "No. Don't leave. Don't do this."

"Do what, Skye? I'm happy that you're pursuing your passion. I would never tell you not to follow that dream. Maybe it's best that we just let it go now before . . ."

"I leave you?" She folded her arms over her breasts. "That's not what this is. Moving to California was just a thought. It's not a fact."

"Where does it leave us if you do?"

She hesitated.

He closed his eyes and let out a deep breath. "Okay, I see. Maybe it's best that I walk away this time."

It felt like someone had just ripped his heart out of his chest. But he turned to leave.

"Garrett, please. We need to talk about this. Let's talk about it."

He stopped at the door, and turned around. "It's okay, Skye. It really is. We're good. Friends."

"No."

"Take care." Then he left.

"What do you do when the worst possible thing that can happen to you, does?" Skye hugged her knees to her chest. "I'm a fixer. But how do I fix this?"

Sasha sat there, still, watching, waiting for her to continue.

After Garrett left last night, Skye had tossed and turned, replaying their conversation in her head. But she couldn't find a way to excuse her behavior. Because *she'd* done this. She'd purposely kept their conversations at a minimum while away and fed him a line of bullshit when he called her on it.

"I . . ." She almost choked on the huge lump in her throat. Her eyes burned with unshed tears. The first one fell and she wiped it away with the wad of Kleenex she had in her hand. When she'd arrived for the emergency session, she'd sat down and sobbed openly, not even caring if she looked vulnerable. Picking at the tattered tissue in her palm, she murmured, "I fucked this up royally."

"Skye, can you tell me why you think this is insurmountable? You've shared with me the huge strides you've made with Garrett in such a short time. Couples argue. Does this have to be the end?"

Shaking her head, she glanced up at her. "You didn't see him." The hurt in his eyes haunted her when awake and asleep. After he'd left, she realized the significance of the date and felt even worse. Because she could have approached the entire thing differently. "I knew he didn't forgive me."

"Have you ever said anything in anger that you regret, that wasn't really true?"

Skye thought about that for a moment. Shrugging, she said, "Maybe. I don't know."

"So, why couldn't he have done the same?"

"Because he's Garrett," was her lame answer. "Sasha, I selfishly went on about everything I had to do that had nothing to do with moving in with him." In hindsight, if she had just told him the truth the night he'd asked, none of this would be happening. She knew Garrett. He wasn't unreasonable. He wasn't the type of man to force someone to do it his way. "I think he would have understood if I'd told him I just wasn't ready. But I had to go and fuck it up by avoiding him."

Sasha sat back, crossed her legs, and rested her hands on her lap. "Why do you think you're not ready?"

"Isn't it too soon to move in together? We just got back together last month."

"Point taken. Just like you're telling me this, you could tell him the same thing."

It's too late. "I don't think so."

"Why?"

"Because I know myself. He was so hurt. Whether he said it in anger or not, he still said it. It was one of my biggest fears when we started this whole thing. In the back of my mind, I always wondered if he would wake up one day and realize he didn't forgive me, and leave me." Even if they talked and he apologized, she'd always wonder when the other shoe would drop.

"Consider the alternative to a conversation with him, then," Sasha challenged. "Living a life avoiding interaction, not being in his company versus sitting down with him and laying it all on the line."

The pang in her heart intensified at the thought of never experiencing him the same way again, never feeling his arms around her or his body against hers.

"Which is worse?" Sasha asked.

Skye already knew the answer. A life without him would be like hell on earth. Because she loved him that much. She also didn't want to be caught unawares two or three years down the line, when her feelings were stronger and their lives were more entwined.

She glanced at her watch. She had to be at the airport in an hour and a half. "I'm scared," she whispered.

"It's a genuine emotion."

"I'm just at this point when I'm attempting to reconcile things that have held me back. I'm changing my name, I had a talk with my mom about her expectations. I literally jumped into a relationship with the one man that could destroy me. And now I'm stuck again, because I know what I want but I don't know if I have it in me to put myself on the line."

"That's definitely something to think about." Sasha smiled. "But something tells me you'll make the choice that has the best chance of giving you everything you ever wanted. Career, family, and love." She ticked off each of those things on her fingers as she spoke. "In the meantime, don't spend too much time beating yourself up for the decision you made. Spend more time doing something about it."

Skye let out a heavy sigh and stood, stretching. "I better go. I have a flight to catch."

"Should we schedule our next appointment?"

Nodding, Skye smiled. "Definitely. But I'll email you."

"Great." Her therapist stood. "Bye, Skye. Try to enjoy Hawaii."

Skye left her appointment feeling a little better, but still not sure where she would land. Or if her and Garrett even stood a chance.

Later, Skye rested her head on the seat. Their flight to Hawaii was due to take off in a matter of minutes, and she couldn't wait to get out of Atlanta.

Zara moaned. "I'm in love with these cookies." She bit into a Biscoff cookie. Usually the airline carried those particular cookies, but her friend had stopped at the store and grabbed several packs just in case they didn't have any. Because she couldn't fly without them.

The flight attendant stopped at her side, and Skye ordered a whiskey. Closing her eyes, she heard the lady across the aisle murmuring something to her seatmate about drinking this early in the morning. Her eyes flashed to the woman, who offered her one of those polite, fake smiles.

Before the flight attendant walked away, Skye stopped her. "Excuse me?"

"Yes, Ms. Palmer?" the attendant asked. "What can I do for you?"

"I'll have two whiskeys." Skye glared at the other passenger, who was still watching her. "Because I'm minding my own business," she added loud enough that anyone who had something to say about her whiskey at eleven o'clock in the morning could hear her.

Zara patted her knee. "Woo woo woo."

Skye couldn't help it, she laughed. "Shut up."

"What's going on with you, sis? You've been cranky all morning. I know it's not the wedding, because you planned the hell out of this thing in less than two months."

The flight attendant set her drinks—as in plural—on her tray. Skye picked one up and took a long sip, making sure she kept eye contact with the lady across the aisle. *Yes, I'm petty, but I don't give a fuck.*

Zara laughed. "Girl! It's not that deep. Forget that lady and talk to me."

Burrowing in her seat, she sighed, then she spilled as much as she felt comfortable sharing on a plane—in a whisper, of course. She wouldn't want the two old biddies on the plane to say anything that would piss her off again.

When she finished her abbreviated version of events, Zara stared at her. "Wow. You did fuck that up."

"Tell me about it," Skye muttered, taking another sip of her drink. "Now I don't know what to do."

"Remember that movie, *The Princess and the Frog*?" Zara asked. "It's one of my favorite cartoons."

Confused, Skye glanced at her friend. The subject change threw her off for a second. "Yeah. Why?"

"She kissed a frog and—"

"He became a prince," Skye said. "I know all of this."

Her best friend shook her head. "See, your ass does not listen. That's your problem."

"Zara, I've watched the cartoon before."

"Obviously you haven't, because you would have known that she kissed the frog and then turned into a frog herself." Zara bit down on another cookie, gulped down a healthy bit of water, then burped. "Anyway, the frog convinced her to kiss him because he thought it would break the spell."

She cracked up. "You're silly as hell for that burp, by the way. But, okay."

Zara shifted in her seat so she could face Skye fully. "So once again, a woman is led astray by an ugly toad."

Skye rubbed her temples. "What does that have to do with me?"

"Ultimately, they get it together and end up happily ever after," Zara continued. "But I love the story because it brought home two very important lessons. Number one, stop kissing frogs, because they'll pull you into the dirty-ass swamp every single time. And two, you don't need the frog to be successful."

Finishing her drink, Skye told her friend to get on with it.

"Like I said, in the end, they worked because she realized she didn't need him. She *wanted* him. Because they complemented each other, brought out the best in one another. Then, they lived happily ever after."

Skye blinked, waiting for the sage advice she thought she would get from her friend. When Zara started happily munching on cookies again, she asked, "Your point, Zara?"

Zara froze. "Oh, sorry. The cookies be calling me, sis." She cleared her throat. "I'll bring this analogy home now."

"Good." Skye rolled her eyes.

"You love me." Zara waggled her eyebrows.

"I do, but can you please get to it?"

"The way I see it, you already kissed the toad. Thank God you got out of that mess," her friend added under her breath. "You've already proven that you don't need a man to become the best Skye you can be. You left a comfortable, lucrative position to start your own company. You're kicking major butt in your career. Now, it's time for you to work on the other stuff, the person who makes you feel at home. Give yourself permission to take what you want. Because you and Garrett? That's the real thing. You work well together; you bring out the best in each other. Don't walk away from that. If you do, you'll regret it." Zara let out a satisfied sigh. "Now, let's talk about wedding cake. I hope you got something good."

Skye laughed. "This baby has kicked your greedy gene up a notch."

"Girl, I know. Like, I'm full now but it's easy. I just keep on eating."

"You're crazy. But you're mine. Thanks, Z-Ra. I love you."

"Love you, too."

Chapter Nineteen

One night in Vegas was all Garrett needed to never let Duke plan anything again. Maybe five or seven years ago, he would have been okay with strippers and booze for twenty-four hours straight, but not anymore. He preferred the quiet of his house to debauchery, any day of the week. And he wasn't the only one.

X had retreated to their suite hours ago to video chat with Zara. And Garrett wished he hadn't been such a fool. An emotional, punk-ass fool. He sat down on a pool chair, pulled out his phone, and started a game of chess with Patrick.

A few minutes later, Duke plopped down on the seat next to him. "Bruh, you look pitiful sitting out here in a full suit at the pool."

Chuckling, Garrett looked down at his club clothes. "I'm going to bed anyway."

"Can I ask you a question?" Duke said.

Eyeing him, he nodded. "If I say no, would that stop you?"

Duke pretended to mull over that question. "Nah. You know me."

The words transported Garrett back to the many times

he'd told Skye that. Apparently, she didn't know him as well as he thought. "Go ahead, man." He drank some of his bottled water.

"Why do I have a roommate that I have no chance of fucking?"

Garrett choked, spraying water over the seat. "What the hell?"

Duke smiled. "I had to ask."

"You could have warned me."

"Again, you know I don't do that shit. Straight, no chaser, is the only way to go."

Garrett shook his head. It didn't take rocket science to connect the dots. When they'd booked the hotel in Maui, he and Skye were sharing a room. Now, they weren't. Since Duke was her one of her best friends, she'd asked to stay with him. Which shouldn't bother him, because he knew the nature of their relationship. But it did. *Because she's not with me.*

"She's staying with you," Garrett said. "I didn't know that."

"I didn't either until an hour ago. She texted me and told me not to bring any nasty hoes to the room."

Garrett barked out a laugh. It was definitely something Skye would say. "Sorry, bruh."

"No, don't apologize. What the hell happened?"

"She's not ready. Why should I wait around for her to get ready?"

"That's bullshit, man. Skye always overthinks things, fucks up sometimes, puts her foot in her mouth a lot, and then comes back stronger than ever. That's her. You fell in love with *her*, right?"

Garrett nodded, unashamed to admit it to Duke, to anyone.

"So you know her. If I was a jealous friend, I'd hate to admit this, but you know her better than I do. I've seen the two of you together, then and now. What I saw then were two young people falling for each other in a pure way. Your youth and unfortunate circumstances prevented it from lasting, and that's okay. What I see now are two people who have done some shit, seen even more. Both of you are accomplished and loyal to a fault. And y'all love each other. You accept all her quirks and don't mind watching stupid-ass *Star Wars* movies back-to-back. She accepts that you're not really the life of a party and rocks with you anyway. It's a win-win, if you ask me."

Garrett frowned. "Thanks."

"Hey, I call it like I see it. You're a house-and-movie type of guy. I'm just that guy."

Chuckling, Garrett said, "Shut the hell up, man."

"Listen, I love Skye. She's very important to me, been there for me more times than I even want to count. She's been through a lot. I want to see her happy. And she's happiest when she's with you. Trust me, I've been there for the others."

They'd both seen more than their share of heartbreak. At the same time, he couldn't get their conversation out of his mind, the way she'd hesitated like she didn't know if she would leave him. The sting felt like rejection and he'd been rejected enough in his life.

"She hurt you," Duke said.

It didn't surprise him that Duke knew what went down between him and Skye. "When did you talk to her?"

"I haven't." He shrugged. "That text was the first I heard from her in a week."

Now he was surprised. If Skye wasn't talking to Duke, who was she talking to? He stared at his phone. He'd thought about sending a text so many times since he'd walked out, but his pride had prevented him from doing so.

"I don't need to talk to her, though," Duke continued. "I've been with you for the last day. And while you're not a party animal, you're never like this."

Garrett studied Duke quietly. "I asked her to move in with me."

Duke nodded. "That's cool. But I'm just going to tell you that you should've known better."

He blinked.

"She's not ready for that yet. She needs a chance to sufficiently freak out before she says yes. Doesn't mean she's not ready for you."

Garrett grumbled a curse. In his haste to protect himself, he'd failed to take into account her feelings. Moving in together *was* a big step, huge for Skye. And he'd totally discounted her fears.

"Damn," he muttered.

"Yeah," Duke agreed. "You probably fucked up. I'm sure she did, too. My mother used to say as long as you're alive, there's a chance. And you'll probably fuck up again. But that's life."

Garrett smiled to himself, then looked at Duke. "Thanks, bruh."

"No problem." Duke stood. "Now, go somewhere. You're killing my vibe."

* * *

The next evening, Garrett and the fellas arrived in Maui and were immediately whisked to the sprawling resort on Wailea Beach. They were greeted with tropical-flower leis by staff.

Like several of the guests, Garrett and Skye had reserved a two-bedroom villa, which was situated on another part of the resort. After he checked in, he received a welcome basket that had Skye written all over it, and was shuttled to the gated community on the property.

His villa featured a view of the Pacific Ocean, a separate living area, and kitchen. It was like a home away from home. They'd splurged on it because it was private, away from the main resort. He'd envisioned nights on the private lanai, curled around each other, making love in the night air.

But his villa was empty. Sighing, he set the welcome basket on the countertop. She'd thought of everything. Inside was bottle of bourbon, two Cuban cigars wrapped in gold foil, cookies, and some other items. Garrett picked up one of the cigars and lifted it to his nose. She'd splurged on the brand, had taken great care to ensure the guests had a memorable experience.

Garrett looked around the villa. Briefly, he considered downgrading. No use in having the huge space to himself. Or he could invite Max and Dame to take the second bedroom. He nixed that idea fairly quickly. The last thing he needed was to find his sister doing anything without clothes with her boyfriend.

Garrett texted Max: Are you here yet?

Yep. Going to head to the pool was her quick reply.

The resort had several pools, and he asked where she'd be specifically. Then he left to go explore a little. According to the itinerary found in his welcome basket, the families were hosting a private luau that evening. He'd see Skye there. Knowing her, she'd look as stunning as the view from his mountainside villa.

After his conversation with Duke in Vegas, Garrett had decided he needed to talk to Skye. He wasn't sure that conversation should happen in the middle of the luau or at any of the wedding events. They needed privacy, time to truly listen to each other. It was the only way they'd come out of this together.

Garrett found Max at the Hibiscus Pool, which was reserved for adult guests.

"G!" She waved him over to her.

"Hey, Max." He glanced over at Dame and greeted him with a handshake. "Having fun?" he asked.

Max beamed up at him. "Yes. It's so beautiful here. I think I want to stay forever."

Garrett laughed. "How was the flight?"

"Long. We had a delay in Birmingham due to weather. But other than that it was pretty uneventful." She stood, pulling on her coverup. "I saw Skye earlier."

Garrett hadn't told his sister about what happened with Skye. But judging by the way she was studying him, she suspected something.

"Really?" He tried to sound unaffected by the mere mention of her name, but he failed miserably.

"Okay, so I know something's going on with you two." She hooked her arm in his. "Let's go for a walk." She told Dame they'd be back in a little while.

They set off for an unknown destination, walking in silence mostly. Eventually, they ended up at the beach. He pulled off his shoes and they continued their quiet journey.

"G, I don't want you to take this the wrong way, but you are so damn stubborn."

Garrett eyed her. "What are you talking about?"

"You act like you're so unaffected by everything, but I know you are."

"I'm fine, Max."

"No, you're not. You look sad, and this is supposed to be a happy occasion."

He hadn't known he looked sad. He made a mental note to smile more at dinner tonight. "I'm okay," he repeated.

"Skye looked sad, too."

That made it even worse. "Really?"

Max nodded. "What happened between you?"

Garrett chose honesty and told his sister what happened between them the other night. "I left and we haven't talked since then."

"Wow, G. That *is* sad. But why haven't you talked to her? You always tell me to be direct. What's different about this situation?"

He couldn't answer that, because he didn't know how they'd gone from in love and spending every night together to no communication at all. It was an argument that went left, and had brought up his own insecurities.

"I had a bad day," he admitted. "It was Mom's birthday."

Max shot him a sad smile. "It *was* a bad day."

His eyes widened. "I thought you were good."

She bit her lip. "I just wanted you to think that. I had a mini crying fit that morning. Dame was there to help me. He listened and didn't try to tell me I was wrong for feeling what I felt."

Garrett wanted to know what she'd been dealing with.

More than that, he needed to help her if he could. "What were you feeling?"

"Rage," she replied, her voice flat. "Every year, I go through a range of emotions." She squeezed a hand into a fist.

"Me too."

"When I think about her, I don't have a lot of good memories. I remember darkness and uncertainty. I remember pain."

Garrett remained silent. Shortly after he'd moved into the house, he'd found out Max had suffered abuse at the hands of their mother, too. Not as bad as he had, but bad enough. For a long time, he'd blamed himself for leaving her, for believing that her father would protect her.

"I hate that you had to go through that," he said.

"I've mostly made my peace with it. Usually, I don't think about those years. I try to concentrate on the good years. And, G, every single one of my good times was because of you. Your visits to Houston and summers in Atlanta with you . . . I don't know what I would have done without that."

Max had thanked him before for being there for her, but this conversation felt different. "I'm just sorry I wasn't there with you," he said.

"You always say that, but you were a victim, too. You did what you thought was best at the time." She stopped, squeezed his arm. "G, if it weren't for you, I wouldn't be in college, I wouldn't be a swimmer, I wouldn't be me. I owe you my life," she whispered, her voice thick with tears. "I love you, G. You're my brother, but you're also my father."

Garrett stumbled backward, taken aback by her words. "Max, I—"

"No, G, don't do that," she commanded. "You always told me to tell my truth. This is my truth. I don't really remember my dad much. He worked a lot. You're really the only father I've had. A parent is someone who puts their kids first, sacrifices for them, roots for them . . . You've done all that and more. The most important thing is you love me unconditionally. I always knew there was nothing I could do to make you stop loving me, and that helped me soar."

"Max, you . . ." He swallowed rapidly, tried to get ahold of himself. "I'm so proud of you."

She smiled then. "That means the world to me."

He brushed a tear from her cheek and pulled her into a hug. When he pulled back, he ruffled her hair. "Thank you. When I think about kids, I think about you, all wide-eyed and innocent and hurt. You're my sister, but you're my baby girl. And I love you very much."

Max flung her arms around him again. "After this, we have to man up, okay?"

He laughed. "Okay."

They pulled back, eyed each other, sucked in a deep breath, and gave each other some dap. Then they started to walk again. Garrett felt lighter, more grounded than he had in hours.

"G?"

He glanced at her. "Yes?"

"So, can I just reiterate that I said I'm your daughter *and* your sister?"

"Yes," he said, wondering where this was going.

"As your sister, I have to tell you . . . get your head out of your ass and go get Skye back. She makes you better, she makes you happy. I don't worry about you when you're with her."

Garrett shook his head. "Max—"

"Nope, I don't want to hear it." She held her arms out and twirled. "We're in paradise. Anything is possible."

He chuckled. "I'm glad you believe that."

"I do."

"You know what I believe?" he asked.

Frowning, she asked, "What?"

"That you can't beat me back to the pool." He took off running, cracking up when she ran after him, muttering curses along the way.

Skye stretched across a lounge chair on the patio of her villa. *Well, Duke's villa.* The countdown was on. Everything was all set, the guests were arriving. Zara needed a nap, so she decided to come get her some alone time.

Grand Wailea Maui, a Waldorf Astoria resort, was a little slice of paradise set in lush tropical gardens. The stunning view of the Pacific Ocean and Wailea Beach made her feel calm, at peace. It was the first time she'd felt that way since her argument with Garrett.

Zara had done a good job of keeping her distracted. Rissa arrived last night, and they'd spent the morning at the spa, lying by the pool, and just enjoying each other's company. Soon, her bestie would be married.

Over the next few days, she'd planned activities for the guests leading up to the rehearsal dinner and then the wedding. If all went well, it would be a truly epic event. She only wished she was celebrating with Garrett.

Both Zara and Sasha had given her food for thought. And she wanted to reach out to him, but every time she opened the Messenger app, she froze. When she finally got up the nerve to type something, she would ultimately delete it. She'd stopped and started so many texts, she'd lost count.

She heard the door slam shut behind her. It could only be one person.

"Skye Muthafuckin' Palmer-Starks!"

Giggling, she stayed where she was. He'd find her soon enough. It didn't take long. Minutes later, he was next to her, looking down at her. She glanced up at him. "Hey, asshole."

He grinned. "What's up?"

"What took you so long? Your flight landed a while ago."

"I stopped at my parents' villa. The whole clan was there."

Skye had seen most of the Young siblings today. They'd all arrived at different times, but she'd spent a significant amount of time at the main resort that day, making sure everything was set for the luau.

"The welcome dinner is in an hour."

He held up a white card. "I got your little itinerary in my welcome basket."

Skye had ordered gourmet baskets, filled with liquor and cigars, popcorn and baked goods, bottles of water and sparkling rosé. Each basket had a post-recovery wedding kit that included ibuprofen and Visine, among other things.

"I have to say I'm a little upset you didn't include homemade cookies," he added. "I'm so disappointed in you."

Laughing, she stood and gave him a hug. "I live to disappoint you." She shoved him with her hip and went into the villa. "Now, get dressed so you can walk me down to the luau."

An hour later, she stood at the entrance to the private area, greeting guests as they arrived. Staff members were also at the entrance, offering lei greetings and directing people to the open bar. Tiki torches lined the area and music filled the space.

Skye had given out so many hugs and kisses. She'd also smiled so much her face might be stuck in that position. But she enjoyed seeing the people she loved in one place.

Max rushed up to her. "Skye Light!" She hugged her. "You look beautiful."

"Thank you." Skye grinned, brushing a finger over one of Max's curls. "You're gorgeous, too."

"I told G I might not want to leave Maui."

"I get it," Skye agreed. "It's so peaceful here."

Max pulled Dame up to them. "Where should we sit?"

Skye waved to Dame and pointed to the hostess near the tables. "She'll show you to your seats."

"Great. I'll talk to you soon." Max and Dame walked off.

Suddenly nervous, Skye smoothed a hand down the front of her long maxi dress. She'd styled her hair up tonight, so she ran her fingers through the curls at the top of her head and hoped she still looked good.

Garrett walked in a few minutes later, looking so smooth and fine she almost fell over. He was dressed in natural-colored linen pants and a white linen shirt. When he spotted her, he approached. She noticed the women doing the leis stop and stare at him. They beckoned him over, greeting with wide, flirtatious grins. She couldn't blame them. He was fine.

"Hello, Skye." His eyes fell to her. She couldn't figure out what she read in them, but it wasn't ire, it wasn't disgust. It was . . . hot as hell. So hot her cheeks heated under his perusal.

One look into his brown orbs and her body reacted, her heart sang. "Hi," she breathed. "How are you?"

"Good."

He smells so good. She flattened a hand over her stomach and exhaled slowly. "There's a hostess over there that will show you to your seat."

He nodded, a small smile on his lips. Squeezing her bare arm, he said, "Talk to you later."

Skye's skin burned for what seemed like forever. Just from that one touch, the warmth of his hands against her arm. She watched him walk away.

"You're staring." Duke stood next to her, a glass of something in his hand.

"Shut up," she muttered.

"For someone as smart as you are, I don't understand why you just let things go down the way they did."

"What do you know about it?" she asked.

"More than you think."

She eyed him. "Who did you talk to?"

"Nunya."

"Duke, get out of here."

"Seriously, Skye. He basically told you he didn't trust your ass not to leave him and you just let him walk away thinking you ain't shit? If that doesn't deserve a conversation, I don't know what does." He sipped on his drink. "By the way, I need the room tonight. So you're going to have to go back to your original arrangements."

She gaped at him. "What? Duke, you can't kick me out for some woman," she whisper-yelled. "I would never do that to you."

"I'm sorry, this is for your own good. And my sex life."

"Really? You're really doing this?"

"Absolutely," he said with a hard nod. "Because you sat

there and made the same damn mistake you told me you didn't want to make again."

Skye grinned at an older couple as they made their way over to the tables. "I'm not leaving the villa," she hissed. "You need to find another hard or soft surface to do your thing."

"You're out of there," Duke insisted.

"You get on my nerves," she said through clenched teeth.

"It's okay. Why don't you go on over there and tell him you need a key to the villa?" He pushed her lightly, catching her off guard. Thankfully, she didn't fall. That wouldn't have been a good look. "Go on."

She whirled around, scowling at him. "I hate you."

"I love you."

Skye muttered a string of Tagalog curses at her friend. "Get out of here." She pushed him. Of course, he didn't budge.

"You know that Olivia Pope thing you got going on doesn't work on me."

"I can't stand you. Bye, Duke. I'm not going anywhere."

"Yes, you are." He walked off. "Be good, Skye."

The luau started with an imu ceremony, followed by dinner. The night ended with a Polynesian dance show and Samoan fire-knife dance finale. Guests milled around for a while, chatting and laughing, but Skye was tired. She hadn't had any contact with Garrett during the luau, but she couldn't keep her eyes off of him. Not during the toasts, not during the performances, and not when he snuck out a little earlier than everyone else.

Skye took the shuttle back to Duke's villa. During the dance show, her best friend had stuffed a napkin into her palm with Garrett's villa address on it. She knew Duke would never actually kick her out, though. No matter how tough he talked. More than likely, her friend would find another place to lay *his* head that night, leaving her alone to wallow.

Maybe he's on to something, she thought.

But could she go to Garrett, lay everything on the line, and risk him turning her away? She'd never know if she didn't try. Decision made, she pulled out her phone and sent a text to Duke: The house is yours. I still can't stand your black ass.

Duke's response came a few seconds later: You'll thank me later. Love you, too.

Smiling, Skye packed up her bags and left the villa.

Garrett's villa was only a short walk from Duke's, so it didn't take her long to get there. She approached the door and set her suitcase down. Sucking in a deep breath, she knocked on the door. A moment later, the door swung open and she was face-to-face with Garrett.

"Hi," she said, with a wave.

His gaze dropped to her suitcase. "Hi."

"Can I come in?"

Garrett hesitated for a moment, then stepped back and let her in. Skye didn't know what would happen, but a spark of hope bloomed in her spirit. She was in Garrett's villa, and if she had her way, she wouldn't leave.

Chapter Twenty

Garrett didn't know what he'd done to deserve this. It was like God had answered his unspoken prayer and dropped her right into his lap. But he wouldn't question it.

"Everything okay?" Garrett asked, taking her suitcase from her.

She breezed past him. "Yes." Instead of stopping in the living area where he'd been sitting, she stepped outside on the lanai.

He followed her to the edge, where she stared out at the ocean.

"I love it here," she whispered. "It's beautiful."

Garrett raked his gaze over her, from her hair to her toes. "So beautiful."

Only he wasn't talking about the island. When he'd seen her earlier, he was rendered speechless. She was mostly covered, with only her back and her arms visible, but she still managed to be the sexiest woman in the room. As always, keeping his eyes off of her had been a struggle. Finally, he'd stopped even trying.

The night breeze blew her hair slightly and he fought the urge to pull the pins out and let it fall down her back.

"Zara almost killed herself on that pork tonight." She giggled. "I told her she needed to stop eating it."

Garrett laughed. X had zoomed past him to chase after Zara when she bolted out of the luau, presumably to get to the bathroom.

"That girl is so greedy," Skye said. "But she was stunning tonight. Glowing."

Zara isn't the only one. "She's a beautiful woman."

"I actually cried when she tried on her dress again today. I can already tell I'm going to be a mess during the ceremony."

"You'll be fine."

"You always say that," she countered.

"Because I mean it."

She shot him a sidelong glance, then turned her attention back to the water. "I hope you don't mind me coming here. Duke kicked me out, and I . . ." Her voice trailed off. "I could tell you I didn't have anywhere to go, but that would be a lie. I could have stayed there, I could have gone somewhere else, but I didn't want to."

Her confession nearly knocked the wind out of him. "What's going on, Skye?"

"Nothing." She didn't move to look at him. "I was just wondering if we could have five minutes?"

You can have forever. But he didn't say that. Instead, he said, "I think we can make that work."

A soft smirk played on her lips. "You knew it could never be just five minutes between us."

It wasn't a question, but he answered her anyway. "Yes, I did."

"How did you know that?"

"Because there's no part of me that will ever be satisfied with just a little bit of your time."

"I've always felt the time we spend together not talking, but just being together, is the best," she admitted softly. "Over the last few days, I missed that."

"I did, too."

She grinned. "Remember that cross-country trip we took to Cali?"

Garrett laughed. "How could I forget? You convinced me to camp out at the Grand Canyon, and then changed your mind when you kept seeing deer and squirrels."

Camping wasn't his thing, but he'd purchased a tent, sleeping bags, lanterns, and a host of other shit for the experience. Because he'd wanted her to enjoy it. Soon as she'd seen the animals, though, she changed her tune in a hurry and he'd packed everything up and drove off.

Skye tilted her head back, laughing. "For some reason, I have a fear of deer. I could never even watch *Bambi.*"

"I know. But at least you can say you tried."

"Right? I still tell people I camped out at the Grand Canyon. I just leave off the part about it not being the entire night."

"It was long enough to count."

Skye swallowed visibly. "That night, I knew I'd never be the same if things didn't work out between us."

Garrett watched her, waited for her to continue.

"The way you handled my panic attack . . ." She shrugged. "My parents love me. My family loves me. But you . . . you cherished me. You protected me. You made me feel safe and wanted and loved. You've always done that for me, even when I didn't act right or treated you wrong. Even when you were hurting, you always made sure I was good."

Speechless, Garrett just stood there, staring at her while she looked out at the ocean.

"The thing is, I don't want to miss those times anymore," she said. "I don't think we should *have* to miss being together. But I feel like we should have this talk. Ya know?"

She was talking in circles, but he didn't care. He was just happy they were together.

"I was wrong," she confessed. "I let fear convince me that we needed to slow down, that I wasn't ready to move in with you. I let my past—*our* past—destroy our future."

"It's not destroyed."

Silence. She hugged herself, swayed on her feet.

Since he'd been on the island, he'd come to the conclusion that his love for her could never be destroyed. Even space and time, relationships and disasters, hadn't prevented him from falling for her again.

If she hadn't come to him, he would have gone to her. Because one thing was painfully clear, his life didn't work without her. And now it was his turn to tell her what was on his mind.

"That day was a bad day," he said softly.

"I know," she admitted, her voice shaky. "I remembered. I wanted to call you back, but I didn't know if you wanted to hear from me."

"I probably wouldn't have answered. I was pretty angry."

"At me."

"At everything. I feel like I'm at a crossroads. The complicated feelings I had for my mother seemed to well up that day, and I *did* take it out on you."

"But my first inclination shouldn't be to run away or hide. Or treat you bad as some sort of twisted defense mechanism."

"Skye, you should have been able to tell me that you weren't ready to move in together without me taking it the wrong way."

"And you should be able to ask me to move in with you without me running away, or making up excuses that don't matter."

He chuckled. "I guess we agree that the argument went too far."

Smiling, she said, "I guess so." She sighed. "You asked me what was going on."

"And you said nothing."

"That's true. Nothing is going on, because my life is nothing without you." Then she turned to face him, her brown eyes shining under the moonlight.

Garrett sucked in a deep breath, her words shooting through him and igniting every nerve ending in his body.

She stepped into him. "Garrett, I can't apologize enough for making you feel that I wasn't ready for you, that I didn't want you, that I didn't love you as much as you love me. I do love you. So much. And I'm ready. I'm ready to take everything you want to give."

Releasing his breath, he leaned his forehead against hers. "Skye," he whispered. He searched her eyes. "Are you really saying this to me?"

She nodded. "I should have said it sooner."

"You said it," he said. "That's all that matters." He cradled her face in his hands and kissed her. When he pulled back, he smirked at her. "You need another five minutes?"

She gripped his shirt with her fist. "I need a lifetime."

"You got it."

Tugging her to him, he pressed his lips to hers. She moaned, wrapping her arms around him, holding him to her. He picked her up and carried her to the bedroom. Laying her on the bed, he stripped her naked.

"So beautiful," he murmured, taking her in. "So mine."

"I am yours," she said. "Now, take your clothes off and do me."

Garrett did as he was told, climbed onto the bed, and thrust into her. They made slow, sweet love. He savored this, he loved this. *I love her.*

"Love you," he said.

"I love you, too. I don't want you to stop."

He tugged her nipple with his teeth, then sucked it into his mouth. "It's okay," he whispered. "We have all night. Come."

She came then, shuddering beneath him and moaning his name. Then, he let himself fall.

"Knock, knock." Skye stepped into the men's dressing room the day of the wedding.

Garrett glanced at her reflection in the full-length mirror he stood in front of and said, "Hey, baby."

Things had moved quickly with so much to do to prepare for the big day. Yet, even as she'd thrown herself into the last-minute details, she'd managed to carve out private time with Garrett.

Garrett had scheduled a private botanical tour of the resort property one afternoon, and she'd convinced him to sign them up for scuba and snorkel lessons with Max and Dame one morning. They'd dined, they'd laughed, they'd made love, and they recommitted to one another.

Skye sauntered over to him and kissed him. "Hey, yourself." She finished tying his tie. "You look good."

He grinned down at her. "So do you." Wrapping an arm around her waist, he pulled her closer and brushed his lips against hers. "I think blue is your color."

Zara had chosen cobalt blue for her primary wedding

color. Initially, Skye had dreaded the bright color, but her mother had really outdone herself on the design. The long mermaid gowns were perfect for the occasion.

"Don't get used to it," she smirked. "I'll be back to basic black tomorrow."

"And you'll be back to naked after the wedding."

"Can you take that shit somewhere else?" Duke entered the room. "There'll be enough sappy love crap during the wedding."

Skye laughed. "Oh, shut up." She snatched Duke's tie from him and tied it for him. "Stop being a hater."

Duke smiled. "I will when you thank me for that tough love."

"What can I say, I don't know what I'd do without you."

Her friend's gaze softened. Then he cleared his throat. "If you don't get out of here with that sentimental shit, I'm going to kick you out. X is already acting crazy as hell. I don't need this right now."

Skye smacked his shoulder lightly. "Hey, I'm trying to be sincere."

"Be sincere next year. Right now, I need to keep my game face on." He shoved her. "Go. X needs you."

"Ugh, you make me sick. Bye, fool." She pushed Duke, kissed Garrett, then headed toward the private room in the back where she knew X was getting ready.

Uncle Jax was seated on the far side of the room, while X paced the floor, muttering something she couldn't make quite make out.

Skye shot Uncle Jax a questioning look. Her uncle gestured for her to step in.

"X?"

Her cousin froze. "Skye." He turned around, a grin on

his face. "I'm really doing this," he said, nodding rapidly. "Today."

"Yes, you are." She approached him and he hugged her.

"I'm marrying my best friend, my lover, my Zara. We're having a baby."

Skye pulled back and smiled up at him. "Yes, you are. I'm so happy for you." Smoothing a hand over his lapel, she added, "You two are made for each other."

"We are, aren't we?"

"Absolutely."

"Thank you, cousin. We wouldn't be here without you."

Skye knew he wasn't only talking about the wedding, and she found herself getting choked up at the sentiment, the sincerity in her cousin's gaze. Skye had done her share of meddling, saying the right thing to each of them at various times to get them to realize they were better together than apart. And in a few hours, she'd be watching two of the most important people in her life pledge themselves to each other forever.

"You're welcome," she whispered, trying not to cry and ruin her makeup.

X sucked in a deep breath. "How is she?"

"Beautiful and nervous. She's Zara."

He laughed. "Tell her I'll be waiting at the end of the aisle, tell her that I can't wait to start forever with her."

Skye's makeup was officially doomed. She fanned her face with her hand, hoping to stave off the tears. X dabbed the corner of one eye with his handkerchief.

"Thanks," she muttered. "I'll make sure I give her the message."

"Good. Love you, cousin."

Exhaling, she nodded. "Love you, too."

Skye spent the next hour handling business. She spoke

with the on-site wedding coordinator, fixed the flowers on the arch, and made sure the caterer hadn't cooked anything with peanuts, because one of the wedding guests was allergic. She also asked for a special favor from the concierge, who'd assured her he'd get it done.

Finally, she stepped into Zara's dressing room. Her best friend's mother and Rissa were in there, making sure the bride was happy and calm . . . and fed.

Zara's face lit up when she spotted Skye. "Hey."

"Z-Ra." Skye inched closer, unable to stop the tears from falling. Her friend was beautiful, stunning in her wedding gown. The long mermaid dress fit perfectly, baby bump and all. "You're gorgeous."

"Thanks," Zara said, biting into a carrot stick. "Mom said I couldn't have a cookie. So I had to settle for this."

Skye laughed. "You're crazy. But Mama Regine is right. No cookies. You'll have cake later."

"With raspberry filling, right?" Zara asked.

"Of course," Skye assured her. "Are you ready?"

Zara nodded. "I am. How is he?"

"He told me to give you a message." Skye told her exactly what X had said. Then all of them cried. Luckily, the makeup artist was still there to save the day and fix their faces.

"Thank you, Skye," Zara said. "I know I've said it before, but I can't say it enough. You're my best friend and I love you to death. I'm glad you worked things out with Garrett. Because you deserve every bit of happiness you can stand. And more."

"Shit, you need to stop." Skye dabbed her eyes again. "I can't cry anymore today. I love you, too. Now, let's go."

* * *

Xavier and Zara were married at dusk in front of their family and friends. Haiku Mill was the perfect venue for their intimate ceremony. The weather was beautiful and Zara stunned in her one-of-a-kind Allina Smith gown. X recited heartfelt vows to love, honor, cherish, and feed his bride. Zara promised to love, honor, cherish, and play spades forever with her groom. There wasn't a dry eye in the courtyard. Even Uncle Jax shed a tear. Skye had bawled like a baby, and her makeup once again suffered for it.

When the minister pronounced them husband and wife, X handed Zara a cookie and carried Skye's bestie down the aisle. Garrett met Skye in the middle and escorted her out of the area.

After pictures and more pictures, after the first dance, after dinner, Skye toasted the bride and groom. And she cried again.

Later, Garrett pulled her out on the dance floor. As they swayed to the music, she wondered if their life together would always be this perfect.

"What are you thinking about?" he asked.

"Us."

Leaning back, he raised a brow. "What about us?"

"About that shower we took this morning."

He'd taken her from behind under the water. Then, he'd towel dried her until she climaxed again.

With a wicked smirk, he asked, "Ready for round three?"

"I definitely am."

He pulled her closer, and she leaned into him, resting her head on his chest. "I have something for you," she said, looking back up at him.

"Something good? Or something naughty?"

"Something good, *then* something naughty."

Laughing, he asked, "Do I have to wait until we get back to the villa?"

"Nope." She winked and pulled out a small bag that was tucked into her dress.

He eyed it skeptically. "What is it?"

The concierge had come through as promised. She couldn't wait to see Garrett's face when he opened her gift. It was more symbolic than anything. Because she had no idea where they'd end up.

He pulled the bag open and shook the contents into his hand. His gaze flashed to her. "A key?"

"My key. I had it made today."

Garrett turned the silver key over in his palm.

"If you decide to move into my house, you'll already have a key," she explained. "But you don't have to move in with me. I can move in with you, or we can shop for a house. It's just a gesture, to prove to you that I want this, that you can trust me with your—" He kissed her. Hard. "—heart."

"Whatever we decide, Skye, it will be what's right for us."

She laughed, flinging her arms around his neck. "Does this mean you still want to do this?"

"Now, you already know the answer to that."

Grinning, she brushed her mouth over his. "That's right, I do. *Mahal kita*, Garrett."

"I love you, too."

Epilogue

Three Months Later

"Garrett!" Skye walked through the house—their house—looking for her boyfriend. They'd decided to live in her house, because it was bigger. But they hadn't ruled out looking for a home in the near future.

Skye Light PR had launched successfully, and she already had a full staff. She shared office space with Steele Crisis Management. The arrangement allowed for them to have their own distinct work spaces, but share the building.

"Garrett!" she called again.

Frowning, she checked his office. *Empty.* She checked the man cave. *Empty.* He'd texted her and told her to come home, but where the hell was he?

She jogged up the stairs and entered their room. Sitting on the bed was Baby Yoda, dressed in a little white gown and veil. A ring was hanging from his ear.

Skye backed away from the clear sign that a proposal was coming. Turning, she ran right into Garrett, yelping, "Oh shit, you scared me." She held a hand to her chest.

"I'm sorry," he said, gripping her waist.

Glancing back at Baby Yoda, then at Garrett, then back

at Baby Yoda again, she asked, "Um, did you put that white gown on my baby?"

He nodded. "I did put a gown on that rodent."

She laughed, shoving him playfully. "He's an unknown alien species, a Jedi Master."

"Um, yeah, that's not what Baby Yoda is. We still don't know."

Unable to hide her smile, she leaned into him. "You're funny. Hi." She kissed him.

"Hello, Skye." He nipped at her earlobe. "So what do you think of his outfit?"

Once again, Skye turned to look at the stuffed alien. "I don't think white is his color."

Garrett barked out a laugh. "You got jokes."

"Always."

"Well?"

She shrugged. "Is Baby Yoda getting married?"

"No, but I hope Baby Yoda's mama is."

Skye sucked in a deep breath, her heart hammering in her chest. Suddenly, she was hot. She fanned herself. "Oh. So you are . . . ?"

"Look at me." Garrett locked his gaze on her. "Don't panic, don't overthink it. If you're not ready, I understand. It's just going to be on Baby Yoda, waiting for you to put it on, okay? Remember? You know me."

She let out a slow, shaky breath as his hand swept over her back. She did know him, and she loved him dearly. She wanted to make it Baby Yoda official. Skye kissed him. "I do know you," she said. "So I'm just going to say yes!"

She screamed when he picked her up and peppered her face with kisses before crashing his mouth to hers. When they broke apart, her body was already on fire, ready for more.

"Garrett?" she said.

"Yes?" He blazed a trail of kisses over her jawline.

"Put Baby Yoda in the corner."

He smirked. "No problem." He dropped her on the bed, pulled the ring off the alien and tossed the doll onto the chair. Picking up her hand, he slid the ring on her hand. "I love you, baby."

She held out her hand, admiring the cushion-cut diamond. "I love this."

Garrett tickled her sides until she cried out for mercy. "You love what?"

Skye peered up at him, the man that she'd fallen hopelessly in love with years ago and never stopped. "I love you. Now . . . Five minutes?"

"No. Forever."

"Forever."

Don't miss the first book in Elle Wright's Pure Talent series . . .

THE WAY YOU TEMPT ME

Brilliant and ambitious,
the high-powered team behind the Pure Talent Agency manages the best creatives in the business.
In this sizzling new series, they gamble big on every wild-card, industry-outsider client—and on delicious, unexpected, crazy-irresistible passion . . .

The heir-apparent to Pure Talent, ex-playboy Xavier Starks had it all figured out. With an engagement to Hollywood's hottest actress and his innovative expansion plans, he can finally prove to his dad, Jax, that he's responsible enough to step into a leadership role at their company. Until a jilting-gone-viral puts Xavier back in the relentless social-media spotlight, out of the running for partner—and in competition with the last person he ever expected: his very-grown-up childhood friend and girl-next-door . . .

With her acclaimed sports talent roster and unparalleled instincts, agent Zara Reid knows she can take Pure Talent to the next level. To make the most of her mentor Jax's faith in her, she'll go head-to-head and scheme-to-scheme with Xavier to prove she's got what it takes. But suddenly, long days working too close together turn into reckless, insatiable nights. Now, being co-workers-with-benefits means Zara and Xavier must face their secrets, dare to trust—and negotiate the toughest game of all—love.

Available from Kensington Publishing Corp.
wherever books are sold

Chapter One

"I've been here since day one. I've seen the strides made, the battles fought, the victories won, and the losses suffered. As one of this agency's first clients, I believe in my father's vision." Xavier Starks met his father's eyes and smiled. "And I can't wait to lead this company into the future."

"And you're sure about this?"

Xavier paused, mouth open, thumb on the presentation clicker. He glanced back up at the screen showcasing his hard work, the slide that he'd worked painstakingly on in an effort to garner applause. Or at least a smile. What he didn't expect was that particular question from his father. Because he was sure. He was definitely confident in his plan to take Pure Talent to the next level by spearheading a new sports division.

Dropping his arms to his sides, he sucked in a deep breath. "Excuse me? Of course, I'm sure. We talked about this. Sports will change the game, improve our bottom line. I envision a huge marketing campaign, the best sports agents, talented players. What's there not to be sure about?"

Jax arched a brow and glanced down at the small box sitting on the desk. The ring. The vintage marquise-cut diamond sparkled from the box, gleaming at him. His father pointed at it. "This."

Sighing, Xavier picked it up and closed the top of the box before he stuffed it in his pockets. "Does this mean you didn't hear a word of my presentation?"

"I heard you." Jax leaned forward, elbows against the oak desk. "Xavier, you came into my office and showed off this ring you purchased for Naomi. Then you went into your work proposal. Shouldn't we talk about this? You are my son. This is a big deal."

Xavier shrugged. "It is. Which is why I wanted to show you the ring first."

"A ring doesn't make a marriage, son. Are you sure you're ready for this?"

"Yeah, I'm ready. Dad, there is a board meeting in two hours. I need to table the discussion about the ring and focus on the work proposal I have to make."

Pure Talent Agency was founded by Jax Starks in 1989, after he had made a name for himself as a sharp, dedicated entertainment attorney for several African-American celebrities. He'd spent years building his brand, negotiating unheard-of deals in Hollywood for actors who had floundered under different representation. The first order of business was signing Xavier himself as the first child actor of the boutique agency.

With his father's vision and connections in the industry, Xavier landed a sought-after role on one of the most influential sitcoms of the 1990s. Every Tuesday evening, families of all backgrounds watched Xavier grow up right before their eyes as the sharp, inquisitive son of a fictional lawyer and his family.

It wasn't long before Xavier had decided he didn't want the life of red carpets and photo shoots. He didn't want to spend his school year with tutors, instead of teachers, and with costars, instead of his friends. Once he realized that acting was not for him, he'd gone to great lengths to distance himself from his squeaky-clean child star image, eventually settling into a career of his own within the agency as one of the best youth-performer agents at Pure Talent. Now he wanted—no, he needed—to take his career to the next level.

"Expanding into sports is huge for this company," Xavier said. "And I want to be the agent to helm this new venture. I've done the work, I've studied the market, I've made invaluable connections. This is exactly the type of project that I'm looking forward to sinking my teeth into."

Jax leaned back in his chair. "I agree. A sports division is the next logical step. I can definitely foresee us taking this company to a whole new level of success."

"Exactly."

"It's no secret that I'm getting older."

Xavier dropped his gaze. Over the past few months, his father had been talking more and more about retirement, of traveling for pleasure, of enjoying dinner with X's mother without interruptions from clients and staff. As much as he understood the notion, he hated to think of his father getting older. In Xavier's mind, Jax Starks was still a force to be reckoned with in the industry.

"I have to admit that seeing you take the initiative on something like this makes me happy," Jax continued. "You've done a good job on the proposal, your presentation is thorough. I'm very interested in exploring this further."

"Thank you. Your faith in me means a lot, Dad."

"Have you thought about potential agents?"

Xavier finally took a seat. "I have some ideas. I can get you a list this afternoon, after the presentation."

"Great. I see no reason not to move on this quickly. I also have a few names."

Curiosity piqued, Xavier asked, "Care to share?"

"Not particularly."

Xavier barked out a laugh. "I'm not surprised." Without another word, Xavier closed his laptop and gathered his hard copy of the presentation.

"Are you sure?"

Glancing at his father, Xavier sighed. He'd been in this position with his father more times than not, hoping to distract from a conversation he didn't want to have. When he'd mentioned marriage to Naomi, both of his parents had reservations and had made it known in no uncertain terms.

He couldn't say that he blamed them. Naomi was one of the hottest black actresses in the industry. Going out with her was inviting attention that he'd tried hard to avoid for many years.

"I'm sure," Xavier said finally.

"Why? Why is *she* the one?"

"We've been together for over a year."

"That's not an answer."

Xavier shrugged. "What do you want me to say?"

"I want you to tell me why you're proposing to a woman who spends more time on her phone than with you. What is it about her that makes you think marriage is the next logical step?" Jax stood to his full height and strolled over to the mini refrigerator he kept in the office. Pulling out two bottles of water, he offered Xavier one before twisting the cap off of his own. "Being married is much more than a high-profile wedding. I just want to be sure you're doing this for you—and not for an image you think you need."

"I don't need to get married, Dad. I want to. Naomi is talented, funny, adventurous, beautiful. We get along, we have fun together, we enjoy the same food and the same activities. She challenges me to . . ." *Watch reality TV and read fanfiction?* He scratched the back of his neck. "She's amazing."

His father leaned against the desk and assessed him with eyes that saw too much, way more than Xavier wanted them to see in that moment. "But you didn't mention *love.* Do you love her?"

"Love"? Xavier closed his eyes as the chorus to that damn Tina Turner song played in his head. The question in the song taunted him, because love hadn't been a part of his decision-making process. Of course, he cared for her, and he did love her. But not in a fiery, all-consuming "A Couple of Forevers" way. More like a "We've Only Just Begun" way.

Still, he couldn't bring himself to admit that to his father; he knew it would only make matters worse. Because Jax Starks fell in love with Ana Perry-Starks thirty-eight years ago and had never stopped being in love with his wife. Growing up, Xavier had watched his parents build an empire, all while demonstrating unconditional love to each other, even during the hard times. Marrying for anything other than love was a no-no to his mother and father.

"You know I have feelings for her. Otherwise, I wouldn't be doing this. I'm a grown man doing grown-man things. I know you think I'm being impulsive, but I don't take this lightly."

He'd thought about everything, weighed the possible pros and cons. In the past, Xavier had made very questionable decisions, based on emotions and appearances.

"I'm doing the right thing." Xavier stood, picked up his laptop. "Tonight is the night I will propose to Naomi. Everything will be fine. You'll see."

"Fine. If this is what you want, I'm going to support you."

"Thanks. I have to run an errand. I'll be back in an hour."

Xavier left his father's office and hurried to his own office to drop off his things. Grabbing his jacket, he told his assistant, Jennifer, to hold his calls; then he rushed to the elevator. He responded to a client while he waited for the car and sent a text to another. When the door opened, he stepped inside. As soon as he exited the elevator, his phone buzzed.

"What's the word, bruh?" Xavier breezed past a crew in the process of decorating one of the many Christmas trees that would adorn the lobby leading up to the holiday in a few weeks.

"Shit," Duke answered.

Since they were kids, Duke Young had been a constant in Xavier's life, since their fathers were best friends. They'd seen each other through stupid decisions, crazy exes, and even an overnight stint in jail.

"Is everything all set?" Xavier's phone buzzed, indicating another call was coming in. He glanced at the screen and hit IGNORE. His cousin, Skye, would have to wait.

"Who the hell do you think you're talking to?" his friend asked. "Of course, we're all set."

Voted one of the hottest chefs of his generation, Duke had blazed a trail in the culinary industry, winning multiple awards and turning the food game on its ears. He'd recently won a reality-television contest for best chef and was currently wielding all kinds of offers, from product endorsements to lucrative job offers to cookbook deals. He'd even managed to snag a deal as an underwear model.

"Did the florist come to the house?"

Xavier had spared no expense, hiring one of the top floral artists to decorate his condo for the proposal.

"She just left," Duke said. "But not before I got her number for tonight."

"You just make sure the entrée is on point, before you hook up with Samantha."

"I got you, bruh. You know that."

"Thanks, man. I need this entire thing to go off without a hitch."

"At least the food will be good." Duke laughed. "That is the only thing that I'm sure about."

"Shut the hell up, man." He'd heard all of his friend's reservations about Naomi and the proposal multiple times since he'd asked him to prepare the meal for the occasion. And after the conversation he'd just had with his dad, he didn't want to hear it again.

"I'm just sayin' . . . Despite the slammin' dinner, the whole engagement thing doesn't sit right with me. But it's your life."

"Exactly, so stop talking about it." The phone buzzed in his ear again. Xavier glanced at the screen. His father. Hitting IGNORE, he said, "Bruh, once you're finished, you can go ahead and go. I'll probably be done here a little early today, because I want to take care of some things at the house."

"I don't just cook a masterpiece and walk away. Part of my process is the presentation."

"For someone else, yes. But not for me."

Another call buzzed in his ear. Skye again. For a second,

he wondered if something was wrong. But he quickly brushed that worry off, because she would have sent a text.

Xavier stopped at a coffee kiosk in the lobby, while Duke ticked off all the details for the romantic date he'd planned tonight. He placed his regular order, but paused when the barista simply stared at him. He looked down at his suit to check for a stain or something. "Is something wrong, Rita?"

The petite woman quickly snapped out of her trance. "Uh, no. I'm sorry, X." She hurried to get his drink.

Frowning, he scanned the area and noticed that Rita wasn't the only one staring at him. Conspicuous glances from several people in the lobby got his attention. Stares and whispers weren't new to him. As a former child star with a hit show still running in syndication, being noticed wherever he went was commonplace. But not in the Pure Talent offices. And not the way the various staff members were watching him.

"X, what's up?" Duke asked, interrupting his thoughts.

"Nothing." He smiled when Rita slid a cup of coffee toward him. Meeting her gaze, he noticed her chin tremble, almost like she was going to break out in an ugly cry. "Are you okay?"

She dropped her gaze. "I'm okay, X. Are you?"

Tilting his head, he nodded. "I'm fine." He pulled out a twenty-dollar bill and set it on the counter.

Before he could slide it to her, she placed her hand on top of his. "It's good. Coffee's on me today."

"Okay," he murmured. "Thanks, Rita."

"Who the hell is Rita?" Duke asked.

Xavier blinked. Because for a second, he'd forgotten he was on the phone. "No one to you, bruh. Listen, what did you decide for dessert?"

Duke described a strawberry-and-chocolate torte that he was sure Naomi would love. Smiling, Xavier said, "Sounds like you have everything under control."

"I told you . . . I got this. This is what I do."

"X!"

Xavier turned toward the entrance of the building. Skye waved at him and rushed over to where he'd been standing near the small coffee kiosk. He held up a hand, signaling her to wait a second. Speaking to Duke, he told him to call if he had any issues and ended the call.

"What's up, Skye?"

Breathing heavily, like she'd been running, Skye ran a hand through her hair. "I've been trying to call you."

Xavier opened an e-mail and skimmed a message from one of his client's parents. "I was in the middle of something." He quickly typed out a response to the e-mail and hit the SEND button. "What's going on?" He read another e-mail and pondered the best way to answer the question posed to him.

Skye snatched his phone. "Listen to me."

Frowning, he wondered if he'd missed something. *Has she been talking?* "There's a lot going on. I'm actually on my way out to take care of something for the proposal tonight."

"X, I . . ."

He pulled the ring out of his pocket. "I forgot to show you the ring." He opened the box and smiled, anticipating her reaction.

Skye had been his number one supporter in everything he'd done in life. They'd grown up together, joined at the hip from the time they could walk. Their fathers were brothers and partners in numerous business ventures.

With a hard eye roll, Skye shook her head. "X, stop."

He paused, confused by Skye's reaction to the ring. He'd expected her to hype him up, coo over the size and shape of the diamond. "What? You don't think she'll like it? We talked about this. You told me marquise-cut was the way to go?"

"Will you just shut up about the ring?" Skye scanned the immediate area. "Too many people, too many ears," she mumbled, grabbing his hand and pulling him toward an empty conference room.

Once inside the room, she closed the door and the blinds and turned to him. "X, we need to talk."

Skye worked for Pure Talent in the public relations department. She knew how to handle all types of situations—good, bad, or catastrophic. Her specialty was putting a positive spin on everything, whether she was writing press releases, fine-tuning images, or managing crises. Right now, she was giving him "bad news" vibes. Soft voice, direct eye contact, and straight back.

He eyed her, waited for her to speak. Then he saw it. The slightest tremble in her chin. This was personal, not client related. "What's wrong?" he asked. "Did someone die?"

She shook her head.

"Accident?"

"Okay, I'm going to talk now." She sighed heavily. "And I need you to remain calm, no matter what."

Dread knotted in his stomach. The last time Skye had told him to remain calm, she'd informed him that their uncle had passed away suddenly. "I'm good."

Finally her shoulders relaxed. "You obviously haven't seen Page Six."

"No. Like I said, I've been busy. Why?"

She pulled out her phone. "There's something you need to see." Xavier took the offered device from his cousin and peered at the Page Six headline. "I'm so sorry," she whispered.

The title of the article was the punch to the gut, the huge picture under the article served as the uppercut. The combination of both knocked the wind out of his lungs. He sat down on one of the empty chairs. Muttering a curse, he glared at the screen. He didn't need to read the article to know that he was screwed, that he had been screwed.

Still, he forced himself to look at the "happy couple" on the page. The woman smiled as if she'd recently descended from cloud nine, while the man held on to her waist as if he'd never let her go. It wasn't the type of picture taken without permission. The man and woman had posed for it, made sure the photographer caught her good side. The only problem? He was an asshole and she had recently been voted one of the "30 Hottest Women under 30" in *People* magazine. His woman, the woman he had planned to propose to that night. The title taunted him, and he re-read it three times in a row, just to be sure and maybe to will it away. He closed his eyes and reopened them. *Shit.* It was still there, still pissing him off, still taunting him: NAOMI MURPHY DUMPS XAVIER STARKS FOR PRO-BASKETBALL PLAYER ETHAN PORTER.